Nurses Of The Civil War

A Clean Historical Mail Order Bride Series

Faith-Ann Smith

NURSES OF THE CIVIL WAR

TABLE OF CONTENTS

Mail Order Bride: Mary's Secret

Prologue

Portsmouth, New Hampshire - 1865

"No! You can't do this," Caleb hollered as he writhed against the four hands that bit like vices into his arms.

He was a soldier, strong and able, but he'd been set upon unsuspectingly, asleep in his bed, and there was nothing he could do to escape.

"Let me go, you swine," he spat at the man who stood in front of him, looking on with cold, unfeeling eyes. After all the battles he'd fought these past eight months, *this* is how it would end?

"Lieutenant...Caleb...my dear friend, there's no sense in struggling." There wasn't a speck of guilt in the undercurrent of the man's tone. His back straight, his shoulders squared; he was completely without conscience. If Caleb had been in any doubt, the Beaumont–Adams revolver the man held in his steady hand banished any hope of it.

The man was an evil savage, and Caleb had been none the wiser this whole time. Nay, not only unwise, but almost entirely fooled by the snake. Almost. The inkling of suspicion had prickled the hairs at the back of his neck every time the man came near, and the unsightly scene he'd walked in on the day before finally confirmed his intuition. But he'd fought next to the man and had been forced to trust him with his life on more than one occasion. And now he would pay the price for his ignorance.

He could have accepted death at the hand of the enemy on the battlefield; he would even have welcomed it if he could have taken the grayback scoundrel with him as he went. But not like this.

"You'll never get away with this," Caleb seethed, though he knew it was in vain. The cold ice in the man's eyes told him he was impermeable to reason.

"Whatever do you mean, Caleb? You have committed a heinous crime and I only seek to set right your wrong."

Crime? "What crime have I committed?"

"Why, I saw you with my own eyes; such unbecoming behavior of an officer."

"You lie. You saw nothing."

"It is your word against mine, dear friend, and I fear you have no one to vouch for you. I, on the other hand, have an ironclad alibi."

"The girl, she'll vouch for me and lay blame where it is due."

"Pity, but I'm afraid that won't be possible," the man replied without pause, which could mean only one thing.

Caleb ceased his struggle against the hulkish brutes that held him. He was an intelligent man, intelligent enough to know when he'd been bested. He would not cower and beg for his life.

From the moment he had left for the war, he'd known he may never see his home again. He just never imagined it would end like this. No doubt, his name would be smeared irreparably, but there was nothing he could do about that now.

He closed his eyes, bringing to mind an image of home; the house where he'd grown up; the young wife he'd left behind when he went off to war. There had been no love match there, but even still, he harbored so many regrets.

Chapter 1

Boston, Massachusetts - 1869

Mary sat in the parlor of her uncle's home, her back stiff and her hands clasped in her lap to hide the tremble she'd been unable to still. She felt just as out of place as she had the first day she'd arrived, and equally as unwelcome.

It did not matter that she'd lived there since she was fourteen years old; she would never come to see it as home. It was just as well. If she'd ever sought to view it as such, no doubt Uncle Robert would have welcomed the opportunity to put her in her place.

The two men who sat across from her looked perfectly at ease, chatting amicably while they sipped their steaming hot cups of tea. Hers sat untouched on the low table in front of her.

"I can't imagine any young woman rushing off to immerse herself in so much brutality. You have an overly strong constitution it seems, Miss Kenleigh," Mr. Wendell commented to her with a disapproving glare, drawing her back into the conversation that went on around her.

She opened her mouth to respond to the man's observation, but was promptly interrupted.

"Nonsense," Uncle Robert exclaimed on her behalf, though not for her benefit. "My dear niece was merely roused to compassion for our brave soldiers. I doubt the gore and brutality of the situation ever crossed her mind. She is too quick to act at times, I confess, but I'm certain it is just a plight of youth."

"That is good to hear," the man replied and then posed another question to her uncle, something about her penchant for irrational action since she'd come home.

Mary ceased to listen, knowing that even though she appeared to be the topic of conversation, her presence was not necessary.

And yet, her presence was very necessary, at least as far as her uncle was concerned. He'd taken her aside the morning prior and informed her of what was to come. He'd told her the fine— and wealthy—Mr. John Wendell would be coming to visit on the morrow and with a specific purpose in mind: he intended to propose marriage to her, and her uncle demanded in no uncertain terms that she accept the man's proposal.

She'd turned down the previous suitors who had sought to shackle her to them in the year since her return from the Fairfax Street Hospital in Virginia. She would have thought that knowing a woman had been up to her neck in blood for months on end would have dissuaded the regal gentlemen of Boston, but that seemed not to be the case.

And now, her uncle would have no more of it. He wanted her wed and out of his house, reminding her yet again how he had never wanted her there to begin with. Well, that made two of them, but exchanging one overbearing brute of a man for another was not what she considered an acceptable solution. She remembered the love in her father's eyes when he would look at her mother, and she'd never intended to settle for anything less.

Unfortunately, she had no choice. Uncle Robert had threatened to put her out of his house if she didn't accept the proposal of Mr. John Wendell, a heavy-handed cad, if the plethora of gossip around the city was to be believed.

She'd railed at her uncle, despite her better judgment, but it had all been for naught. The ultimatum still stood: she was to marry Mr. Wendell, or find herself homeless and penniless within the same hour of his proposal.

And so she sat across from him now, waiting for the wretched words to spew forth from his lips.

Mr. Wendell was an attractive man, for sure—tall and strong with chiseled features. His wavy, golden blonde hair could deceive one into thinking he was little more than a boy, despite his thirty-one years.

"The weather is unusually warm for this time of year, Miss Kenleigh," Mr. Wendell commented, his attention returning to settle directly on her.

"Indeed, it is." Did he think she was incapable of discussing a topic more intelligent than the state of the weather?

"Would you care to take a walk through your uncle's garden with me?"

Tension knotted in the pit of her stomach. She searched the room for some plausible excuse—*any* excuse.

"I daresay the garden is not so large that we will ever be out of your uncle's watchful gaze," he supplied quickly, presuming her hesitancy arose from the impropriety of their being alone together.

"As you wish, Mr. Wendell." She heaved a heavy sigh. There was no excuse or escape to be found, and therefore, no sense in prolonging the inevitable. She'd wracked her brain since she'd stormed away from her uncle yesterday morning, each time coming back to the same conclusion: he had her trapped.

But this wasn't so difficult, was it? She'd spent three years caring for the injured, the maimed, the ill and the dying. Certainly, she could force herself to endure *this*. She wouldn't worry about what came next; how the next few moments would tie her irrevocably to a man she barely knew and couldn't help but despise.

She would only focus on these next few moments, forcing herself to put one foot in front of the other, and when the time came, forcing the wretched words of acceptance past her lips.

She rose and Mr. Wendell was there, wrapping her arm around his, leading them to the foyer and outside.

He didn't say a word as they walked around the property to the vast spread of gardens behind the house, and a flicker of hope flitted through her mind. *Perhaps he wanted nothing more than to stretch his legs.* Even a few minutes trapped in the same room as her uncle left her feeling caged like an animal, in need of escape. Mr. Wendell may have been no more immune to her uncle's cloistering presence than she was.

A moment passed, and then another, and her hopes rose higher. *Uncle Robert had completely misinterpreted Mr. Wendell's intentions; what a relief!*

"Miss Kenleigh," he startled her from her inner thoughts. "There is something I would very much like to ask you."

Drat! She'd been foolish to hope, to cling to the inane possibility that her uncle had been wrong.

She forced her gaze to meet his as he came to a halt next to the pink-shell azaleas. Though little more than buds so early in the spring, in just a few weeks, the trusses of pink and white flowers would be in full bloom. Would she be there to see them, or would her uncle insist on speeding her to the altar?

"I have spoken to your uncle, and with his blessing, I would like for you to become my wife."

No words of love. Of course there weren't; she and Mr.

Wendell were barely more than acquaintances. She was nothing more than a pretty face with a sizeable dowry—a rarity in these modern times—and a lineage replete with English peers.

Her throat was dry, so much that when she opened her mouth, no words came out. But this was what she needed to do to survive. She'd never been a coward before, and she would not let her uncle reduce her to such pathetic behavior. "Yes, I will marry you, Mr. Wendell."

"Excellent!" His eyes roamed over her while revulsion rose high in her throat.

All her hopes and dreams were dashed on the rocks in a single moment. She would never know the kind of love her mother and father had shared. It was all gone.

****

Mary awoke swiftly, the frightening images of her nightmare following her out of slumber. The same images had haunted her from her first day at the hospital in Virginia. So much pain and suffering, and no matter how she tried, she could not relieve it all.

She drew in a deep breath as she wiped the sweat from her brow. Her friends had thought her foolish, volunteering as a nurse when they'd all hidden away from what was going on around them.

She'd felt inclined to agree with them that first day. Walking into the triage area amid a group of new nurses, so much of her had been tempted to turn around and run all the way home. But a young man had caught her attention as she'd stood there trying to recall the merits of her decision to volunteer as a nurse.

"Help me," he'd called. "Help me, please," he'd cried again, staring directly into her eyes.

And that was precisely what she'd done, springing to action and doing what she could to bring down the man's raging fever. He'd lost an arm on the battlefield the day prior, and fever had already begun to rage in his body.

Not once did she question her decision again after that, not even two days later when the young man succumbed to his fever. Three years later, she could still remember his face so clearly, etched in her mind along with the face of every other soldier she'd cared for in her three years at the hospital.

A sudden knock at her door made her jump, pulling her away from her nightmare, though she knew it wouldn't be far away for long. It would be there to greet her again that night, just like it had almost every night since she'd returned to her uncle's home.

"Good morning, Miss." The bright and cheery middle-aged woman smiled to her as she entered the room, expertly balancing a heavy tray.

"Good morning, Margaret," she greeted in return, banishing her memories to the back of her mind where she kept them most of the time.

The pungent aroma of coffee wafted through the room and served to expel the final remnants of sleep. She always did prefer coffee to her uncle's tea, though it was rather unladylike of her, in his opinion.

"Your uncle's bustlin' about this mornin', so I thought you might like your breakfast here," Margaret informed her, though it wasn't necessary. Mary ate breakfast in her room most days, preferring the quiet solitude to her uncle's company.

She pulled herself upright in bed as the woman settled the tray on her lap. Breakfast looked the same as it did most mornings and she ignored it for the moment, turning her attention to sweeten the coffee, and then downing a hefty swallow of the strong brew.

Unlike most mornings, there was a newspaper folded on the tray and she peered at it curiously. Of course she could read, but ever since the war, she'd had no interest in the goings-on of society. Bad news tended to fill the pages of the local papers, and she had no use for any more of that than was necessary. So, it was rather unlike Margaret to include a crisp, fresh copy of the newspaper with her breakfast.

"I won't be needing this, Margaret, but I thank you for the breakfast."

"You never know what good news might be waitin' for you, Miss Mary," the woman replied with a mischievous grin.

Mary couldn't help but smile back, despite having no idea what Margaret was up to. "And how can you be so certain of that, may I ask?"

Margaret's face turned solemn, all traces of mischief gone from her expression in an instant. "I can't deny that I overheard you talkin' with your uncle the other mornin', and I saw you and Mr. Wendell in the garden yesterday afternoon. If I'm not mistaken, that uncle of yours has left you in a mighty...uncomfortable situation."

Margaret was silent then, either waiting for confirmation, or for Mary to tell her it was none of her business. But Mary couldn't do that. Though not family, Margaret had been there since Mary's birth, hired by her parents as Mary's nurse, and the woman had stayed with her all these years.

Since the death of her parents, she was grateful for Margaret's presence in her life. While her uncle was cruel and devious, Margaret was kind and sincere. Mary had always been able to turn to her for comfort and compassion when her uncle was at his worst. She would have already told Margaret about her uncle's ultimatum and the resultant betrothal, but she hadn't wanted to speak the words aloud yet. As if somehow by saying nothing, some small part of her could delay the reality of her situation.

"You aren't mistaken, Margaret. I'm afraid it is as you say."

Margaret was quiet for another moment, the expression on her face one of grave contemplation as if she were trying to deduce the lesser of two evils.

"You know I've only ever wanted what's best for you; that I've never acted against your best interests."

"I know that, and I've been absolutely blessed to have you here with me, Margaret." While true, what in heavens did that have to do with a newspaper?

"The newspaper...it has advertisements in it that I thought might be of interest to you."

Mary raised an eyebrow, curious about the woman's meaning.

"Marriage ads," Margaret filled in quickly.

Marriage ads? She'd heard of them, matrimonial advertisements from men out west looking for brides back east. But Mary's problem wasn't that she couldn't find a husband—she didn't *want* one.

"You do realize, Margaret, that I've been saddled with a fiancé already? What need have I for another?"

Margaret shifted uncomfortably, and Mary could see her mind working, trying to choose her words carefully. Suddenly, her expression changed, and Mary watched as all pretenses fell away.

"Mary, I've loved you like you were my own child, and I can't stand the idea of my dear child bein' married to that evil rake."

"Margaret!" Had the woman ever spoken so harshly in her life?

"I'm sorry, but it's true. Gossip isn't always right, I know that, but I know in my heart that this Mr. Wendell is a scoundrel of the worst kind."

Mary would protest, but she felt the same way. She was quite certain John Wendell didn't have an honorable bone in his body. "And how do you suppose..."

She closed her mouth suddenly, realizing what Margaret was up to. Margaret was trying to provide her with a way to escape both her uncle and Mr. Wendell. All she had to do was marry a man she'd never met in the west. Of course, that also entailed leaving Boston and Margaret behind, and there was no way to know if what she would find out west would be any better than the future that awaited her here.

"You can't possibly be serious, Margaret."

"I've given it a lot of thought, and I am. I am certain you have a much greater chance of findin' happiness there than you do here."

While she'd never consider the idea on her own, it seemed Margaret felt there was great merit to it. Was it possible these marriage ads were the answer to her prayers?

Rolling the idea over in her head, she dismissed it quickly. There was one large problem that hampered the possibility, even if she were to consider it.

"Uncle Robert will want this wedding to come to pass as quickly as possible." She was half-surprised she hadn't woken up to the pastor awaiting her in the parlor to speak her vows that morning.

"So, my dear, you will simply have to convince him to put it off long enough for you to get yourself a proposal from one of these young men," she said with the mischievous light returning to her eyes.

It was possible...if she could find some way to delay her uncle. And his one weakness may be just the thing. If she could convince him an elaborate wedding behooved his social standing, it wouldn't be difficult to convince him that the intricacies of planning a wedding were significant and time-consuming.

She glanced at the newspaper in front of her, realizing just then that the paper had been conveniently folded to present the matrimonial ads right there for her perusal. She scanned through the ads:

"A respectable bachelor, fifty-five years of age, desires to immediately marry a charming young lady between sixteen and twenty-one years of age with skin like alabaster and eyes the color of the ocean..."

She rolled her eyes and moved onto the next.

"Refined, healthy man of 45 years wishes to correspond with an attractive and domesticated young lady with a view of matrimony..."

Scanning through the ads, the small ember of hope was squelched quickly. Every man was in search of a pretty, young girl, less than half his age—no doubt docile and brainless, too. She'd always been told she was pretty, but she was anything but docile, and suddenly, she felt like an old maid at twenty-three years of age.

She sighed. "Margaret, I'm afraid none of these gentlemen offer much more promise than Mr. Wendell."

"Just one, Miss Mary. This one." She pointed to an advertisement further down the page.

"A young man, twenty-eight years of age, in search of an intelligent and amiable woman with whom to share a quiet and happy life. What I lack in fortune, I make up for aplenty with a warm heart..."

"You are an intelligent and amiable woman, if ever there was one, Miss Mary. And even though this one won't be able to provide for you as well as your Mr. Wendell, I've never known you to be a woman obsessed with riches."

She read over the brief advertisement again, and then again. Was it possible this man was the solution to her problem? Margaret was right; wealth had never compelled her to consider one suitor over another, despite the obligations her uncle felt she had to the Kenleigh name. But to leave Boston, travel across the country and tie herself to a man she'd never met?

Perhaps it was crazy enough that it just might work.

And with that thought, the cooling embers of her shredded hope reignited. While it was natural to fear the unknown, in this case, it was difficult to imagine the unknown being worse than the certainty of the bleak future with Mr. Wendell.

Now, all she had to do was convince the man in the advertisement to choose her above any other young lady who responded to his advertisement. The truth of her situation was hardly the stuff that would make a gentleman leap to an offer of marriage. No, if she was going to go through with this, she'd have to present herself in the most appealing light possible. Her father used to tell her the most outrageous and silly stories when she was a child; how difficult could it be to concoct one of her own?

"Margaret, I believe I have a letter to write," she stated resolutely before she changed her mind. "And," she added as Margaret nodded and started toward the door with her mischievous smile firmly in place, "may I be assured of your discretion in this matter?"

"Of course, Miss Mary. I'll deliver your letters myself."

All that was left was writing the letter, filling it with enough fable to win an offer of matrimony.

"Dear Sir," she began.

"I am writing to you in response to your advertisement in the matrimonial news section of the Boston newspaper. I was most pleased to discover a gentleman in search of an intelligent and affable young lady, and I look forward to meeting such a unique and respectable character.

My name is Tessa Jenkins. I am a librarian in the city of Boston, where I've spent my entire life amid a warm and loving family. But I fear it is not in Boston where I was destined to find a match. You see, as captivating as the city may be, I have always longed for a quieter existence..."

On and on, she continued, filling one page and then another. From her name and occupation to the current state of her familial relations, so many of the things she had written were blatant lies, but it couldn't be helped. Not if she hoped to escape her current situation.

She re-read the letter to herself, folded it carefully and slipped it into the envelope Margaret had provided. As if the woman was born with a sixth sense, she returned to collect the letter mere seconds after Mary had placed it on the tray on her lap.

"I'll see that this letter gets on its way this very mornin', Miss Mary." She paused briefly as a flicker of doubt passed through her amber-colored eyes. "That is, if you're certain..."

"I can assure you, Margaret, that I am positively *uncertain* about this, which is why I need you to take this letter and deliver it now before I change my mind."

She offered a tremulous smile—it was the best she could muster at the moment. Lying to a man she'd never met in order to obtain a proposal of marriage was surely something no young woman would feel certain about. It was devious and selfish—the most selfish thing she'd ever done, in fact—but it was the only way to escape the inevitable misery that would accompany a marriage to Mr. Wendell. Once safely out of the reach of his heavy hand, she would find a way to make amends for the wrong she was about to commit.

****

Alone in her uncle's library, Mary read the man's reply.

"Dear Miss Jenkins," she whispered the words aloud.

Several weeks had passed since Margaret had delivered the deceitful letter on her behalf, and she had all but given up hope of a response. With a nervous flutter in her stomach, she continued to read.

"I was genuinely pleased to receive your letter. I imagine, as a librarian, you possess an avid interest in books, and I thoroughly share that same affection for the written word.

I am familiar with the excitement the city has to offer, having grown up in Portland, Maine, but I must confess, it pales in comparison to the serene tranquility and the unpainted landscape of the west..."

Perhaps Margaret's idea hadn't been so bad. The man was eloquent, shared her love for reading and he painted a compelling picture of life out west. She continued to read, and the moment she finished the letter, she sat down to write her reply while a combination of relief and anxiousness mingled in her veins. It was a relief that the man had taken interest in her, but it may still be for naught. Her uncle had agreed to a late-August wedding, but with the time it took for her correspondence to reach the frontiersman, and for his to reach her in return, she worried she would not garner a marriage proposal in time. Still, she had to try.

But what was she to write? Should she tell Caleb Knight how very accustomed she was to hard labor? That she'd toiled relentlessly, day and night, for nearly three years in the Fairfax Street Hospital? That since her parents had died, she'd been more of a prisoner in her uncle's home than a lady of leisure?

No, she shouldn't tell him any of it. There was too much risk he'd be repulsed by her work as a nurse during the war, and she'd already told him hers was a happy and loving family. It was better to stick to the neat and tidy life she imagined belonging to a librarian.

Closing her eyes and praying that, one day, she might find a way to be forgiven for her transgression, she allowed her pen to float across the blank page in front of her, filling it with more of the same lies and deceptions she'd written in the first.

She didn't read it over when she was finished; she was painfully aware of every fib and falsehood she'd written. Stuffing the letter into an envelope, she went off to find Margaret once again before she could change her mind.

The pattern continued, waiting anxiously for Mr. Knight's responses and then guiltily scrawling whatever stories would speed him toward the end she sought. First one exchange, and then another, and then one more. Each letter she wrote made her feel worse than the one before it. Caleb Knight was kind and courteous with a gentle nature and a sense of humor; at least, that was what she'd come to learn from his letters.

She was doing what she had to do to survive; she knew that, but every word became more difficult to write, her conscience slowing her hand more and more.

The last lie she'd written had been the most difficult. She'd been in the middle of an enthusiastic sentence, writing that she was very much looking forward to bettering their acquaintance, when her conscience had nearly stopped her hand entirely. It was one thing to lie on paper, but quite another to imagine coming face to face with the man, pretending to be the woman she'd concocted.

But she'd already started down this path; she wouldn't turn back now.

****

Time flew by more quickly than it ever had before, and every minute that passed tightened the knot in her stomach a little more. With just two weeks remaining until her impending wedding, Mary waited anxiously for Mr. Knight's latest response, both hoping for and dreading a proposal at the same time.

And then it came.

Margaret handed her the envelope, the woman's own hands shaking. They were both well aware there would be no time for more correspondence. If there was no proposal written in the letter in her hand, her marriage to Mr. Wendell would be inevitable.

"Aren't you goin' to open it, Miss Mary?" Margaret prodded anxiously.

Always before, Margaret had delivered the letters from Mr. Knight and then proceeded to leave her alone to read the correspondence in private. This time, Margaret fidgeted nervously beside her, her eyes transfixed on the envelope as if she could see through it, or influence the words written on the page if she stared at it long enough.

Taking a deep breath, Mary opened the envelope carefully, painfully aware that the thin slip of paper inside would decide the course of her future.

"Dear Tessa," he began more informally than he had addressed her before.

She scanned through the brief paragraph of courtesies and trivial conversation. Though she couldn't help but smile at his quick wit, her heart sunk a little more with every sentence.

But there, in the last paragraph on the page:

"I hope you don't find it too forward of me, but we began our correspondence with a mutual interest in a matrimonial end. Through your letters, I have learned that you are a quiet and gentle woman; a woman I believe would be happy here with me. I hope you have come to see the potential for a favorable match as well. It is my pleasure then to ask you, Tessa Jenkins, if you would do me the great honor of consenting to be my wife..."

The letter fell from her fingertips and fluttered to the floor.

Someone wanted her for *her*, not for the dowry she could bring them, the lineage of peers from which she descended, or the attractiveness of her features. Caleb wanted to marry *her*.

Except...Caleb Knight didn't want Mary Kenleigh. He knew absolutely nothing about Mary.

Caleb wanted Tessa Jenkins...the woman she'd concocted from thin air, and the woman she would have to become to escape John Wendell.

Margaret's gaze darted back and forth between Mary and the paper on the floor, and tears welled in the woman's eyes. "I'm so sorry, Miss Mary. I should never have suggested this route...If I'd just kept my mouth shut..."

"He proposed, Margaret," she whispered.

"Oh child, that's wonderful!" Margaret hugged her tightly while Mary's arms remained frozen at her sides. "But, then, why do you seem so distraught?" She pulled back and looked at her intently.

Margaret had no idea what Mary had written in those letters; that she hadn't written an ounce of truth in all their correspondence. "I suppose it's all just so overwhelming." It wasn't a complete lie.

"Are you havin' second thoughts, Miss Mary? You don't have to go through with this."

Yes, she did. She'd made up her mind before she'd written a single word to Caleb Knight. "Of course I'm not having second thoughts. This is exactly what I've been hoping for. I just..." she hesitated, swallowing against a lump in her throat. "I just know this means I won't have you there with me."

It wasn't untrue. It was a fact she'd been deliberately avoiding since Margaret had proposed the idea. She would be leaving behind the only person who had been a staple in her life; the only person in the world who cared about her. But from what she'd heard, Mr. Wendell treated his house staff no better than he treated the women in his company. She was doing Margaret a favor by not making the woman choose that sort of life in order to stay close to her.

She bent to retrieve the letter on the floor, and then stood, straightening her shoulders, knowing this was the best course of action for the both of them.

"It's all right, Miss Mary. You'll see. God willin', we'll be reunited again," Margaret crooned soothingly. "You get yourself settled there with your new husband, and maybe I'll come join you. This old woman could use a little adventure, don't you think?"

Mary smiled. Whether the woman spoke the truth or not, she had to believe it was so. It would make what she had to do that much easier to bear.

Returning the letter to the envelope, her fingers touched upon something inside, something she hadn't noticed before. But she saw it there now—the passage to her future.

On the hope that she—Tessa Jenkins—would accept his proposal, Caleb had included the ticket that would bring her to him. It wasn't a ticket for a train, which could require multiple stops and a long and uncomfortable wagon ride to her destination.

Caleb Knight had paid for her passage from Boston to California by clipper, the fastest sailing ship she'd ever heard of. With the ticket was a note explaining that a single ship would sail her from Boston, around Cape Horn and directly to San Francisco, where he would be waiting for her when she arrived. He'd gone to the trouble—and no doubt, the great expense—of making the trip as comfortable as possible for her.

But one more piece of information stood out to her: the date she was to sail. It glared at her from the page and made her stomach knot painfully.

Her wedding day.

The ship was scheduled to leave the same day she was expected at the altar.

She couldn't possibly do it. She'd be a fool to try. How on earth could she set sail for a new life in California at the exact same time she was to be married to John Wendell?

"Margaret…" Her voice was barely a whisper, "the ship sails rather close to my impending wedding," she forced the words out, holding back just how close it was.

"Oh."

That was it? All Margaret had to say was 'oh'? It seemed anti-climactic in comparison to the crushing defeat roiling within her.

"I suppose you'll just have to make a quick getaway, won't you, dear? Just imagine the look on Mr. Wendell's attractive face when he realizes he's been left by his bride so close to the wedding."

An image of the arrogant Mr. Wendell appeared in her mind,

a look of stunned outrage marring his handsome features while he stood at the altar alone. A bubble of laughter rose from within, and Mary pressed a hand against her lips to contain it. Perhaps it was the rise and fall of too many emotions in the past several weeks, because there should be nothing humorous about the situation. If she didn't make a clean escape, she had no doubt Mr. Wendell would make her pay dearly for the indignation she'll have caused him.

So, she would just have to make sure her escape was flawless, nary a telltale sign to lead them on her trail. Margaret already knew far too much, and she felt guilt for putting the woman in a position that required her to lie, but she couldn't undo that now. All she could do was ensure Margaret had no more information that could force her further into that uncomfortable position. It would also be helpful when there was a modicum of truth in her words when she told Mr. Wendell and her uncle that she had no idea Mary would go running off the morning of her wedding.

Chapter 2

This was a mistake. Caleb knew he'd made a terrible mistake. What had he been thinking? Tessa Jenkins sounded lovely, but he wasn't interested in *lovely*. In fact, he would prefer her to be stern and humorless, or young and brainless.

No, that wasn't true. He couldn't stand the thought of a foolish woman wandering about his home.

But he'd rather she didn't share his love of reading or his quest for a quiet life far away from inquisitive eyes. In her letters, she'd seemed kind and compassionate with a hidden strength he couldn't quite put his finger on. It was nothing she said in particular, but rather the tone of her words. It was a characteristic he found admirable in a woman, so often brought up to consider herself the weaker sex.

But what he thought of Tessa didn't matter. He needed a nanny, not a wife. Unfortunately, there was no hope of finding the former. He'd tried, but without the promise of matrimony, it seemed there was no woman of decent character willing to make the trek out west. And since there was no way he could ensure Adam's safety and his own back east, out west was where he had to stay.

He stood at the docks, watching the smooth-sailing clipper pulling into the port. It would have been better if he'd come alone. He would have had the entire length of the ride back to his house to break the news to her gently. But there was no one he was comfortable leaving Adam with, and so this particular surprise would have to be thrust upon the young woman rather abruptly.

At least it was rather unlikely she'd turn around and re-board the clipper; it wasn't sailing back to New England anytime soon. In fact, it was bound for a month and a half-long trek to Hong Kong before it would return. He'd scheduled the trip carefully, making sure she'd be forced to give him a chance. Well, he didn't care one way or another if she gave him a chance, but the two weeks before the next vessel would set sail for New England should be more than enough time for a young woman to fall helplessly in love with Adam.

The ship dropped anchor a few moments later and Caleb squinted his eyes to see the passengers as they began to disembark. He could have moved closer, but he felt more comfortable here, watching from a distance to see if he could pinpoint the young woman by the description she'd given. It hadn't been much—she was tall for a woman with auburn hair and pale green eyes.

He'd never cared for redheads. The brassy orange of their hair reminded him more of rust than anything else, but again, it didn't matter. She wasn't for him; she was for Adam.

Unfortunately, the few women that left the ship all had bonnets and hats covering their heads, so it was difficult to tell which one might be the woman he'd been writing to for months.

But then he found her. One errant lock of fiery red escaped the tall, slim woman's bonnet and he knew in an instant it was her.

He also knew that he'd never again think of redheads the same way.

The wayward strands that would not be tucked back inside her bonnet—no matter how hard she tried—were not the color of rust. No, they were the vivid red of the autumn leaves in Portland, Maine.

He sorely missed autumn in New England, the most beautiful landscape nature provided. But it seemed Tessa Jenkins had brought a piece of that landscape directly to him.

He watched as she finished her descent and then stood still, looking back and forth amid the crowd. He didn't move for a moment, but quite quickly, he realized he wasn't the only one paying attention to the auburn-haired beauty standing alone on the docks.

Taking Adam's hand, he hurried through the crowd before any one of the less-than-gentlemanly men there gave her a poor first impression of California, or worse, one of the discerning men there sweet-talked her into accepting a different offer of marriage.

"Miss Jenkins," he called from several yards away just as a seedy looking fellow started toward her. The man backed off quickly as he caught sight of Caleb's solid, intimidating frame. The woman turned her head toward the direction of his voice, and Caleb came face to face with the most vivid green eyes he'd ever seen. They weren't pale as she'd described; they were like crystal, and it made him angry.

Of course that was irrational, but he didn't want her to be lovely, or strong, or beautiful, or to have the most captivating eyes he'd ever seen. He didn't want her to appear flawless but for a small scar on her neck that wouldn't have been noticeable but for how it stood in stark contrast to her perfection. He wanted a woman to care for Adam, and nothing more. This marriage was to be one of convenience and nothing else.

He chanced a glance down at Adam who clung loosely to his hand, and wasn't pleased to see the boy smiling brightly at the woman. Of course, that was ridiculous, too. It should have pleased him immensely that Adam was immediately impressed with her. He wasn't thinking logically and that had to stop. He'd lied through his teeth to convince the young woman to come all this way because he needed help, because Adam needed a mother figure. Glaring at the young woman wasn't going to help his cause. He needed to convince her to stay—despite the fact she had no idea he had a child, nor that the child was to be her sole responsibility.

"Good day, Miss Jenkins. I'm Caleb Knight," he greeted her cordially, which seemed almost as ridiculous as his irrational displeasure over Adam's smile. He'd offered to marry this woman, addressed her by her given name in his letter, and learned a great deal about her over the past several months through their correspondence. And yet, she was suddenly Miss Jenkins once again.

"Good day, Mr. Knight." She smiled warily as her gaze darted back and forth between him and the boy at his side.

Alright; this was it. "Miss Jenkins, may I present to you Adam Knight. My son."

Panic flashed in her beautiful eyes, but she seemed to cover it up quickly. Right there on the docks, she lowered herself down to Adam's level and held out her hand to him.

"Good day, Adam. It's a pleasure to meet you."

The boy's grin grew wider and a tiny giggle escaped his lips as he slipped his small hand within the woman's grasp. "Good day, Miss Jenkins," he replied, his clarity of speech impressive for a boy only four years of age.

She rose to her full height, and he realized she hadn't been kidding when she'd said she was tall for a woman. Though not as tall as Caleb, her eyes were level with his chin whereas most females barely made it to his shoulders. He liked that she was tall, that she would need only to tilt her chin upward for him to sweep in for a kiss.

Dash it all! What was he thinking? This first meeting was going even more poorly than he'd expected, and mostly because the lovely Tessa Jenkins was the one surprising him at every turn.

"It seems we have a great deal to discuss, Mr. Knight. Might I suggest we make our way from the docks?"

"Are you certain you wish to accompany me?" he asked, though why on earth he'd pause to give her the out was beyond him, particularly when he'd gone to great lengths to ensure she would have to give Adam a chance to woo her heart. He hadn't known the woman a full two minutes and already she was making him forget himself—and his purpose for being there. A nanny for Adam; that was all he wanted.

"Yes, well, it seems the ship on which I arrived will not be returning to New England any time soon," she noted with an undercurrent of accusation in her deceptively light tone.

He tried to smile, but no doubt, his chagrin marred the attempt.

"Are you going to come home with us, Miss Jenkins?" Adam piped up enthusiastically, still too young for decorum and too innocent to recognize the tension that hung in the air between them.

"I do believe that is the plan." She smiled brightly as she spoke to Adam.

And then she turned to him, still wearing the bright smile, though he noticed it had lost some of its authenticity now that it was pointed in his direction. "I wonder at the propriety of the arrangement, Mr. Knight. Should there not be a chaperone to accompany us?"

He'd considered that, and though propriety wasn't as much of a concern in the west, he knew it was vastly important back home, particularly for a young lady. "There is a second building on my property, not much more than a shack, but I would be content to make myself at home there, Miss Knight, until you feel comfortable...moving forward. Or else, we might stop by the church on our way. I have spoken with the pastor and he knows of our situation—"

"Yes, I suppose that would be best," she answered a little too quickly. He'd surprised her with a child, and she was still eager to proceed? She wasn't even going to take advantage of the time he was offering her to become better acquainted with him or Adam? Was it possible for this woman to have been swayed so much by his inventive letters, or did Miss Jenkins have other reasons to tie herself to him so quickly? And if she did, would that stop him?

He'd gone in search of a caregiver for his son, so it made no difference to him what secrets she kept hidden from him, but if there was any chance her secrets could put Adam in danger, then the arrangement was unacceptable.

He eyed her speculatively, trying to ignore her delicate features and looking past them to the woman beneath. He'd learned the hard way to trust his gut when it came to sizing up a person. There was no maliciousness lurking in her crystal eyes. There was pain and guilt, both intense enough that he was half-surprised they hadn't swallowed her up. But no, he was quite certain no evil creature was hiding deep within her. And that was enough for him.

"Very well, then allow me to escort you, Miss Jenkins." He motioned in the direction of his carriage several yards away, and she hesitated for only the briefest of moments before she started in its direction.

Within the hour, he would be a wedded man, and Adam would have a woman to care for him.

Chapter 3

Not two hours had passed since she had stepped off the boat, and she was married. A married woman. And apparently married to a man who already had a child—though he hadn't mentioned a word of it in all the letters he'd written.

She'd been tempted to turn around and get back on the ship bound for Hong Kong the moment he'd introduced her to the adorable, young boy—or at the very least, berate the man for his deception—but she'd held her tongue. Who was she to reproach Caleb Knight when she hadn't been honest about a single detail of her life? At least there was a decent chance 'Caleb Knight' was the man's real name.

And then, when he'd proposed, they proceeded with the wedding that very day, she couldn't turn him down. Once she was married, there was absolutely nothing John Wendell could do— even if he did somehow manage to discover her location.

Still, all of a sudden, she found herself with a husband and four-year-old boy, and she couldn't help but wonder what else he'd been less than forthcoming about. Had his letters been filled with as many blatant lies as hers? Could he be just as much of a scoundrel as John Wendell?

No.

Of course, there was no way for her to know for certain, but her intuition told her Caleb Knight was not a bad man. Though he held himself aloof, it was impossible not to see the love that shone in his eyes when he interacted with his son. How bad could a man be if he cared for his child so thoroughly?

The carriage slowed and she saw a house come into view just up ahead. It wasn't at all what she'd been expecting. He'd spoken of a simple existence and meager accommodations in his letters, but the house that stood in front of her was beautiful. It was perhaps only a third of the size of her uncle's manor, but there was a plethora of windows, and the decorative woodwork lent an air of welcome to the home.

"I do not believe you did the house justice in your letters, Mr. Knight. It's beautiful."

They hadn't spoken a word to each other since speaking their vows in the church. She'd had no idea what to say, and his thoughts seemed to have taken him elsewhere. Even now, he glanced over at her, but it took a moment for her words to register.

"Thank you," he murmured and then returned his attention to the road in front of him.

No one could accuse the man of idle chatter. Perhaps, like her, his thoughts had turned to the evening ahead of them. She'd never been a married woman before, but she knew enough about it to know what was expected of her on her wedding night. Her stomach churned at the thought, but she thrust the thoughts from her mind.

Less than two minutes later, he came to a halt in front of the house and descended from the carriage without a word. Adam had fallen asleep next to her sometime after leaving the church, and his small head rested against her ribs while his hands rested in her lap. She gathered him up as carefully as she could, but before she could stand, Caleb was there, bending down to relieve her of the weight in her arms.

"I'll bring him to bed and then return to collect your things. Feel free to take a look around," he told her. His voice was little more than a whisper next to her ear, and a shiver raced down her spine. She nearly gasped aloud in response. What on earth was that?

But already he stood towering over her, looking at her with an expression she couldn't decipher. He turned away a moment later and stepped down, balancing Adam in one arm easily. She rose and hesitantly took the hand he offered up to her. As she alit from the carriage, she deliberately ignored the tingling sensation that originated where he touched her and traveled up her arm.

He strode ahead, inside the house and she followed slowly, taking in the sight of the man in front of her. Though she had no idea what to expect, she could not have anticipated the man who had come to collect her from the docks. He was tall and broad-shouldered, with dark hair and piercing blue eyes. She had no doubt, had they been in Boston, Mr. Knight could have had his choice of any of the fine ladies there.

He disappeared inside the house and she turned her attention to her surroundings. The scenery was so different from New England, and yet it held its own appeal. It was warm and fresh, untouched in comparison to the busy streets of Boston.

She hesitated once more as she reached the threshold. This was her home now; she was a married woman. She had deceived this man into believing she was someone she wasn't, and he'd made her his bride. Relief and guilt flooded her together, guilt nearly overshadowing every ounce of relief. She'd taken advantage of a man and his young son in her selfish need to escape John Wendell, but what could she do about that now? Confess and wait for Caleb to ship her back where she belonged? No. She would find a way to make up for her wrongs because she couldn't go back now.

"Are you hungry, Miss Je—Mrs. Knight?" he corrected himself as he shot her a curious glance.

She was still standing at the threshold, trying to force her feet to carry her inside.

"There's nothing prepared, certainly nothing one would count as a wedding feast, but I'm sure we could put something together," he offered, still eyeing her curiously.

"I'm fine, thank you."

"Of course. You've probably had a very long day and are anxious to get to bed," he surmised.

She had been tired just seconds ago, but suddenly, she was fully alert. It was their wedding night, and she was not ready to consummate their marriage whatsoever. "Actually, I am a bit hungry. If you'll show me where the kitchen is..."

He smiled knowingly and it looked like he was struggling not to laugh. "You do realize you'll have to come inside if you'd like me to direct you to the kitchen. I suppose I could give you directions from out there, and you can try slipping in one of the windows..."

"No, of course that won't be necessary." With a deep breath, she forced her feet to do what they'd been unwilling to do thus far, and in the blink of an eye, she was inside Caleb's home. *Her* home.

"There, that wasn't so bad, was it?" he asked, still smiling.

"Yes, well, it isn't often that I'm left unchaperoned in the company of a man."

"I can see that," he bit back another peal of laughter. "But I'm not just any man, now am I? I believe it isn't the least bit improper for a young bride to be left alone in the company of her husband. In fact, I believe the impropriety would come if a man and his bride weren't afforded any privacy. Wouldn't you agree?"

The meaning of his words hit her quickly. "Mr. Knight!" He looked ready with another quip on his tongue, so she circumvented it in a hurry, "I believe you were going to show me the way to the kitchen," she reminded him.

His smile fell away and his expression was stern. "Yes, you are correct," he motioned to the hall at his left, and she followed. She wasn't unfamiliar with the domestic chores of cooking and cleaning—something she'd done more than once as part of her duties as a nurse.

Their conversation turned to California's weather as they ate and she was amazed at the differences. She hadn't once considered that she might rarely again see a snowfall when she'd set out from Boston.

"You must be tired, Tessa," he commented again when the meal was finished.

There seemed to be no other excuse to delay the inevitable. "Yes, I believe I am," she said behind her hand as she stifled a yawn.

"I'll show you to the bedroom," he told her, staring at the empty plate in front of him.

She nodded, though she didn't know why since he wasn't looking at her. But he stood up and strode across the room without a backward glance. She followed...because what else could she do? It only took a moment to reach the bedroom door, and she placed her hands over her stomach, as if the action could somehow calm the butterflies that fluttered inside.

"If you have need of anything, I'll be in the room next door—Adam's room. Otherwise, I trust I will see you in the morning." He nodded to her curtly and left her there at his bedroom door while he turned into the room next to it.

A flurry of confusion assailed her—and she wasn't easily prone to confusion. They'd just gotten married, and yet, on their wedding night, her groom intended to sleep in a different room? Was he being kind, giving her a chance to settle in and get to know him? It would be sweet of him, except she didn't get that impression. His words had a finality hidden in his tone. He wasn't leaving her alone on this night in particular; he was announcing what was to happen that night and every night after—absolutely nothing.

Chapter 4

Caleb moved about the kitchen quietly, trying to avoid waking the woman who'd become his wife just a few short hours ago. He was putting off the conversation that would come inevitably once she was awake. He'd seen the look of confusion on Tessa's face when he'd left her standing outside his bedroom. He could hope she'd simply fall into the kind of easy, uncomplicated existence he'd intended for them, but he'd be a fool. If she was the kind of woman who went with the flow of things, she wouldn't be there now, uprooting herself from her loving and comfortable existence in New England for whatever unknown promises were to be found with him in the west.

Every hour that passed left him thinking more and more that he had absolutely no idea what he'd gotten himself into. Finding a wife in order to garner a caregiver for Adam had seemed perfectly reasonable at first. But now, with a beautiful wife in his home, he questioned his former logic.

"Good morning," a gentle voice spoke from the doorway behind him.

He turned abruptly, jarred from his thoughts. It had been some time since a woman had been there to greet him in the morning, and it disturbed him—more because he liked it than anything else.

"I wanted to speak with you before Adam woke up..." she began, her tone hesitant.

"Yes, of course," he replied, though the last thing he wanted at the moment was a conversation. Was she going to inform him that she intended to annul their marriage and return home? Would she inquire about his intentions for their relationship as husband and wife? Would she grill him about the unexpected presence of his son? Though he should have been prepared for any one of them, when she hadn't broached the topics the night prior, he had hoped to put off the battle this morning—at least until he'd had his morning coffee.

"Why did you not tell me you had a son?" she asked softly, though there was none of the accusation in her tone that he would have expected.

"I did not lie to you about Adam. I simply failed to mention him in our communications." An omission of this magnitude was just as severe as a lie, but it seemed his plan was to emphasize the difference.

"That is true."

That was it? No woman would accept such a pathetic shell of an excuse unless...she could understand all too well one's motivations for lies and omissions. Tessa was definitely hiding something of her own. As much as he couldn't help but to wonder what secret the fiery beauty was keeping, he wouldn't ask, at least not yet. He'd expected a thorough inquisition, if not an outright battle, over Adam. He would consider himself lucky to have avoided it, and leave it at that. There was, however, one topic he felt compelled to discuss—for his own best interest as well as hers.

"Tessa, now that you know about Adam, I believe there is one more thing you should know."

She looked up at him and nodded, waiting expectantly, but he could see the connections she was making by the look in her eyes. She was most certainly intelligent, and that pleased him far more than he was willing to admit, and it wasn't the time for such observations even if he was.

At the moment, there was no point in being anything but blunt. He owed her that much. "I haven't any need for a wife; I have need for a mother for my son."

"As you wish, Mr. Knight," she replied more quickly than he'd expected, but he could see the shock of both pain and relief in her gaze, though she worked to cover up the emotions in her expressive eyes. "If you'd be kind enough to tell me what is expected, I believe I will prove to be a worthwhile caregiver for your son."

And so it was done. He'd acquired the caretaker he'd been seeking for Adam. He should be elated, so why did it feel as if he'd just suffered a crushing defeat?

Chapter 5

"Well, Adam, what do you suppose we do all day?" she asked the child as he finished his breakfast. The impish grin he replied with gave her the impression he'd have no trouble keeping her busy from dawn to dusk.

And her impression had been correct. The energetic four-year-old proceeded to introduce Mary to every nook and cranny within the house, and then gave her a tour of the property. He was an honest youngster—she had to give him that. He spent the entire time explaining to her all the things he was not permitted to do. Like when he struggled hard to open the barn door and walked inside, all the while explaining to her he wasn't allowed in the barn. Or when he introduced her to the small garden behind the house by picking a handful of flowers for her—which, he told her, he was definitely not allowed to do.

If she was going to be responsible for caring for the child, she'd have to explain to him that rules would have to be followed in her care as well as his father's, but given that it was their first day together, she supposed a few leniencies weren't uncalled for.

And by the time the day had run its course, it seemed Adam had tired of his mischievous adventures, and was quite content to follow along behind her as he recanted stories of his life since arriving in California. The best she could figure from Adam's descriptions, he and Caleb had only been in California for a little over a year. And even more surprising, Adam hadn't lived with Caleb for much longer than that. Apparently, he'd lived with Caleb's parents prior to that, but he couldn't recall much from those early years. Interesting information, nevertheless.

She wondered if he'd been a soldier in the war, but then, he'd never said anything to that effect in his letters. If not the war, then where had he gone off to? By the flippant way he seemed comfortable leaving Adam in her care, she'd presume he didn't care much for the child, but the look she saw in his eyes told her otherwise.

"Good evening," a deep voice startled her from behind just as she and Adam were settling down for dinner.

"Father!" Adam squealed and zoomed across the room into Caleb's outstretched arms. Yes, he definitely cared a great deal for the boy.

She hadn't been certain whether he'd return in time for the meal or not. She supposed it was a good thing she'd decided to plan on his presence there just in case. "We were just sitting down to dinner," she announced, rather unnecessarily, but she'd felt compelled to say something as he'd stood up straight and his gaze settled directly on her. It was strange; none of the men her uncle had encouraged to come calling ever did this to her—

making her glaringly aware of his nearness and painfully attuned to the effect it had on her.

He nodded, holding her gaze a moment longer before taking his place at the table. "Did the two of you have a successful day together?" he asked in her direction, but Adam was quick to jump in.

"Yes, we did. We did have a succ-ess-ful first day together," he enunciated carefully. "Miss Tessa knows all the things I'm not allowed to do."

"Does she, now?" Caleb replied with a mischievous grin. No doubt, the father knew exactly how Adam had explained all the rules to her.

Adam proceeded to recount the day's activities, careful to leave out their trip to the barn and the flowers he'd picked from the garden.

"I'll be along to help you with your prayers in a few minutes," Caleb told his son as Adam got down from the table.

The dining room grew quiet once the boy had left. "I should go see to Adam," Caleb spoke up after a moment of silence. He sighed as he placed his hands against the table and prepared to heave himself upright.

"I could...I mean, if it's too much of an imposition then certainly not..."

"Would you like to say goodnight to Adam, Tessa?" he asked softly, settling himself back in his chair and looking at her strangely.

She nodded and left the room quickly, though she could feel Caleb's gaze on her with every step.

"I got started already," Adam told her as she opened the door to his room. "But you can come help me," he told her, looking very serious.

She nodded and knelt next to him at the side of the bed. She clasped her hands in front of her and closed her eyes, waiting for him to continue, which he did just seconds later with great aplomb.

"May God bless my father, and my grandmother, and my grandfather, and the dog that used to run down their street...and the animals in the barn...and the flower garden behind the house 'cause I picked some flowers from it when I wasn't s'posed to. And may God bless the cat I play with sometimes, and Mr. Tuttle who works for Father, and his horse 'cause it was sick. And may God bless Miss Tessa 'cause I think she's really nice."

He crawled up into bed then and looked up at her expectantly. Adam had just included her in his prayers. Why the kind gesture had overwhelmed her, she didn't know, but she struggled to swallow against the lump in her throat and blinked back the tears in her eyes.

"Are you going to tuck me in, Miss Tessa?" he asked expectantly.

"Yes, of course." She pulled up the thick, plush cover from the foot of the bed and tucked it around his small body. He smiled contentedly.

"Do...do you know any songs?" he asked nervously. "If you don't, that's all right," he added quickly.

"I know the lullaby my mother used to sing to me when I was your age."

"Yes. Yes, please!" he shouted eagerly.

It was the same lullaby she sang to the men at the hospital who were scared or in pain. Her voice wasn't quite as beautiful as she remembered her mother's being, but it seemed to help soothe her patients, nonetheless.

Her mother's face flashed behind her eyes as she began to sing, and then the face of that first wounded soldier she'd met her first day as a nurse. And then the soldier she thought of most often. And then a plethora of other faces, each of them sad, or scared, or hurt, but she'd determined to commit every one of them to memory. Unfortunately, they often appeared at times when she most wished they'd stay away.

Tears gathered in her eyes, but she continued to sing, stroking the young boy's hair. He snuggled deeper into his covers and sighed contentedly. By the time she was finished, the gentle rise and fall of Adam's small chest told her he was fast asleep. She smiled through her tears, brushing them away as they welled over and trickled down her cheeks. She leaned in slowly to avoid disturbing the mattress and laid a gentle kiss on the boy's forehead.

"I'm glad you're here, Miss Tessa. I think God has answered my prayer," he whispered sleepily.

She stood watching him for another moment and then backed toward the door slowly, but as she turned to leave, she ran straight into the solid wall of Caleb's chest. Her hands flew to her mouth quickly to stifle her cry of surprise.

"You're very good with him," he observed in that same gentle tone he always seemed to use when he was talking about his son.

But he was looking directly at her, his eyes searching hers for... *something*. She'd looked down in a hurry, but knew there was no way he hadn't caught sight of the tears in her eyes or those streaming down her cheeks.

She'd never cried in front of another person before; not after her parents died, or her first patient, or the countless number of men who died in her care after. Always, she would hold back her tears until she was alone.

"If you'll excuse me, Mr. Knight," she whispered as steadily as she could and flew past him. Fortunately, she only had to make it a few steps away, throwing open the door to his...her bedroom and closing it behind her.

She leaned back against the door, looking towards the ceiling as she forced her lungs to take slow, steady breaths. Just as she'd managed to get her breathing back under control, a knock sounded on the door behind her. She wiped her cheeks and opened the door, because what else could she do?

"I hadn't meant to upset you, Tessa," Caleb told her the moment the door was open, obviously thinking he'd been responsible for her watery state. "I had only intended to pay you a compliment."

"Yes, I know that. Thank you. Adam is a very easy boy to care for. You did nothing to upset me." She fidgeted beneath his gaze, waiting impatiently for him to leave, but he didn't. He continued to stand there outside the door. "Is there anything else I can do for you, Mr. Knight?"

"Well, for starters, you can start calling me Caleb. Given that we're married now, I believe it is more than acceptable."

"Are we?" she asked softly before she could stop herself.

He opened his mouth to reply, but snapped it closed without making a sound. He stood there for another moment, his eyes boring into hers while she tried to figure out what it was he was thinking. And then she watched as something changed. Where there'd been gentleness and concern in his gaze a moment prior, now there was none of it. In fact, there was nothing. It was like he'd erected a solid wall between them, and she knew right then he wasn't going to provide her with an answer.

"Yes, well, it's been another very long day. I believe I'll turn in now. Good night, Tessa." He turned and left, just as he had the night prior.

She didn't know much about Caleb Knight, but what she did know was the man's demeanor changed so quickly and so often, whiplash would be inevitable in her near future if she tried to keep up.

Chapter 6

Caleb was awake before the sun the next morning, and the handful of mornings after that, pacing across Adam's bedroom floor. This wasn't going well. It wasn't going at all like he'd intended. Sure, Adam had taken to her right away, and she seemed to genuinely enjoy Adam's presence. That was all well and good, but he wasn't supposed to give a darn whether or not she had tears in her eyes singing his son a lullaby. And he certainly shouldn't have had any reason to hesitate when she'd asked about their...relationship.

He should have been straight with her, just as he'd been before. Instead of using it as an opportunity to reinforce what it was he wanted, he'd held the words on the tip of his tongue. And not only could he not force the words out, he hadn't been able to focus on anything but her full, rosy lips and the way her green eyes sparkled through her tears. He'd been determined to keep Tessa at an arm's length, but truth be told, he'd never wanted to fail at something so badly in his life.

He crept out of his son's room, knowing that if he kept pacing back and forth across the floor, Adam would be awake in no time. Intending to ruminate in silence, he sauntered into the dining room only to find Tessa there already, sipping a cup of coffee. She was the first woman he'd met who actually preferred the bitter brew over tea. It should make her seem somehow more masculine to him, but instead, it only heightened his interest, making him wonder what other idiosyncrasies made up the woman.

"Good morning, Caleb," she greeted him in a cheery, lilting tone. "I wasn't certain what time you'd be up, so I brewed a full pot of coffee if you'd like a cup."

She was offering him coffee? He'd kept himself guarded the past several days, crossing paths with her as seldom as possible, and here she was offering him coffee? Certainly nothing like his first wife who would never have dreamed of doing even a small favor for him without something to gain from it.

"I appreciate it, but please don't get up. I can see to a cup of coffee."

He retrieved a cup and poured the brew, passing on the sugar and cream she'd brought to the table. He'd gotten used to drinking it black over the years, and was just glad it tasted like coffee and not sludge.

"I was wondering if I might expand the small garden in the back, if that's alright with you," she asked as he took a seat next to her, pushing his chair back to keep some distance between them. "Adam seems quite enthralled with it, and I thought he might enjoy seeing the fruits of his own labor once the new plants start to grow."

"Yes, of course." What else could he say?

"The house is lovely. I never imagined a house in the west could appear so welcoming. I think you must have done a fine job transforming it into a home for Adam."

He thought over the things he'd done to change the building since he'd arrived, predominantly small touches he could recall from his own childhood as aspects that had warmed his family's home. "Thank you. I hope Adam feels the same way."

"Oh, I'm sure he does. He idolizes you, you know."

"Is that so? I hardly think—"

"No, it's true. Every other sentence out of his mouth is something you've told him, a skill you've taught him…you speak nothing but words of wisdom in his mind."

"I'm sure you're reading too much into it, but thank you for the compliment, nevertheless."

He'd never really considered how Adam felt about him. He'd spent so much time trying to keep him safe and making up for all the time he'd missed that he hadn't stopped to take stock of what kind of job he'd been doing as a father. As much as he hated to admit it, for the first time, Tessa made him feel that he might have some hope of becoming a worthy father to his son.

"Good morning, Father," Adam greeted sleepily as he wobbled into the dining room and wrapped his arms around him in a morning hug.

"Good morning, Adam," he greeted in return and hugged him tightly.

Adam continued on then, walking the few steps further to Tessa and wrapping his little arms around her neck. "Good morning, Miss Tessa," he greeted her just as easily.

"Good morning, Darling," she whispered as she hugged him back, a look of awe brightening her eyes and parting her lips.

Wow. Just like that, she'd found her way into Adam's heart. It should have been a relief, but it wasn't. If she'd gotten to Adam so quickly, how much longer would it be before she'd worked her way into Caleb's heart as well?

"I have a long day ahead of me, so I'm going to head out early. Be good, Adam," he warned lightly. A quick nod to Tessa as he rose from the table and then he was out of the room in a flash.

But no matter how much distance he put between them, she remained on his mind the entire day. A battle waged in his head, making it difficult to concentrate on anything but the beautiful woman in his home.

And worse, as the day wore on, something else threatened to drive him to distraction. He wanted to be home. He wanted the day to be over so he could see her again, hear her soft voice, breathe in the scent of jasmine that seemed to follow her everywhere she went. He wanted to watch her lips as she spoke his name, and see the light in her crystal eyes when he came near. He wanted...his wife.

But maybe that wasn't what had him rushing through his day so he could hurry back home. For several days, he had left Adam alone with a veritable stranger. And though the boy had taken to her well, there was no guarantee he'd made the right decision for Adam in choosing Tessa as his bride. So, of course he was anxious to get home—just to make sure Adam was faring well in her care.

A full two hours early, he called it a day, almost convinced that it was his concern over Tessa's suitability as a caregiver that had him riding home at a near-breakneck speed.

And there they were, behind the house, elbow-deep in dirt in the small garden. Strangely, he didn't breathe a sigh of relief when he saw them there; it was as if he hadn't truly been worried that Tessa might have been an unsuitable choice. But he was already home now so he saw no need to analyze his motives any further. Instead, he stood there watching as the two of them dug holes and planted seeds and tiny seedlings in the dirt. She spoke to Adam the entire time, but Caleb was far enough away that he couldn't make out the words; only the soft, lilting sound of her voice. She smiled, and Adam smiled, and when she swiped at a blob of dirt on the boy's nose, he scrunched up his face and squealed with delight while she laughed so hard he saw tears in her eyes.

And then it was quiet. Adam was focusing all his attention on his task while Tessa stroked the boy's dirt-streaked hair. And what he saw in her eyes...what was written all over her face made his jaw drop open.

It couldn't be. It just wasn't possible.

But it was unmistakable.

It was love shining in her expressive, green eyes. In a matter of days, Adam had captured her heart. And while it had never surprised him that he'd immediately been overwhelmed with affection for the boy, it amazed him that a complete stranger could be captivated so quickly. Adam wasn't her child, but it hadn't mattered.

And though grateful for her instant affection for Adam—the boy deserved more love than even a father could give—Caleb was also jealous. What would it be like to have Tessa looking at him like that? Patricia had never looked at him with love in her eyes, and he'd never looked back at her that way either. The two of them had been a good match, and he'd been eager to please his family. Since then, he'd learned better than to ever hope for, or offer, dangerous things like trust and love.

"Father, you're home!" Adam hopped up onto his little legs after spying him there and scurried across the yard. "Would you like to help?" he asked excitedly. "Miss Tessa knows all about gardening. She could teach you, just like she's teaching me."

"I believe that sounds like a wonderful idea. Lead the way." Adam grabbed his hand and pulled him back to the small garden.

"Miss Tessa, can you show my father how to plant seeds, too?" Adam bounced excitedly, still holding onto Caleb's hand with both of his.

"I'm sure he would enjoy that, Adam, but perhaps we should let your father rest. He's only just arrived home."

She was trying to give him a way out, though whether for his benefit or hers, he didn't know. Nevertheless, Adam looked too excited to disappoint him, so Caleb got down on his knees and let Tessa guide him through the steps of digging a hole, tossing in some seeds and filling the hole back up with dirt.

She explained each step to him—for Adam's benefit, no doubt—but laughter lit up her eyes the whole time. She must have found the lesson in gardening just as humorous as he did. Of course, luck would have it that he was so busy paying attention to the tone of her voice and the way she moved her delicate—and dirt-covered—hands that he lost track of where he'd been digging and dug up a handful of seeds that had only recently been planted.

"You can't dig them up that quickly, Father," Adam explained seriously. "Miss Tessa says that these things take time and we have to be patient."

"An important lesson, for sure," he agreed with his son, merriment alight in his own tone.

Tessa covered her mouth with the back of her hand to stifle a laugh but when she pulled it away, she'd become the most adorable woman he'd ever seen, with dirt streaks across her cheeks and a dab on her nose. He'd never think of playing in the dirt as an unworthy pastime for a woman ever again.

"I think we're just about finished, Darling. Why don't you go wash up for dinner."

Adam nodded, not the least bit perturbed that this particular fun was over for the moment. "I think you need to wash up, too, Miss Tessa." Adam reached out and swiped his small fingers across her cheeks, not doing much more than smudging the streaks there.

Adam then jumped up and rushed toward the house, leaving Caleb kneeling in the garden less than a yard from Tessa.

"I'm sorry," she spoke after a moment of silence. "I hadn't thought you would be home so early or else I'd have had Adam cleaned up and dinner would be ready."

"It's no trouble. It was nice to see him enjoying himself."

She rose to her feet and swiped at her face just as Adam had a moment prior, but the results were the same: more smudging. He stifled a laugh as he stood up, but he wasn't entirely successful and she glared at him in mock disapproval.

"Now, Mr. Knight, where are your manners?"

"My lady, you are covered in mud and you inquire about my manners," he spoke as his lips quivered in a poor attempt to conceal his humor.

She laughed, abandoning her efforts. "Yes, well, I suppose I've just spent too much time getting covered in all sorts of—" her mouth snapped closed and all humor fled her expression.

What was that?

"I think I should wash up and see to dinner. I'll see you inside," she finished quickly and then hurried past him and around to the door to the house.

She just spent too long getting covered in all sorts of *what*? What on earth would a librarian have spent so much time getting herself covered in? And why had her demeanor changed rapidly, mid-sentence? Tessa was certainly a conundrum; one he had increasing interest in unravelling.

Darn it! He'd done it again. He'd allowed himself to get carried away in her smiles and her laughter and...her. He should have no interest in unravelling Tessa—none whatsoever.

She seemed to have recovered herself by the time he joined them inside and a bright smile lit her face once more as she talked to Adam. It remained there all through dinner, though she kept her attention on Adam the entire time.

"Will you help me with my prayers, Miss Tessa?"

"I'll be there in a moment," he cut in before Tessa could respond, just as he had each night since the first.

"Yes, Father," the boy replied, not even attempting to hide his disappointment.

Adam was truly taken with Tessa, and Caleb would have been inclined to give into his son's wishes to make him happy, but he'd seen the tears in her eyes that night after she'd sung her sweet lullaby. Something had upset her deeply, and though he shouldn't care, he couldn't deny he didn't want to see her upset like that again.

Tessa was quiet beside him, although he could see the question in her eyes, wondering if she'd done something to displease him. He felt compelled to offer some sort of explanation, but he held his tongue. He didn't owe her an explanation, did he? This was his home, Adam was his son, and if he wanted to be the one to tuck him in at night, that was his right. At least, that's what he told himself as he pushed away from the table, nodded succinctly and left the room.

Adam was still sulking when he joined him in his room, but he recovered quickly as they knelt at the side of his bed. And by the time he tucked him in beneath his blanket, he was smiling sleepily, reaching his arms out for a hug.

"I like Miss Tessa very much, Father. Don't you?" he asked innocently.

"Yes, I do." *Far too much*, he thought.

He left the room a moment later, closing the door quietly behind him. She was right there, coming down the hallway to his...her bedroom. She came to a stop a few feet in front of him, fidgeting awkwardly as if she was trying to find something to say. Against his better judgment, his feet moved by their own volition, closing the distance between them, but just as he was about to lean in, an image flashed through his mind. Stone walls. Nothing but stark, stone walls—it was his brain's way of tipping the scale.

He turned abruptly and retreated to his son's room—his current bedroom—cursing the pile of blankets that served as his makeshift bed. If he was going to make this a permanent arrangement, he'd have to see about finding a more comfortable bed.

He laid down, not bothering to get undressed for bed, but sleep would not come. An hour passed, and then another, and he continued to lay there, wondering how on earth he'd thought his plan could have been anything but a disaster. Of course, at the time, he'd had no idea she would be the most beautiful woman he'd ever seen; that she'd be the kind of person who could come to love his son in a matter of days; that she was a woman he was beginning to think deserved a husband who could devote himself entirely to her happiness.

And that brought him to another question. Tessa could have had any man of her choosing, he was certain of it, so why had she been looking for a husband in matrimonial advertisements? She was hiding something—he was equally certain of that. What kind of secret could possibly have reduced her marriage options in New England to none?

Every fathomable reason flitted through his mind. She could be a murderess fleeing the law, an escaped convict or a woman who conned men out of their fortunes. But none of them fit. There was no look of a criminal or of violence in her eyes, and she couldn't possibly know he wasn't the poor miner he'd claimed to be. The possibilities continued to roll about his mind as his eyes finally grew heavy.

He had just begun to drift into the realm that existed between awake and asleep when a scream ripped through the air. He was on his feet in a flash and gave one quick look to make sure Adam was alright before he dashed out of the room. In the hall, he knew right away where the scream came from and he didn't hesitate when he reached the bedroom door, throwing it open and darting inside. Hellish visions flashed through his mind as he sought to peer through the darkness. He imagined her near-lifeless form, drenched in blood like so many of the bodies he'd seen littering battlefields.

"Tessa!" he yelled in panic, but her scream continued to fill the room and pierce his ears. His eyes had adjusted to the dark by the time he reached the bed, and he couldn't help the sigh of relief that escaped his lips as he saw her there, thrashing wildly but unharmed. She was asleep, her heart-wrenching scream a byproduct of a nightmare, though he couldn't imagine what evil thing tormented her in her sleep.

He perched himself on the edge of the bed and shook her gently. Within seconds, she came awake, sitting upright in a flash.

"Tessa, it's alright. It was just a bad dream," he whispered soothingly.

She nodded, but he could see the tears cascading down her cheeks. Without thinking, he pulled her to him, wrapping her in his arms and rubbing her back soothingly. She buried her head against his shoulder as quiet sobs racked her body.

Though she was taller than most women, she seemed so small in his arms; delicate, almost fragile. It wasn't an impression he'd gotten from her before, which meant she kept this part of her well-hidden. She'd seemed immensely strong to him, maybe not in the same physical way a man was strong, but in other ways, as if it would be nearly impossible for the world to bend her to its will. This part of her, though, could be easily crushed, and suddenly the thought of anyone ever attempting to harm any part of Tessa made his blood boil.

The fierce protectiveness that coursed through his veins was unwelcome. He didn't want to feel this way, and he leaned away from her, hoping that putting distance between them might help to remove the unwelcome feeling. But it only served to make it grow stronger, as if the only way to placate it was to keep her close, to keep her where he knew she would be safe.

His movement must have jarred her back to reality because she pulled away, her teeth beginning to tug on her bottom lip as they often did when she was nervous or uncomfortable. Strange, that he was already beginning to recognize such small details about her. Strange...and terrifying.

"I'm quite alright now," she spoke, her voice little more than a whisper and not the least bit convincing.

"Are you sure, Tessa?" He should be making a hasty retreat, but instead he lingered, wanting to see that she was actually alright.

"Yes, quite. My apologies, Caleb, for disturbing your sleep."

"No apology necessary," he whispered as he reached out to caress her damp cheek. He stopped himself though, a mere inch away from her tear-soaked face.

"If you have need of me, you know where to find me," he told her gruffly and hurried out of the room.

He laid back down in his makeshift bed and then proceeded to toss and turn the entire night as Tessa made an appearance in every thought, dream and nightmare that filled his mind.

Chapter 7

A day passed, and then another, and then several more. No more nightmares plagued her sleep, and Mary was grateful for that—even if it meant she'd slept less in the past week than she usually would in a single night or two. She would stay awake as long as she could, and then sleep fitfully, waking every hour or so. At least it kept the nightmares at bay. In truth, the memory of Caleb's arms around her had threatened her composure far more than anything in her dreams.

For the first time, she'd felt far removed from the gruesome memories that haunted her mind. Even the memory that haunted her sleep most often couldn't hurt her in Caleb's arms. The memory of a man, a man she'd cared for over two days and two nights, at his bedside almost constantly. He'd been delirious with pain when he startled her, wrapping his good arm around her with a knife in his hand, holding it against her, threatening to hurt her if she let the doctor take his arm.

"I'll take both yer arms if ya don't let her go," another soldier had threatened from behind him, thrashing him over the head with a rifle musket seconds later. His hand and the knife fell away and he collapsed sideways on the bed.

The doctor still took his arm, but it was for naught—he died a week later from infection. The worst part, though, the part that haunted her most often, was the other soldier, the one who had saved her life. He'd valiantly come to her rescue, but there had been nothing she could do to save him. He'd wasted away from a serious infection as well, and it wasn't fair. It wasn't fair that the man who saved her died in the same manner as the man who'd threatened to take her life.

But in Caleb's arms, she'd felt a small sliver of peace, as if something in his embrace was telling her it was alright to move on. She would never tell him that. Caleb wanted no part in an actual marriage and she wouldn't make herself so vulnerable to a man who didn't want her. It stung to know she would never know the kind of love she'd witnessed between her mother and father, but nor would she ever know the heavy hand of John Wendell.

And what Caleb had provided her with would be enough— Adam. The little boy had stolen her heart so quickly that she hadn't even realized he had it at first. Though he was not her son, she loved him as if he was. Could she complain that her life was not what she'd hoped it would be when it was so much better than she'd not so long ago feared?

So, with that in mind, she smiled at Caleb. They'd just finished dinner and Adam was chatting about his activities that day. Caleb was there each morning for breakfast and dinner now. Their early morning conversations had become comfortable—an enjoyment she looked forward to each day—but later in the day, his demeanor could change so fast it would make her head spin. Even so, once he left each morning, she couldn't help but secretly watch the clock, waiting for the time he'd return. And at the moment, he seemed to be in good spirits. But as Adam's bedtime neared, the room grew quiet.

"Why don't Miss Tessa and I both help you with your prayers this evening, Adam?" Caleb suggested.

She feared her head had been elsewhere and she'd missed a question from Adam, but the boy seemed more than content with his father's reply. Still, ever since that first night she'd tucked Adam into bed, Caleb had taken over the task, insisting she relax while he spent the last few minutes of the day with his son. She hadn't persisted, afraid she might be overstepping some invisible boundary, but it was Caleb who made the suggestion she join them tonight.

Adam stood excitedly and grabbed her hand, pulling her up and across the room with him while Caleb followed behind them. Once the boy had changed his clothes and washed up for bed, the three of them knelt beside his bed and waited while Adam gave thanks for everything in his life from his father and Tessa to the seeds which he hoped would soon begin to force their way through the ground in their garden. He was such a happy boy.

"Will you sing again, Miss Tessa?" he asked when he was settled in bed.

She nodded reluctantly and forced a smile. Caleb was still right there standing next to her, and it didn't look like he had any intention of leaving any time soon. Awkwardly, she positioned herself on the edge of Adam's bed and let the song flow from her lips. Caleb's nearness made her self-conscious, but that was good. It helped to staunch the flow of images that flooded her mind as she sang. Still, her eyes teared up. She couldn't help it, but she kept them in check, refusing to let them fall until she was finished.

"It's the song that makes you so upset. Why?" he whispered as they left the room and Caleb closed the door quietly behind them.

"It was the song my mother used to sing to me. When she died—"

"Died? Didn't you say in your letters that you have a happy family?" Caleb asked with sudden suspicion in his eyes.

She hadn't even thought to guard her answers, and it felt like it had been a lifetime since she'd written all those lies. "Yes, we are," she tried to cover quickly. "Those of us remaining. Unfortunately, my parents died when I was young. My aunt, my...uncle," she hesitated, forcing the last word, "They took me in and they are good people. They were always kind to me," she lied.

The suspicion never left his eyes but he nodded. She was at her bedroom door then—so quickly she'd come to see it as her bedroom—and he paused. He didn't speak, he didn't move. His eyes met hers for a brief moment, but then traveled lower, settling on her lips. He wanted to kiss her; she knew it, though she had no idea how she could be so certain. But any doubt faded quickly as he leaned in and his lips grazed across hers, once, twice, before she felt the full weight of his lips against hers.

But he pulled away abruptly, and his eyes met hers. At first there was confusion in his gaze, but it disappeared quickly as the wall he so often erected between them came up. She sighed, knowing what came next.

"Good night, Caleb," she whispered and hurried inside the bedroom, closing the door on the man who seemed determined to keep her shut out.

Her lips still tingled as she changed for bed and slipped beneath the covers. She was exhausted, in part from a long day of toiling around the house with Adam, and in part from the ups and downs that seemed inherent to residing under the same roof as Caleb. She closed her eyes, anxious to escape the emotions that roiled within her, and after so many nights of inadequate sleep, she drifted off quickly.

In her dreams, once again, the man held a knife to her, and though it hurt immensely, she fought hard against the panic that welled inside. She had to keep her wits about her if there was to be any hope of soothing the angry man. She kept her hands at her sides, speaking in soothing tones, reassuring the man he would be alright. The man didn't budge; not until the soldier sent him sprawling, out cold. The moment the hand and knife fell away, she spun around, but it was not the man who had wielded the knife lying on the bed in front of her; it was the soldier who had saved her. He lay broken and bloodied on the bed, begging her, "Help me. Save me, Mary. I saved you, didn't I? How can you stand by and let me die?" She tried, and she tried, staunching the flow of one wound only for another to appear. She cried out in sorrow, in frustration; in terror that the soldier's blood would forever be on her hands.

"Tessa!" the soldier called to her as she worked to cover his wounds, but that wasn't her name. Why was he calling her that?

"Tessa, please wake up," he called again, his eyes pleading.

And then there was nothing but darkness. Darkness, and warm, strong arms surrounding her. Her breath came rapidly but as those arms continued to hold her, it slowed.

"It was just a bad dream, Tessa," he told her as he had the time before, his hands beginning to rub in slow circles across her back. Her breathing resumed its normal cadence and she melted against him. She was safe, and far away from the brutality of war. So safe. But then he started to pull away.

"Caleb...would you..." she began without thinking.

"What is it, Tessa?" He stilled, rubbing her back once more.

"Would you stay with me?" she asked, her voice barely a whisper.

If his hands hadn't stopped moving, she'd wonder if he'd heard her at all. And then he was silent for so long, she wondered if he'd fallen asleep sitting up. But then he nodded against her and lowered her down to the mattress, keeping his arms around her.

Feeling his warmth and the strong wall of his body behind her, she closed her eyes. More content than she could ever remember, she drifted off to sleep.

Chapter 8

Caleb awoke to see the sky only just beginning to lighten through the window and he knew instantly that he'd made a mistake. He wasn't alone, nor was he sleeping on the pile of blankets he'd slept on the past several weeks. He was in his bedroom, and Tessa was lying there cradled in his arms, blissfully asleep. He'd only meant to lay there for a minute or two, until she'd fallen back to sleep, but it'd felt so nice, he must have fallen asleep, too.

He needed to get out of there; he needed to put distance between them. Because right then, waking up to her was feeling just as right as it had felt to fall asleep next to her. As carefully as he could, he slipped his arm out from underneath her and slid off the bed. But he couldn't resist looking down at her, seeing her features relaxed in sleep, knowing she was sleeping peacefully now because she'd sought comfort in his arms.

And he realized right then, it was too late. All the effort he'd put into keeping his distance, to staying detached from and disinterested in Tessa... he'd been fooling himself all this time. If he was being honest with himself, he'd known from the beginning he was doomed to fail.

But there was more to Tessa than she was letting on, and that could spell serious trouble for him. He had no idea what secret she was keeping, whether it could wreak havoc on his life and Adam's.

He contemplated his own secrets; what Tessa would think of him if she knew? But thousands of miles away from home, it was unlikely that his secrets could impact her life.

Could the same be said of hers? If she was on the run, then what would happen if her past ever caught up with her? What if someone came to take her away?

He crept out of the room, peeking into the next room to make sure Adam was still sleeping soundly. He'd only just made it down the hall and sat down at the dining table with his coffee when a knock sounded at the door, an odd noise to hear so early in the morning. It seemed to echo through the house more than the sound ever did during the day. His heart thudded in his chest, so loud he wondered if it was still the knock at the door sounding in his ears.

Had his worst fear just knocked at his door? It couldn't be. He'd left absolutely no trail to his whereabouts.

He listened, making sure Adam and Tessa weren't stirring, and when he was met with silence, he stood, retrieving his Smith & Wesson before creeping quietly toward the door. What would he do if the person on the other side of the door had come to collect him? There was no way he would allow anyone to separate him from Adam—ever—and, he realized, he would not allow himself to be separated from Tessa either. But could he shoot a man in cold blood? End a life in order to maintain the life he'd created for his small family? In war, it had been different; he'd fought and killed for the good of his country. But for his own selfish desires?

Still uncertain of his answer, he tucked the Smith & Wesson into the back of his pants and opened the door. What he found on the other side was not what he'd been expecting. The man was well-dressed, with an air of confidence and disdain surrounding him. But he was a slight man, no taller than Tessa and nearly as fragile-looking, and he held no weapon in his hand.

"Can I help you?" he asked, forcing a calmness in his tone he didn't feel.

"My name is Clarence Wilkes. I'm here in search of a woman, sir."

"Aren't we all?" Caleb joked, a tentative modicum of relief flitting through his veins at the man's words. He was looking for a woman, not an escaped man.

"Yes, well, one in particular, actually," Clarence replied uncomfortably, a light blush creeping across his cheeks in response to the way his words seemed to have been misinterpreted.

More relief filled him with every passing second, and so Caleb held his tongue rather than rattling the man further.

"Her name is Mary Kenleigh, sir," Clarence explained, "and I am searching for her on behalf of her fiancé—John Wendell."

Caleb froze, though he tried to appear unperturbed while every ounce of relief drained from his body. He knew that name, a name that had haunted him for years. But he couldn't let Clarence see how he'd been affected by it. He tried to cover himself quickly. "I can't say that I've heard of either of them, I'm afraid."

The man scrutinized Caleb's expression, and Caleb was careful to hold the man's gaze unwaveringly. Clarence nodded a moment later, obviously satisfied with his findings. He then held up a small picture...a picture that looked strikingly similar to the woman sleeping in his bed. No, not similar...exactly like the woman in his bed.

Tessa was John Wendell's fiancé? Her name wasn't even Tessa. Was this some kind of sick game? Had John and Tessa...Mary...concocted this scheme together? Had they plotted to reel him in, make him fall for the woman and then pull the carpet out from under him? It was despicable enough that she'd do that to him...but to Adam? Did she have no idea how much his son had grown to care for her already? Or did she not care? He'd been certain about her affection for his son—had he been so wrong?

Caleb was angry, ready to scream so loud he'd blow the roof off the house, but the man's next words trapped his rage in his throat.

"If you happen to see her, I'd appreciate it if you would contact me. Her fiancé would like his...property returned to him as soon as possible."

If Tessa had been a knowing participant in the scheme, why would there be someone looking for her?

And the way the man had referred to her as 'his property' reverberated in his mind and sent a chill down his spine. Was it possible she'd been betrothed to John Wendell against her will? Had she fled her home in order to escape the wretched fiend? If so, Caleb was beginning to understand what secret she'd been hiding. And why.

And though he was angry that she'd deceived him, he couldn't find it within himself to blame her. How could he? Had he not gone to equal lengths to escape the man and the destruction he'd wreaked on his life? Nevertheless, she'd practically brought the very man who had destroyed him to his doorstep. The only way to ensure his safety and Adam's was to send her back. Once John Wendell had his fiancée returned to him, he would have no reason to continue poking around the west.

Clarence handed him a card with a New England address written on it as Caleb opened his mouth to speak...but no words came out; he couldn't force them out. God help him, he couldn't hand Tessa over to that evil man.

"Thank you," he said instead. "I will be in touch should I happen to see her."

"I'd appreciate that."

Clarence eyed him once more, and Caleb forced a calm, unassuming demeanor. These last few seconds was all he had left to convince the man he would not find what he was looking for there.

"Father?" Adam's sleepy voice called to him from a few yards back.

"Good morning, son. I'll join you in the dining room in a moment," Caleb replied over his shoulder. "As you can see, Mr. Wilkes, I have a son to tend to. If there's nothing else I can do for you..." He was amazed at the nonchalance in his own tone. If he managed to pull this off, he'd have to congratulate himself on his performance later.

"No, nothing further. Thank you for your time. Good day, sir."

"Good day to you as well," he replied and then stepped back and closed the door slowly, watching as Clarence turned away and made his way back to his carriage. He thought back over the conversation and considered the man's body language. Whether Caleb had given a good performance or Clarence was too daft to recognize the truth, he didn't know. Either way, he was relatively certain the man had no idea John Wendell's fiancée slept within that very house.

He listened as the man rode away and breathed a sigh of relief when he was no longer within earshot. It was over. Adam was safe. He was safe. But what was he to do about Tessa...Mary?

Before he could even contemplate it, she appeared from the hallway. Had she been awake through the conversation? Had she heard the entire exchange?

She strode over to him, her spine straight and her head high. If it weren't for the way she nibbled at her bottom lip, he would have no clue she was ill at ease. He would rather have had more time to consider how to proceed from here, but it seemed that was not an option.

"Caleb," she began as she came to a halt in front of him. "I want to apologize for last night...for...I should never have..." she fumbled with her words.

She had no idea what had just transpired at his front door. Her uneasiness was the result of her asking him to stay with her last night. For the second time in as many minutes, he breathed a sigh of relief. He would have to confront her on the subject, but for now, he was free to consider his next step.

"I assure you, it's quite alright...Tessa. Don't let it concern you." Without another word, he strode to the kitchen to replace his now-cold coffee, forcing at least a modicum of his concentration onto the task in front of him. Already, the morning had been fraught with far too many revelations. First, it had hit him how very strongly he cared for Tessa, and then he discovered she wasn't Tessa, that she'd lied to him about everything...her name...her reason for seeking a husband. It was likely she'd never been a librarian, and he was already quite certain her account of her family had been anything but truthful.

So why didn't he hand her over to Clarence Wilkes, or at the very least, send her away?

Because the things he knew about her were far more important than her name or her occupation. He knew she was kind and compassionate, strong and yet fragile, full of life, but still haunted. He knew he cared for her more than any woman he'd ever known, and that she would make a better mother to Adam than the boy's own mother ever would have.

He needed to think, and he couldn't do that with her so near...so beautiful...

"Please see to Adam's breakfast. I'll be going out," he offered brusquely as he strode from the room.

Chapter 9

Mary had no idea what to make of Caleb's sudden abruptness, not that it was entirely unfamiliar. But he'd seemed uneasy from the moment she'd approached him in the hall, and that uneasiness had grown exponentially by the second until it was a palpable force between them. By the time he'd made his hasty retreat from the room, she wasn't sure if she should breathe a sigh of relief or whimper in protest.

She didn't want this sham of a marriage; feeling Caleb's arms around her the night before had taken away any doubt. She'd believed she could be content to live a loveless life, but it had been a lie, just like everything else she'd told herself and Caleb these past few weeks. She couldn't be content, not when the man whose love she craved was there as a constant reminder of what she could not have. And yet, her only alternative was to leave them, to leave the little boy she'd come to love as well. She could not do that either.

And so, she was left with no options, just as trapped as she'd been in her betrothal to John Wendell. At least with him, she'd known she would never want his love, even if the man was capable of such human emotion—which she seriously doubted.

Adam's jubilant voice broke through her silent crisis. "What are we going to do today, Miss Tessa?"

"What would you like to do today, Adam?"

The boy seemed to think long and hard, but before he could reply, a knock sounded at the door. It couldn't be Caleb. Why on earth would Caleb be knocking on his own front door? A sizzle of apprehension ghosted over her skin, raising the tiny hairs at the back of her neck.

"Adam, wait here," she told him as she hurried out of the room and to the door. Perhaps it was an innocent caller, another wife in the area who'd spied Tessa and Adam and wanted to introduce herself. That was entirely plausible. But what if it wasn't? She could ignore them and hope they would go away.

The knock sounded again.

"Who is it, Miss Tessa?" Adam yelled from where he remained seated in the dining room. There was no way to pretend there was no one home now. Stealing her shoulders and breathing deep, she reached for the handle, ignoring the way her hand trembled.

"Hello, Mary," the man spoke with an evil leer as she opened the door.

Oh no. He's found me! She moved to slam the door closed, but he shoved it open, making her stumble back. He was in the house, closing the door before she could regain her balance.

"I'm a married woman, Mr. Wendell. There is no point in you pursuing—"

"I know full well what you've been up to."

"P-please just leave," she whispered.

"Of course," he replied, far too agreeably. And then, she saw the Beaumont–Adams revolver in his hand as he raised it, settling his aim directly on her chest. "If you'll just accompany me, I'd be happy to leave right now."

What could she do? Little Adam would come looking for her at any moment.

"Put it down, John," a husky, male voice spoke clearly from behind her. He must have come in through the rear entrance.

She spun around to find Caleb standing just a few yards from her, holding a vicious-looking weapon in his hand, too, which was pointed directly at John.

"I don't think so, Caleb, but don't worry, I won't leave you to pine after her this time."

"Father?" Adam's voice spoke from the dining room, but she could hear his small feet approaching quickly.

She looked at the two men incredulously. *How…how can they possibly know each other?*

And then it all happened so fast. The loud sounds reverberated in her ears. Adam cried out, and she screamed.

Caleb fell to the ground in front of her while at the same time, a loud thud sounded behind her as John sunk to the ground.

She grabbed John's weapon from where it fell, but then hurried to Caleb, converging on him at the same time as Adam. She looked over the boy quickly, but he was unharmed. Caleb, on the other hand, had blood seeping from a wound to his thigh.

A quick glance back at John told her Caleb hadn't been taking any chances; he'd aimed for John's chest and hit his mark dead on. Ignoring the late man behind her, she sprung to action, tearing away Caleb's pant leg until she could find the wound. A quick inspection told her the bullet had gone clean through. She wouldn't have to dig around inside to find the bullet, thank goodness.

Tearing a strip from her dress, she wrapped it around his leg, pulling it tight to staunch the flow. Adam stood nearby, tears silently falling down his cheeks.

"It's alright, Adam. Your father is going to be just fine. I just have to patch him up a little. Do you think you could help me?"

"H-how?" the boy stuttered.

"I need you to fold down the blankets on the bed and get me some extra pillows from your room. Do you think you could do that for me?" she spoke calmly, knowing it was the only way to reassure Adam.

He nodded and backed away slowly, turning to do her bidding after a few steps.

She looked down and Caleb's eyes were open, though he was rubbing the back of his head. He must have hit it hard when he'd fallen.

"Do you suppose you could walk if I help you?" she asked, wanting to get him away from there quickly before Adam returned.

Caleb nodded and she stood, offering her hand to help him up, but he waved her away and stood on his own, hobbling toward the bedroom after checking to see that the man he'd shot was indeed dead. The body lying on the floor made a gruesome scene, but she couldn't think about that now. She'd seen plenty of gruesome scenes before, and this one was no different—at least, that's what she had to tell herself until she'd seen to Caleb's leg.

She followed him to the bedroom, surprised that he could manage so well on his own, but she insisted on helping to lower him onto the mattress and arranged his leg on the pillows Adam had brought for her.

"Thank you, Adam. Now, I know this is difficult, but I promise your father is going to be just fine. Right now though, I need to focus on fixing his leg."

Adam nodded solemnly, and scurried to sit down on the chair next to the bed, watching intently. She turned her attention to the luggage she'd yet to unpack, pulling out the small case full of useful things she'd collected as a nurse.

"This is going to hurt, I'm afraid," she told him, biting at her bottom lip as she applied the poultice that would keep the wound from becoming infected.

"How is it you know what to do?" Caleb asked with a grimace, though he was also searching her eyes like he so often did.

She opened her mouth to lie, but no words came out. She couldn't do it; she couldn't lie to the man she loved—to the man who had saved her life—a moment longer. If he hated her for it, if he sent her away, then so be it, but she could not continue to deceive him.

"I volunteered as a nurse during and after the war for three years. I was never a librarian," she confessed, willing him to forgive her.

He was silent for a moment, not even flinching as she tended to his leg. "The nightmares..." he asked, though it sounded more like a statement than a question.

She nodded, keeping her gaze focused on the task in front of her.

"Your family?" he asked, this time, with a question in his tone.

She'd come this far. She wouldn't turn back now. "My parents died in a tragic accident when I was fourteen, and I was sent to live with my uncle. He's a wretched man who never wanted me there, and he was intent on marrying me off as quickly as he could. He didn't object to my volunteering as a nurse because it got me out of his house, but when I returned..." She hesitated, remembering the awful fight with Uncle Robert.

"When you returned, his interest in marrying you off resumed, and you were not...pleased with his choice."

She nodded, although he made it sound like she'd acted like an obstinate child, rejecting the man of her uncle's choosing. "Caleb, the man..." How could she make him understand? And how could she explain that he was, in fact, the man who lay dead in the next room? "He was an evil fiend, and—"

"I was arrested, Tessa," he interrupted. "A man I fought beside betrayed me and had me convicted of a crime I did not commit. He had me thrown in prison."

He wasn't rejecting her...he was opening up to her, but what he told her made her heart ache for him. "Why would he do such a hideous thing?"

"I found out later he had known of me prior to the war. He wanted my wife and intended to have her until our betrothal was announced—though, I learned later that did not stop him, nor Patricia."

Mary's eyes grew wide, her jaw dropping as she covered her mouth in shock.

"Little did he know, when he had me imprisoned, I'd recently received word that Patricia had died just weeks after giving birth to Adam."

"But then...how are you here now? Why are you no longer in prison?"

"There was a riot; a fire in the prison. I should not have been able to escape, but the guard...he was kind. He had spoken to me often in my years there, even though the prison demanded silence. He pulled me out of the fire, but instead of heaping me with the rest of the prisoners, he let me sneak away."

He was silent for a moment, but she had a feeling he wasn't finished. She waited quietly, applying a final dressing over his wound.

"I traveled home to Portland, collected my son who had been in the care of my parents since Patricia's death, and came here without telling a single soul where I was going. I was fairly certain all the guards at the prison would believe I was dead, but the man who had put me there...I could not trust..."

"I understand, Caleb." She tried to tell him that she held no animosity for his deceptions; how could she?

"My name is Caleb Westmoreland."

Her head shot up, recognizing the name instantly. "You're from Maine...you said you were from Portland...I've heard of the Westmorelands there." She'd heard of them because, just like the

Kenleighs, the Westmorelands were one of the most prominent families in New England.

"Yes, but that is not all, Tessa. My name is Caleb Westmoreland, and the man who betrayed me...is John Wendell."

No! The man she'd run away from was the same man who had nearly destroyed Caleb's life. And by her running off to marry Caleb, she'd brought John Wendell right to his door and nearly cost him and Adam everything. She hadn't understood why he'd chosen that moment to tell her the things he'd been keeping from her, particularly why he'd cut her off when she'd been in the midst of doing the same, but now she understood. Their pasts were intertwined. How could he ever forgive her for bringing the villain there?

"Oh, Caleb...and I brought him right here..."

"You couldn't have known, Mary," he offered, grimacing as she adjusted the dressing.

Mary? She'd never told him her name wasn't Tessa. "How do you know..."

"A man came by the house this morning looking for John Wendell's fiancée. He showed me a picture of you. I thought I'd put on a good show, but John must have been nearby and recognized me."

"You could have handed me over...you should have—"

"I couldn't," he whispered emphatically, and suddenly, the

love that shone in Caleb's eyes was unmistakable.

Feeling bolder than she'd ever felt in her life, and drawing on the bravery she'd found within herself during the war, she leaned down slowly, watching his eyes every second. She waited for the wall, for the distance he so often put between them, but it didn't come.

She stopped no more than a hair's breadth from him, feeling his warm breath against her lips. Still no wall. What she saw there instead warmed her heart. She closed the gap, touching her lips lightly against his, once, twice, mimicking the way he'd kissed her the night before. And as her lips settled over top of his, she felt his arms around her, holding her close to him.

She had no idea where they would go from there; whether they would continue to call the west their home, or make their way back east now that John Wendell could no longer wreak havoc on either of their lives.

But it didn't matter. The only thing she'd ever wanted from a marriage was suddenly hers. She had the love of the man she adored with all her heart.

A Westmoreland and a Kenleigh, she thought ironically as Caleb held her closer.

What would her dear uncle say if he ever found out she'd made such a match all on her own?

THE END

Mail Order Bride: Annika's Courage

City Point, Virginia - 1865

Chapter 1

The stench of war permeated every one of the hospital tents. It was unmistakable now. When Annika had first arrived twenty-seven months prior, she hadn't been able to put a name to the pungent odor that had assaulted her senses. But she knew it now. Ever-present and always threatening to overwhelm her, she fought it back constantly with the same ruthlessness.

"Miss Neville, I need you here right now," a doctor called to her from two beds over.

She rested the cool cloth on her patient's forehead and scrambled between the narrow walkway to where the doctor had appeared a moment before with a new patient. Riddled with bullet wounds, the man wasn't long for this world. She recognized the difference now between bullet wounds and stab wounds—not that the difference mattered much; each one could rightfully claim wielding its lethal blows on countless men. She looked down at his pain-stricken face and a lump formed in her throat. The man was barely a man, a boy of no more than eighteen years.

She dove in without a word, helping to staunch the flow of blood, but she knew her efforts would be for naught, so, at the same time, she did the only thing she could for him. Leaning in close, she met his eyes and forced a smile to turn up the corners of her lips.

"It's alright," she whispered soothingly. "You're safe now, and we're going to do all we can for you."

"I...I fought bravely. My father..." the young soldier rasped in between ragged breaths.

"Your father would be proud of you. I'm certain of it," she offered, knowing it was the justification the boy needed to help ease his transition.

His eyes glazed over seconds later, and she knew without checking for his pulse that he had left her. She ceased her efforts before the others, but their hands stilled on his chest a moment later as they realized what she'd already known.

"That's all then," the doctor told her before turning and walking away, leaving it to her and the other nurses to clean and prepare the boy's body. So common had death become that the doctor didn't seem the least bit perturbed by the scene he left behind him. It was her biggest flaw in this place, unable to erect the wall so many of her fellow nurses had. It was a necessity to survive amidst so much violence and suffering, but she'd yet to master the skill. Still, she never let it show. Never.

With the help of Betty, the nurse who had been at the hospital the longest, she wheeled the gurney toward the far corner of the tent, laying a sheet over top of the boy to conceal his lifeless body.

"Is there a Miss Annika Neville here?" she heard a man's deep voice boom from outside the tent a moment later.

An ominous weight fell upon her and it threatened to hold her in place, making her legs protest against every step. Fighting the heaviness, she forced herself across the tent and outside in search of the source of the deep voice. The man looked no different from any other soldier who had come to the hospital, but a shiver raced down her spine when she spied him standing there, back straight and shoulders squared.

She closed the distance between them and mimicked his stance, hoping it would fill her body with a courage she wasn't sure she possessed. "I am Annika Neville," she told him, her voice not quite as unsteady as her insides felt.

"Miss Neville, my name is Lieutenant Charles Branscomb. I was sent to inform you that your father, Colonel William Robert Alexander Neville, has been declared missing in action, and is presumed dead."

The man's monotonous, unfeeling tone made her wonder if she'd perhaps heard him wrong. But then his armor cracked and her hope was squelched. "I'm very sorry for your loss, Miss. I knew your father briefly, and he was a fine and brave man. I...I requested that I be the one sent to inform you because...because it was my life, and the lives of my fellow soldiers that your father gave his life to save. If it weren't for him, neither I, nor five other men, would be standing today."

She nodded. She'd begged her father in her last letter to be careful, to cease his heroic antics. He was all she had, and now she had no one. "Thank you, Lieutenant Branscomb. I appreciate your coming all this way."

She wanted him to leave. It wasn't that she wished him dead, wished that her father had left him and the other men to die. It just wasn't fair. None of it was.

She could see he was already trying to mend the armor, carefully arranging his features and looking beyond her rather than at her now. She couldn't blame him. She wouldn't want to be standing there if the roles were reversed.

****

The following weeks passed in the same heart-wrenching blur as the weeks and months before, and then it happened.

The war was over.

Everyone at the hospital rejoiced; everyone except for Annika. Of course, she was glad the war was over—no more senseless violence and death—but what was there for her now? She would return home and her father would not be there. She would never find him reading in his study, sipping coffee in the dining room or strolling through the elegant gardens behind the manor.

In the weeks following, the tents were dismantled as the remaining soldiers healed enough to travel home—those that recovered at all. On her final day there, she stood looking around the barren field. It was empty, all evidence of the place's tragic history gone. But she could see it clearly, the wounded soldiers, the feverish shells of men they became when infection took them. She would never forget. And it was as if the soldiers who had been there followed her home, filling her mind and haunting her dreams on the long trek home. As she looked up at the great manor that had been her home since childhood, she prayed for peace. She prayed for some way to find her way with so many horrid memories in her mind and no father to offer her comfort or guidance.

She knocked on the door—her own door. It had been so long since she'd last been there that it felt almost foreign to her. But the moment the door opened and the woman who'd cared for her since childhood appeared in the doorway with so much love in her eyes, Annika knew she was home and felt a tiny spark of hope that her prayer might be answered.

"Hello, Martha," she breathed a small sigh of relief as the middle-aged woman gathered her in her warm embrace right there on the front steps.

"Oh, honey, I've missed ye' so much," the woman exclaimed, pulling her tighter in her arms.

"I've missed you, too." Her nurse since Annika was nine, Martha was nearly as dear to her as her own mother had been.

The two of them fell into their easy camaraderie, catching up on all the time they'd missed. She carefully averted the conversation when Martha inquired about what it had been like to be a nurse. She'd rather discuss the difference in weather and find out all that she'd missed at home. She was glad that she'd volunteered as a nurse, that she'd been there to do what she could for all those suffering soldiers, but she wasn't prepared to share her ghastly tales. Not yet.

It was almost a reprieve when a knock sounded at the door an hour later and Martha rose from where she sat across from her in the parlor to see to the caller.

"Good morning, Miss Neville," a man appeared at the entrance to the parlor a moment later, and Martha bobbed her head, stepping back far enough to avoid listening into their conversation, but close enough to oversee the exchange.

"Good morning, Sir," Annika replied, trying to recall how she knew the man in her parlor.

"My name is Oliver Fitzpatrick. I was your father's lawyer. I apologize for my delay in calling on you. I'm afraid I've been away from the city the past few weeks and was only just informed this morning of your father's...of his...passing," he stumbled over his words, unable to find a gentler way of phrasing what he could have stated plainly. She was painfully aware of her father's death.

"It's quite alright, Mr. Fitzpatrick. I've only just arrived home myself. What can I do for you today?" It had taken her a moment, but she recognized him before he'd spoken his full name, having seen him at the house several times in the year before her father left for the war.

"Well, I'm here regarding your father's will," he told her as she motioned for him to take a seat in the chair opposite hers.

"You see, it was quite a rather odd situation, very unlike what is custom these days. I must tell you that I urged him against this—"

"Please just have out with it, Mr. Fitzpatrick," she cut in as calmly as she could. The way the man sat so uncomfortably and fidgeted with his hands made her nervous.

"I hate to be the one to inform you, Miss Neville, but the majority of your father's estate has not been left to you."

It was a blow that struck her no differently than a fist in the stomach, but she tried to cover her surprise. If her father hadn't trusted her with his fortune, then who did he leave it to? Who would ultimately be made responsible for her well-being? He had no relatives that she knew of, no sister or brother who could take over the manor...

"May I ask to whom my father bequeathed his estate?"

"No," the man replied bluntly.

She stumbled for words at the unexpected response. "No?"

"What I meant to say is I don't know. I was put in charge of the small stipend left to you, but I do not even know the name of the lawyer your father charged with the remainder of his...fortune."

"I see. Thank you, Mr. Fitzpatrick."

"I'm afraid you don't, Miss Neville. You see, I have been left with instructions...after a period of one year following your father's death, the manor is to be transferred into the hands of this other lawyer and you will be required to vacate the premises."

"Oh," the sound came out with her breath. What on Earth had her father been thinking? Perhaps he thought she'd have married long before he passed on from this world, but her father was a shrewd man. Certainly, he hadn't overlooked the possibility that she might still be living in his home.

"Now, please don't think it too forward of me," the man's words jarred her from her thoughts. "But given the circumstances, I might have a solution. While usually these things would take time...If you would consent to be my wife..."

"Oh, Mr. Fitzpatrick, I would certainly never force upon you my own problems in such a manner. It is kind of you to offer, but I'm afraid I must decline."

"Right. Right, of course," he replied, looking flustered, making her think that his proposal hadn't been entirely a gallant offer in the face of her troublesome situation. He certainly wasn't the first young man to make an offer of marriage to her.

"If there's nothing further..." she started as she rose from the settee.

"No, nothing further." He rose a moment later, thrusting a handful of papers into her hands. "I'll leave you with these," he said and then crossed the room in long, fast strides, leaving her behind to catch up. She barely reached the front entrance by the time he'd retrieved his coat, thrown open the door and stepped outside.

"Good day, Miss Neville. I wish you well."

"And to you, Mr. Fitzpatrick."

She closed the door behind him, leaning against it to hold herself up. What had her father done? What was she supposed to do now? Where would she go?

"Miss Annika, are ye' alright?" a worried frown furrowed Martha's brow as she appeared in the hallway.

"I'm alright, Martha. It's just...It's just some bad news, I suppose."

"What kind of bad news?"

"It seems my father has left me in a rather difficult situation. Most of his estate, including the manor, has been left to an unnamed party."

"Oh, I see... Well, that *is* a difficult situation," Martha agreed, though she seemed to lack the staggering shock Annika had felt at the news.

"This doesn't surprise you?"

"Well, nothing yer father did had ever surprised me. He was always a complicated man. Don't ye' worry. I'm sure ye'll figure somethin' out. Ye've got his quick wit."

"I suppose you're right. I can always look for work. I was never much overjoyed at the prospect of wiling away my hours sewing and embroidering as some brutish rich man's wife."

She'd lived through so much tragedy and horror, she had hoped returning home would bring about a respite from the turmoil. A small break from the terrors that had plagued her mind day and night for nearly three years. But that place of solace she'd awaited for so long would soon be ripped from her, too.

Chapter 2

Gabriel paced back and forth across the gleaming wood of his small study, reading and then re-reading the papers in his hand. He'd read over the same words at least a dozen times, but they seemed no more real to him now than they had with his first pass.

William was dead. After all the time he'd spent fighting alongside him, he'd never imagined it could really happen. They'd talked about it, coming to that ridiculous agreement should anything take the man from this world. He felt the loss now more than he thought he would, mourning the passing of not only a brave soldier, but a good friend.

Placing the papers down on the small desk, he dropped himself into the chair behind it and breathed a heavy sigh. If he'd stayed, maybe he could have saved William; he'd pulled him from the battlefield once before. But Gabriel had fought and bled for his country, and the injury to his leg had rendered him useless as a soldier—at least temporarily—and by the time he'd recovered enough to stand alongside his fellow soldiers, the war had been over.

With most of his family lost to the war, he'd taken the meager savings he'd mustered up and headed out west, never expecting to hear about William or their agreement ever again. In truth, he hadn't thought about it at all these past months. Had he really agreed to such an outrageous arrangement? He tried to recall William's reasoning, but it escaped him, just as it had when he'd made his proposal. The man had seemed desperate, though how on Earth a man of his wealth could fathom himself desperate for anything, Gabriel didn't know.

But it didn't matter. Gabriel was a man of his word. He'd never had much money, never had much he could offer a person aside from his brute strength and the strength of his promise. And so, if he made a vow to do something, he did it, no matter the personal cost.

There was nothing left for him to do but honor the commitment he'd made to William. The man had made good on his end, providing him with more money than he could ever possibly spend in this lifetime—or ten more. And because of that, he should feel elated, but he didn't. A man's life was worth more than any amount of money, wasn't it?

The only reason Gabriel was now a wealthy man was because a good man had died. And before he'd met William, Gabriel had been able to do little more than sign his own name. But in the days and weeks in between battles, the man had taught him to read and write, educated him in economics and politics, and explained to him the mechanics of running a business...any business, from a plantation to a shipping endeavor to a homestead. Wasn't the sheer knowledge the man possessed worth more than the enormous sum of money?

He pulled a stack of papers from the drawer of his desk and settled himself to his task—even if it was the most absurd thing he'd ever done. He wrote one letter after another, filling each one with exactly what William had asked of him. It was one of Gabriel's more unique talents: he remembered things in ways that others couldn't. He could review an entire battle plan just once, and later remember every facet of the strategy with flawless detail.

He remembered every one of William's lessons and could recite the name of every man he had fought beside over three long years. As such, William needed only to tell him what to write once and Gabriel remembered every word of the thirty-two letters he'd been asked to send.

As each page dried, he folded it carefully and inserted it into an envelope, sealing it along with another incredulous shake of his head. William had been so certain his plan would work, he'd felt no need to strategize a backup, but that left Gabriel in a terrible predicament. If the man had been wrong, how on Earth would he follow through with the rest of the plan?

Chapter 3

Annika awoke long before the morning's sun rose above the horizon. She'd spent the past several hours of the night tossing and turning, and so it was with bleary eyes she greeted the day too early. She'd grown accustomed to it, but still she longed for the sleep of her childhood, calm and full of fanciful dreams. She'd been so innocent then, so unaware of the violence of which humanity was capable. But after having witnessed it first hand in the hospital, it permeated her mind, if not in her waking hours, then while she slept.

At first, she'd tried to go back to sleep after a nightmare had wrenched her from her slumber, but she'd learned it was for naught. The nightmares would only return to her when she closed her eyes. And since she was better able to keep the memories at bay while awake, she slept as little as possible, preferring to take a nap here and there rather than submitting herself to hours of tortuous dreaming.

Of course, no one was aware of her predicament. There was no one but Martha and Mrs. Potter, the cook in the household, and she didn't feel the need to burden either one of them. That meant keeping up pretenses, though; allowing Martha to help her change and ready herself for bed each night, and greeting her each morning as if she'd wiled away the night hours fast asleep. Last night, she'd been so tired when Martha had left her room that she'd buried herself deeper in her covers and given herself over to sleep, despite knowing what awaited her there.

The news of her father's will had weighed on her heavily these past several weeks, particularly because she hadn't the slightest idea what she was going to do. This home was the only remaining link she had to her father, and it was going to be taken from her in just a few short months. She could look for new lodging and find herself employment, but could she live so near the house she'd grown up in, never allowed to wander through it and remember the happy years there with her father?

Her alternative was to move away, but to where? Aside from the years she'd spent at the hospital, she'd never ventured anywhere in her life. And a move to a new city would be costly with no guarantee she would find the work she needed to sustain herself, Martha and Mrs. Potter.

What could he possibly have been thinking? With no more answers than she'd found the other hundred times she'd asked herself the same question, she thrust the topic from her mind. No good would come from wondering why, only in figuring out what to do now.

In a little more than an hour, Martha would be awake and she would turn her attention to getting some sort of plan underway...any plan for the future. She would look for work here in Boston, and consider a move to a new city when she had more than a meager stipend to her name.

"Good morning, Martha," she greeted the woman right on cue an hour later as she peeked her head into her bedroom. She pretended to yawn and stretch as she spoke, keeping up the pretense of a sound night's sleep.

Twenty minutes later, she descended the stairs to the dining room where Mrs. Potter had set down her breakfast. Next to it was the morning paper, and like every morning, she turned her attention to it before the food on her plate. It was a fool's errand, no doubt, but she couldn't help but look for news that would tell her something about her father. He'd been presumed dead, but until she knew for certain, she wasn't willing to extinguish the tiny embers of hope that he was still alive, still trying to make his way home to her.

But the newspaper was different this morning. It was folded to a different section as if it had already been read. She peered at the section in front of her, and her breath caught in her throat. It had been opened to the matrimonial advertisements. She'd passed over the section many times before, but had never paid it any attention. But now...it meant that Martha was looking for a husband. Martha was going to leave her, too. She thought back over the conversations they'd had the past few weeks. Martha had talked about new adventures, transitioning to a new life, but she hadn't given much thought to what the woman had said.

But then, if Martha hadn't said anything about her search for a husband, perhaps she'd been uncomfortable, too loyal to admit to her that she wanted to leave. If Martha wanted to leave, then Annika wasn't going to be the one to stop her. She wouldn't be the one to interfere with the kind woman's happiness. Martha had been there for her since she was a child, caring for her like a mother when Annika's own mother had succumbed to illness.

And if she could find the advertisement Martha was most likely to have responded to, she could take it upon herself to write to the man. But what kind of man would interest Martha into marriage? She scanned through the advertisements on the page, many of them so similar. Almost identical, in fact. It seemed every man out west was looking for an extraordinarily young and pretty wife with little brain and a substantial amount of money. She was suddenly glad she hadn't bothered with the section before, but couldn't imagine any one of these men being worthy of Martha.

And then she found one, like a diamond glittering amid the rough rock around it. He was a man of reasonable means looking for an intelligent, strong and amiable woman. He said nothing about wanting a young girl fresh from the schoolroom. And though Martha was an attractive woman, it pleased her that the man had said nothing about a need for a pretty thing to grace his home.

If it were possible to judge a man's character by the few lines of words on the page, then this man was the one most likely worthy of Martha. She would write to the man for her and wait to see if there was a reply before telling her. She would keep the letter simple, vague, sharing as few personal details as possible to leave that part of their getting acquainted to Martha. All she had to do was entice the man to respond. She would hand over the letter to Martha then, and let the woman share whatever she chose with the man.

And that was precisely what she did, but as she reached the bottom of the page, she hesitated. What name would she use to sign the letter? Her own, she decided. That way she would know if the man replied and could break the news gently to Martha. If the man did respond, it would be a simple thing to correct the name later. And the moment the eloquent letter was finished, she tucked it in her sleeve and snuck out to deliver it as quickly as she could, laughing at her own devious plan. It had been quite some time since she'd indulged in such intrigues. Though it was dishonest of her, she meant well, and she was certain she'd be forgiven.

****

The weeks flew by in a blur. Annika had applied to the only jobs for which she was qualified, but her search was not going well. It seemed since the cessation of the war, many young women were eagerly vying for places in the workplace as nurses, governesses and even nursemaids. As much as she hadn't wanted to branch out to other cities so soon, she might very well have to in order to sustain her small household. Then again, all of Mrs. Potter's family was in Boston. She might choose not to accompany Annika to a new city, and with Martha looking for a husband, she could very soon find herself in a new city, in a new job and all alone.

Even thinking about so much loneliness threatened to consume her a little more each day, which rendered it no surprise that she'd completely forgotten about her letter to the man out west until a response arrived with the mail that morning.

She darted off to her father's study—her favorite room in the house, especially since he'd been gone. She felt his presence there most, remembering the plethora of times she'd sat across from him while he'd read the newspaper, worked on his ledgers, read to her and talked with her. She could almost imagine him there at times, his deep voice recounting stories of his youth and telling her about her mother, the woman he'd loved and lost too soon.

She sat down at his big oak desk—not behind it, but in front of it, where she'd always sat as a child—and opened the letter with trembling fingers. If the man appeared at all decent, she would hand over the letter to Martha. How long would it be then before the woman moved away? Would it be weeks? Months? Could she hope to still have a full year with Martha?

Forcing her fingers to continue their task, she withdrew the letter from the envelope and gave two silent prayers; one for Martha, that the man might be her match, and one selfish prayer for herself, that he wouldn't be.

She read the man's letter with bated breath, giving her thanks to God that he answered the less selfish of her prayers. The man talked about his passion for books, sharing a love for some of her own favorites. He was an orphan, having lost both his parents as well as his brothers in the war. She felt a strange affinity for the man, knowing how devastating it could be to lose one's family. He'd left behind his home back east and headed west for a new life—something she only wished she was courageous enough to do.

Her first impression of him from his advertisement had been right; he was most certainly a fine choice for Martha. In truth, she couldn't have crafted a more suitable husband. Whatever displeasure Martha would feel from learning she'd gone behind her back, she'd forgive her easily when she read the letter from the man—from Mr. Cole.

She went to stand, but hesitated and sat back down in her chair. What was it that made her hesitate? From the limited information she had, she'd concluded Mr. Cole was likely a reputable man. Did she question whether he had the potential to make Martha happy?

Just then, two things struck her at once. First, she shouldn't have been meddling in Martha's personal affairs, and second, she was more than a little interested in the man herself. Which one made her pause, she wasn't certain. If she had no interest in the man, would she still be sitting in her father's study? If Martha had welcomed her involvement, would she have easily handed over the letter? A little bit of well-meant deception seemed to have placed her in a difficult predicament.

She was quickly remembering what had halted her intrigues as a child—they always got her into trouble. But for this particular indiscretion, there was a clear solution, unlike so many of her childhood antics. Or perhaps she'd matured significantly since then and finding the right solution wasn't as difficult as it had once been.

Rising determinedly from her chair, she left the room in search of Martha, and found her quickly, dusting the furniture in the parlor.

"Martha, I'd like to talk to you," she announced without preamble. It was better to come straight to the point rather than circumvent it and risk losing her nerve.

"What is it, my dear?" she asked, looking up from her task.

"I've done something I should not have, and I feel it's important to discuss it with you now. You see, several weeks ago, I noticed the newspaper open to a certain section. I speculated that you had...developed an interest in seeking out a husband, and I sought to help you with that task. I realize now I should not have done so, but I fear it is already done."

"I can't imagine ye've done any harm, and it was kind of ye' to think of me. Though, I must confess, I had not been of the mind to marry."

"Then why was the newspaper open to the matrimonial ads?"

"That, I canna tell ye'. Perhaps Mrs. Potter thinks it's time to settle down with a lad."

"I see." Mrs. Potter was at least sixty years old, if her grey hair and deep lines were any indicator of her age. It seemed unlikely she'd developed a sudden interest in matrimony after staving it off her entire life.

"Does that mean ye've written to one of the men in there?" Martha asked, her eyes alight with something that looked an awful lot like mischief.

"Yes, well, as I said, I thought I was helping..." she stumbled through an explanation, knowing Martha was hiding something, but not certain what that was.

"Would ye' care to tell me about him, if it isn't too bold of me to ask?" The same mischievous light danced in her eyes.

"I suppose, seeing as he was intended for you," she offered. "The man who responded, his name is Mr. Cole. He is an orphan, just like me, and he loves so many of the same books as me. He was a soldier in the war, though I do not know how long he served or his rank. The only title he used in his letter was mister. He was from the east but moved out west after the war. Though he did not say as much, it seems to me that he was perhaps in need of a new direction for his life after so much loss."

"It sounds to me as if ye're kindred spirits, my dear," Martha responded easily.

"No, Martha. Mr. Cole was not meant for me, but for you."

"As I told ye', I appreciate yer effort, but I'm not interested in findin' me a husband. Lookin' after yer pa all those years was enough for me."

"And you did a fine job, with both my father and myself. I know he cared about you very much."

"Thank ye', Miss Annika."

The sadness that flitted through Martha's eyes caught Annika's attention, and something occurred to her just then, something that had never crossed her mind once in all the years she'd been in Martha's care. Martha had spent more than a decade caring for her father since mother's death. She'd never once considered taking a husband—at least as far as Annika was aware—and looking back over the years, small things caught her attention now that never had before: the way Martha gazed up at her father; the occasional brush of her hand against his arm; the infinite patience in her tone no matter how obstinate her father would be; and the way she always spoke kindly of the man. They were all signs of a woman in love, weren't they? Annika didn't have any firsthand experience with the condition, but she'd read about it and heard about it aplenty, from books and friends who had fallen in love.

"Martha, were you in love with my father?" The question fell from her lips before she could stop it, and a light blush stained her cheeks over her inappropriate question.

"Aye, my dear, I believe I was." Martha's gaze grew wistful, and Annika immediately regretted bring it up.

"I'm sorry, Martha. That is none of my business."

"Nay, it's alright. Now what about this young lad who's managed to catch yer attention?"

"Oh no, I don't think that would be wise. He's in California, and I couldn't possibly venture so far from home."

"Why not, if ye' don't mind me askin'?"

"Well, there's you...and Mrs. Potter...and..." Without her father, was there anything else holding her to Boston? But wasn't that enough? How could she possibly consider leaving Martha? She'd been devastated to think Martha intended to leave her. How could she do the same thing to the woman?

"We'll be just fine, my dear. Mrs. Potter has her family, and I'd miss ye somethin' awful, but I always knew this day was comin'. Ye' were always too beautiful for me to think ye'd stay without a husband for long. I just thank the Lord ye've stayed with me this long. But don't go passin' up happiness on my account."

"I'd miss you, Martha. You're like a mother to me."

"I'm honored, my dear. I've always thought of ye' as my own daughter, which is why I need you to write to this Mr. Cole and see what comes of it."

"I'll think about it."

"Very good, my dear. Now, if there's nothin' else, I'll finish up the dustin'. That Mr. Edgewood intends on stopping by today, and I'll not have him thinkin' I've let the manor go to the dogs."

She'd completely forgotten about Mr. Edgewood—yet another eager, young gentleman. He wasn't the first to call on her since she'd returned from the war. And long before she'd volunteered as a nurse, her father had welcomed the slew of unmarried men vying for her hand in marriage. Despite his desire to see her happily wed, she'd told her father then that she had no interest in any of the men who knew nothing more of her than her pretty face and her family's overflowing coffers. And her opinion had not changed. No doubt, word had spread of her unexpected financial crisis, but that changed nothing. It meant that instead of her family's money and her pretty face, it was only her physical charms that brought them to her door.

"I think I might lay down for a while."

"Certainly, Miss Annika. But perhaps ye'd like to see to that letter."

"I said I'd think about it, Martha, and nothing more." Despite the sternness in her tone, she smiled at the woman's eagerness.

And despite her assertion, she stopped in her father's study to gather up a pen and paper on her way to her room. The moment she closed her bedroom door, she began to pace, the letter from Mr. Cole and Martha's words at the forefront of her mind. An hour ago, she would never have considered corresponding with a man from the west—especially not in the pursuit of marriage. Had his letter really affected her so much that she would consider such an outlandish idea? Perhaps it was her lack of sleep catching up with her because she was apt to say yes if she thought about it honestly.

What was even more surprising was the way her legs carried her toward the small table and chair by the window. She stared down at the paper she'd placed in front of her, wondering what on Earth she would even say to the man if she weren't writing to him on Martha's behalf. And stranger still was the way her pen began to float across the page, her thoughts seemingly appearing there before her like magic.

"I am very sorry to learn about your brothers. I was a nurse for three years in the war at the hospital in City Point, and I know firsthand its terrible consequences. More than that, only recently I lost my father to the battlefield as well, so I can well imagine your heartache."

She wrote from her heart because her mind seemed to have no say in the matter. It was still pacing back and forth across her room, wondering what step to take—if any.

She confessed her initial reason for writing to him, that she'd been eager to do what she could for Martha's happiness despite her own selfish interest in having her there. Even bolder of her, she admitted his words had compelled her to respond to him herself.

In a matter of moments, she'd filled one page and then another. Perhaps it was the long weeks she'd spent in the house with no one to talk to but Martha and Mrs. Potter, but she'd never imagined herself having so much to say to a man she had never met.

She hesitated once she'd slipped the letter into an envelope, thinking that perhaps she should not have been so forthcoming about her reason for writing to the man. Would he be insulted that she hadn't first written to him on her own behalf, or would he be flattered that his letter had compelled her to do so? No, she wouldn't change a word of what she'd written. She had been honest, and if anything came of it, then she would see it as God's will. If the man cried off, then it was for the best.

That decided, she set the envelope aside and laid down for the nap she'd intended. Never in a hurry to fall asleep though, she allowed her mind to wander, wondering what a new life in the west might entail. And when she hovered on the edge between the realm of sleep and wakefulness, she gave her mind free rein to venture further, wondering what a life with Mr. Cole might be like. Would the hardships that he'd suffered make him more attentive or distant? Was he truly interested in a partner to share his life with, or was he more in need of a woman to keep his house and cook his meals?

She smiled, thinking that perhaps she should have mentioned in her letter that she hadn't cooked a meal her whole life and knew very little about the upkeep of a manor. Her father had taught her how to manage an estate—though she had no idea why, given that he'd apparently intended to strip it from her. What was he thinking, and what would he think of her now to find her corresponding with a complete stranger, thousands of miles away?

What would he think to discover that so quickly, Annika had seriously begun to consider making herself the wife of that complete stranger?

Chapter 4

A week went by and then another, and unlike the last time, Annika was aware with the passing of each day and a knot grew tighter in her stomach in anticipation of Mr. Cole's letter. She'd read the previous one at least three dozen times, thinking more and more he was somehow a perfect choice for her. It was only logical, wasn't it? They shared so much in common that, barring some unseemly discovery, she couldn't imagine finding a better match there in Boston.

When his letter finally arrived, she opened it with a mix of eagerness and trepidation. Had he been pleased by her letter? Had he shared more information about himself in return or inquired more about her? Or had he written simply to tell her he had no interest in furthering their acquaintance?

And when had she become no different than a besotted, young maiden anxiously awaiting a suitor's call? Years of easily turning away one after another who appeared in her father's parlor, and yet this man she'd never met had her fingers trembling like a schoolgirl. It was ridiculous and unnecessary. If they continued their correspondence with one another and anything came of this silly idea, then so be it. Otherwise, her life would continue on just as it had been several weeks prior.

Feeling calmer, she slipped her letter opener beneath the envelope's edge and sliced through the top fold, retrieving the letter with hands that were decidedly steadier than they'd been a moment prior. She opened it and read Mr. Cole's words...and then read them again.

Something was wrong; the words she read couldn't possibly be there on the page. Her mind was playing tricks on her, though why it was playing this particular trick, she didn't know. Squeezing her eyes shut to clear her vision, she opened them a moment later and read the letter once more. The same words appeared there, and she could do nothing but accept she had read it correctly.

"Would you do me the great honor of consenting to be my wife..." She read the words near the bottom of the page aloud to herself.

A marriage proposal had never even crossed her mind in all the things she'd considered might be written in his letter. This was far too soon, wasn't it? She'd conclude it was so, but the other things he'd written made her hesitate. He was so different from the men she'd met, even from the valiant soldiers who she'd cared for in the hospital.

And he'd written about Martha, too; he understood her fondness for the woman who had been like a mother to her for many years and wouldn't think to separate them. Hence, he'd included passage for her to sail with Annika.

But was she really prepared to leave behind her old life and sail off to a new one—with a man she'd never actually met?

"Word from yer man out west?" Martha asked from behind, making her nearly drop the pages in her hand in surprise.

She couldn't very well lie to the woman, but she'd been so shocked by Mr. Cole's letter she had no idea what to say if she inquired further.

"'Tis good news, I hope," Martha prodded when Annika said nothing.

Well, there was no way of avoiding the topic now. She couldn't help but notice the same mischievous light in Martha's eyes that had been there each time they'd discussed the topic of the man out west.

"Mr. Cole has written to me. It seems my last letter to him was well-received," she began stiltedly. It was then that her eyes honed in on the date of their intended passage—just three days hence. Oh my, this was certainly progressing too quickly.

"Ye' should be smilin' then, Miss Annika, not lookin' pale as a ghost."

"Yes, well, it appears Mr. Cole is more eager than I had expected."

Martha stared at her, waiting expectantly for her to continue. But how exactly was she to explain?

Realizing there was only one way to do so, she steeled her shoulders and forced the words out. "Mr. Cole has made an offer of marriage. He has provided fare for the both of us to sail to his home in California in three days' time."

Martha smiled approvingly, as if she'd shared nothing more spectacular than a forecast of good weather ahead. Had the woman taken leave of her senses?

"This does not faze you, Martha?"

"I know in my heart this is what yer father would have wanted. And I've never known ye' to be a coward, my dear. Ye' wouldna' want to be startin' that now."

"Well, I suppose not, but this is all happening too quickly. I know nothing about the man, really. And I hadn't even given marriage serious consideration. You know how I've felt about the matter up to this point."

"But many things have changed, my dear. Yer a woman, full-grown. Ye've experienced war and plenty o' heartache. I wouldna' want to see ye' linger here forever. There's too much life in ye' to keep closed up like ye've been doin'. I think yer Mr. Cole is a fine choice."

"But you know nothing about him. How can you be so sure, Martha?"

"Call it intuition if ye'd like. All I know is ye' should be on that boat, and I'd be glad to be there with ye'."

"You'd come with me, Martha? Truly?"

"'Course I would."

It was a small relief to know that she would not have to face this new life all alone, that Martha would be there with her—if she chose to be on that boat, of course.

"I'll need to think about it, Martha. I know that will not leave us much time to prepare, but I can't possibly make this decision so lightly."

"Take all the time ye' need, my dear—at least for the next three days," she smiled and sauntered out of the room, leaving Annika to stare and wonder how the woman could appear so at ease.

Chapter 5

Gabriel paced back and forth across the docks. As the day had approached, he'd wondered more and more what had compelled him to agree to such a ridiculous arrangement. Certainly, this couldn't be what the man had wanted. But it had to be; he remembered every word of his conversations with William. Undoubtedly, this was William's plan.

Perhaps she wouldn't be on the clipper that would pull into the harbor shortly. He'd followed William's instructions to the letter, but it was out of his hands whether or not the man's daughter took the bait. In part, he hoped she wouldn't. Though he wasn't sure he could bring himself to spend William's money if he didn't follow through on his end of the bargain, he also wasn't certain he could marry this woman.

Marriage for money was not at all unusual, but gone about in this way, something didn't sit right with him. Firstly, he didn't know the woman at all. She could be a hideous, spoiled brat. Perhaps that was why William had determined to saddle her to him—a near-penniless man who hadn't had the misfortune of meeting his daughter. Though, he would admit that she didn't strike him as such. In their brief correspondence, she'd been honest and kind, witty and...something else that he couldn't quite put his finger on. Still, if she was a ghastly beast of a woman, would her decent character be enough to overcome her physical flaws?

"Her green eyes are unmistakable, Gabriel..." William had told him. "She inherited them from her mother, and to this day, I can remember the first time I gazed into Caroline's eyes—brilliant emeralds, I tell you."

Alright, perhaps she had pretty eyes, but every father was boastful of the attributes of his children—particularly when one was in the midst of trying to pawn his daughter off on a fellow soldier. In all likelihood, the woman's eyes were no more resplendent than the dull green of New England's autumn grass. He imagined her mousy brown hair trapped sedately at the nape of her short neck, and William's description of her "slim frame" either meant she was as scrawny as a mouse or else wide as an ox.

Still, there had been something about the tone of her letters, her voice coming through in a way that had him imagining a soft lilt. It wasn't that she struck him as weak. No, not weak at all, in fact, but feminine. But that was absurd—he couldn't possibly glean how the woman sounded from her words on a page.

He saw it then—the clipper—and it drew him from his inner thoughts. It was still far off in the distance, but close enough to follow the final leg of its travel into port. This was it. He was about to meet the woman he was supposed to marry. Marry—him? Was it worth all the money in the world to give up his freedom and commit to a woman he'd never met? Still, a small sliver of hope remained that Miss Annika Neville had chosen to decline his offer and remain in Boston. He'd happily have spent the day on the docks on a fool's errand if it meant he could leave there with his bachelorhood intact.

The ship sailed closer, and Gabriel's strides grew faster as he paced. Before long, the clipper had completed its journey.

Several moments passed but eventually, he watched as a woman stepped out from among the crowd waiting to disembark. She wasn't exactly the young maiden William had spoken of— he'd never imagined William old enough to have a child so far in her years. She was pretty, in a plain sort of way. She had soft features, from what he could tell at this distance, but her mousy-brown hair was pulled back harshly and tied in a knot just like he'd predicted. He would find grassy-green eyes when she drew nearer, no doubt, but it mattered naught. William had told him she'd been a nurse in the war, and with Mrs. Dorothea Dix's demand early on that her nurses be at least thirty years of age and plain-looking, he hadn't been expecting a remarkable beauty.

Still, something wasn't right. He immediately got the impression the woman was not the same unique combination of gentleness and strength she'd seemed in her letters. Perhaps she'd misled him in her letters, and he actually knew no more about her than any other lady he hadn't met in New England.

She looked out over the crowd that had come to gather at the dock, and he was about to wave his hand to garner her attention when she looked away. Something had drawn her attention back the way she'd come. She disappeared behind the passengers who were about to disembark. Maybe she'd taken one look at California and decided the place wasn't for her.

No...she'd gone to fetch her maid—that must be it.

And he must have assumed correctly because she reappeared a moment later. She stepped forward through the crowd, bidding those in front of her to part.

And then he saw her—Miss Neville's maid, Martha. Her glossy brown hair glimmered in the sunlight while wisps that had escaped her delicate-looking up-do whipped about her oval-shaped face with the wind. She was tall and slim, and she held her chin up just enough to appear confident, but not arrogant. She walked through the opening Miss Neville had created.

William could keep his money if he could only have the maid.

He watched as they disembarked, striving desperately to focus his attention on Miss Neville, but his eyes would have no part in it. They remained fixed on the lovely maid and her graceful movements. He raised his hand and stepped forward as they stepped off the boat, and Miss Neville spotted him right away. Her maid led the way then, her slender form coming to a halt no more than a yard from where he stood.

And the most magnificent emerald eyes looked up at him. "May I presume you are Mr. Gabriel Cole?" she asked softly.

Her teeth worried with her bottom lip for just a moment then, and it was all he could do to pull his attention away from her cupid bow lips.

But the maid couldn't possibly have the very same eyes William had described of his daughter. And the maid's voice was a soft lilt, just like he'd imagined of Miss Neville's. And why would Miss Neville's maid be the one to greet him?

Didn't that mean the maid wasn't the maid at all? She was Annika Neville...his betrothed.

Oh no. It felt as if good luck and misfortune had befallen him at once. Annika Neville was beautiful, with a voice that could both soothe and entice a man at the same time.

And he was absolutely certain she was trouble. This woman wasn't some plain Jane one married for money and honor. She was a woman he imagined a multitude of men would have gladly taken as their wife. So, what was wrong with her? How was it that her father had been unable to see her properly married?

"I am he, and you are Miss Annika Neville?" The question was unnecessary; the more he thought about it, the more he knew it was so. The way she carried herself, the perfection of her skin, and eyes that no two people could lay claim to but through inheritance meant she was a lady of refinement, and she was most certainly the daughter of William's emerald-eyed Caroline.

He chuckled to himself, just imagining how Mrs. Dix must have clucked in disapproval over such a comely, young nurse tending to the soldiers.

"It is a pleasure to make your acquaintance, Mr. Cole," she lilted as she offered him her hand. As he took it in his own, a tremor of excitement raced up his arm, and looking in her eyes, he could see she felt it too.

He guided her toward his carriage as he watched the leers and curious glances from the crowd that was assembled at the dock. He breathed a small sigh of relief as they reached the carriage and he helped her inside.

They didn't speak much on the way to his small homestead far away from the docks, but he pointed out places of interest along the way, a gleam of interest lighting her eyes with each one. The woman he now knew was Miss Neville's maid glanced out the carriage with interest, too, but she looked back at her charge almost continuously as if she was trying to assess Miss Neville's comfort or contentedness. The woman was certainly attentive to her charge, which either meant Miss Neville was a woman who had garnered her maid's devotion, or else a surly mistress who had obtained her maid's attentiveness through fear. Which one was it?

The question continued to plague his mind as they reached his home and he alighted from the carriage, reaching back to help Miss Neville and then her maid descend from the lofty height.

He groaned inwardly as the mangy hound he called a pet came racing around from behind the house and barreled straight for them. Miss Neville smiled and it surprised him when she didn't back off, but instead took a step forward.

"Be careful, Miss Neville. He can be rather standoffish with strangers," he warned her as the dog stopped in front of her, not wearing his usual apprehensive expression.

The dog usually barked and paced authoritatively whenever someone approached the property, but he certainly didn't appear threatening. And he seemed even less so a moment later as the dog stooped to lick her outstretched hand and then ducked his head beneath her hand to encourage her to scratch behind his ear. Did the dog seek to make a liar out of him?

"Yes, he seems quite vicious indeed, Mr. Cole," she smiled.

"It isn't often he makes friends so easily...or at all. Dog, inside," he instructed the animal gruffly—who proceeded to ignore him. It seemed his four-legged friend had been captivated by Miss Neville's beauty as well.

"It's quite alright. My father had a dog just like him when I was a child, and I confess, I was rather fond of him."

That was something he was not aware of, and now it didn't surprise him in the least that William had encouraged him to take the dog. And it made him wonder what else William had manipulated to the benefit of his plan.

"Where did you find him?" she asked with laughter dancing in her tone as the hound nuzzled deeper against her hand.

"He wandered into camp one day a few years back and never left. Most of the men ignored him at first, given the dog had no interest in fetching a stick or seeking attention like some of the pets they had back home. But the stubborn mutt wouldn't leave. In fact, he marched right into battle alongside us, and we quickly realized how useful he could be. He did his part each time, sniffing out graybacks and even attacking some of them who got too close. He didn't get himself caught even once."

"Then it seems he's a rather special animal."

"Yes well, I suppose he proved his worth," he told her with a smile. "In the last battle I fought, I had been pinned down, my leg seriously wounded. All I could do was stagger back toward safety. If it hadn't been for Dog's keen senses, I never would have spied the grayback laying wait in the bushes. He knew though. He lunged at the bushes and forced the man out. I figured I owed it to the mutt after his heroic acts to provide him with a comfortable existence."

"All this and you couldn't come up with a better name for him than 'Dog'?" she teased.

"I imagine he doesn't particularly care what I call him, so long as I call him for his dinner," he bantered back, already enjoying her company. And it certainly seemed she'd won the dog's affection. So, what was he missing? What was wrong with her that had made her unmarriageable?

"If you'll follow me, I'll show you to your room, and then when you've had an opportunity to settle in, I would be happy to give you a brief tour of the property," he offered, figuring if he didn't intervene, Dog would quite happily remain there at Miss Neville's feet, seeking her attention indefinitely.

She nodded and stood up straight, giving Dog a final pat on the head. He led the way into the house and down the hall to the bedrooms.

"The house isn't large, Miss Neville, so I'm afraid I'll have to ask that you and your maid share a room, but I've set aside my room—the larger of the rooms. I hope you'll be comfortable." He'd considered having a larger house built with William's money, but he was still a man; he hadn't wanted to establish his future entirely on the man's money.

"That's really not necessary, Mr. Cole. Martha and I will be perfectly content in smaller quarters. The sleeping quarters at the hospital at City Point were primitive at best, and I assure you I am no worse for it."

"Nevertheless..." He opened the door to his bedroom and motioned her inside while his theory that William must have turned his daughter into a spoiled, obnoxious brat crumbled. Primitive nursing quarters? Insisting she'd make do now? That didn't make her sound much like an overindulged princess.

However, the way she'd stubbornly stopped right there in the hall and refused to enter the room had him wondering if perhaps an overly strong will had thinned the marriage pool.

"And I suppose if I continue to insist further it will be for naught," he presumed aloud, curious how she would reply.

"You suppose correctly," she told him while her maid tugged on her sleeve. But the look in her eyes wasn't entirely one of stubborn defiance—though the light in her eyes told him she was enjoying it at least a little. Still, she was uncomfortable.

He nodded, seeing no good reason to argue the point further, and motioned in the direction of the spare bedroom further down the hall. She smiled, as if she'd won a small victory and made her way to the other room.

The woman was a conundrum, but he would figure her out. At first, he'd intended to proceed with the wedding as soon as Miss Neville arrived, but as her arrival had approached, he'd thought better of it. With Martha there, she would have a perfectly acceptable chaperone to placate her sense of propriety. Postponing the date for a week or two would give her the opportunity to re-evaluate her decision before committing to it irrevocably.

And that time would be more than enough for him to dig beneath the surface and solve the mystery. He wasn't certain whether anything he found could make him go back on his word to William, but he wanted to understand the enigma who was to become his wife regardless, to learn why William had such a difficult time marrying her off.

He followed then and deposited her luggage in the room. He'd have to see about finding a cot for Miss Neville's maid. Otherwise, the poor woman would be left to sleep on the floor. He again considered insisting they take the larger room, but thought better of it. He'd allowed her the victory, and wouldn't appear indecisive now.

"I'll leave you to freshen up, Miss Neville. If you have need of me, I'll be in the study down the opposite hall." He nodded curtly and left the room, closing the door behind himself and striding down the hall while the few things he knew about her tossed about his mind. She really was a mystery.

Chapter 6

"So, my dear, what do ye' think of yer Mr. Cole?" Martha prodded the moment she'd closed the door to their small room.

Martha bustled about while Annika contemplated her reply. It seemed too forward and too soon of her to say so, but thus far, she genuinely liked the man. He seemed intelligent and kind. But he also possessed a quiet strength that gave her the immediate impression he would have been a formidable foe to meet upon the battlefield.

Of course, the breadth of the man alone told her he must have been a capable soldier. He was taller and more muscular than any man she'd ever seen, and she was having difficulty denying the effect his physique had on her. He'd merely touched her hand, which sent tiny tingles shimmering up her arm. She'd touched countless soldiers in the administration of nursing care, and never had her body responded in such a manner. But what was she to tell Martha?

"He seems to be an affable man, don't you think?"

The woman giggled like a girl fresh from the schoolroom. "Aye, very affable," Martha replied with a knowing smile.

"You seem very amused," Annika observed drolly. "Would you care to impart to me what it is you find so humorous?"

"It appears yer quite taken with the man, and it seems to me he's equally taken with ye', 'tis all."

"I will confess this first meeting has gone better than I would have imagined, but I think anything more is rather presumptuous of you."

Martha said no more but the knowing grin remained plastered on her face the entire time they unpacked their luggage and transferred it to the closet opposite the bed. Within an hour, everything she'd brought from home was properly stored in Mr. Cole's guest room. But how long would she remain there in the guest room? She'd wanted to ask him about that—about when he intended for the marriage to take place—but she'd felt it too forward of her to pose the question right there on the docks.

Did he want to proceed with the marriage right away? Did he intend for them to have the opportunity to get to know one another? Her tumultuous existence for the past several years, combined with the upheaval once she'd arrived home filled her with a need to know what to expect.

She was knowledgeable enough to know he was attracted to her; the look in his eyes was certainly telling. But his advertisement and his letters suggested he was interested in more than just a comely wife; he valued intelligence and a strong character. Would he want to be sure of those things before he followed through on his offer of marriage?

If he didn't broach the subject over dinner, then perhaps she would. If he intended for this uncertainty to drag out for any amount of time, she at least wanted to be aware of it up front.

An hour after he left her in her room, she ventured out, down the hallway in the direction he'd pointed earlier. The dinner hour was approaching, and though she'd insisted Martha join them, the woman had refused. It seemed silly now to keep them segregated like this. Martha was like family to her, not her servant, and after nearly three years of toiling endlessly and working alongside women of all backgrounds, maintaining that distinction between mistress and maid seemed ridiculous. Nevertheless, she accompanied her, taking her duties as a chaperone very seriously. Annika approached Mr. Cole's study and tapped on the door tentatively.

"Come in," his deep voice called from the other side of the door. She liked his voice; the throaty timbre of it was quite appealing.

She opened the door then, and knew immediately this would be her favorite room in the house. The rich hues and pleasant scent of the wood made her feel right at home, as if she were in her father's study. And the desk which Mr. Cole sat behind was reminiscent of her father's. Not just reminiscent, a near replica, if a little smaller.

He'd been rifling through papers when she'd opened the door, but he set them aside and rose as she entered the room. Martha stayed back at the door, but seemed in no hurry to leave her there.

"I hope you've managed to settle in comfortably."

"Yes, of course—as I knew I would," she replied, a twinkle of victory no doubt lighting her eyes.

"I believe dinner should be ready any moment, if you'll accompany me to the dining room, Miss Neville," he asked, offering her his arm.

She saw Martha smiling approvingly as she stepped back from the door to let her and Mr. Cole pass, and she followed along behind them a few steps back all the way to the dining room. Once there, Mr. Cole pulled out a chair for her and then sat down next to her at the head of the table. All the while, Martha hovered nearby, and Gabriel smiled knowingly.

"Martha," Annika began, "I spent nearly three years in the constant company of men and it did nothing to tarnish my reputation." It wasn't that she didn't want Martha nearby, but rather the way she hovered made Annika feel as if her every movement was being scrutinized. "Certainly, I can keep my good name intact for the duration of a meal."

"Very well, Miss Annika," Martha agreed reluctantly, though she didn't move from where she stood.

"Mrs. Kent, my cook, will be along shortly, Martha. She is a discerning woman, and I'm certain she wouldn't let anything happen that could even border on the tattered edges of impropriety."

And he had been right. Though Mrs. Kent didn't hover in the same, obvious manner as Martha, she lingered by the doorway that led to the kitchen, keeping a watchful eye.

The next several days passed in the same manner, and though she had plenty of opportunities to talk with Mr. Cole, she was looking forward to their wedding day when she could do so without Martha or Mrs. Kent always nearby.

She'd finally worked up the nerve to broach that very topic— nearly a week after her arrival—and it had been as she suspected: Mr. Cole had been giving her time to make sure she was comfortable with her decision. She never would have imagined it possible just a few months prior, but in such a short amount of time, she'd become certain of it, indeed.

And so, when he proposed to her again over dinner ten days after her arrival in California, there was nothing for her to consider. Of course she would marry him. She couldn't imagine any man ever having the ability to affect her so thoroughly if she searched the whole world over.

She'd come to care for him quickly. Some would likely say too quickly, but it wasn't so surprising to Annika. She'd thought very highly of the man who'd written to her, and it seemed he was the exact same man in person as he'd been in his letters.

Chapter 7

Gabriel had never known one man could be plagued by so much guilt. And all in the course of upholding his promise, nonetheless! But as he left the church with his bride on his arm, the heavy feeling threatened to overwhelm him.

At first, when he hadn't known anything about Annika but her name, it had seemed like the honorable thing to do, to follow through with the agreement he'd made with William. But as he'd gotten to know her and their wedding day had neared, he'd questioned the honorable nature of it. She knew nothing of the reason why she was there; why he'd enticed her in the advertisement, using the precise words William believed would call out to his daughter. Why he'd responded to her letters the way he had and proposed marriage to her so quickly—as William had instructed him to do. He remembered the man's exact words: "She's intelligent, for sure, but sometimes that brain of hers is her own undoing."

Annika also didn't know that the only reason he'd sent passage for Martha to accompany her was because William had felt his daughter would be better be able to leave her old life behind if she could bring the woman who had been a comfort to her all these years.

What he didn't know though, was whether he could confess the truth to her now and risk her leaving. In the short time since she'd arrived, everything had changed. Though he hadn't given much thought to marriage before Annika, he would have revelled in his wedding day if their beginnings had been different. He couldn't explain exactly what it was he felt for her. Love? No, that was such a foreign concept, one he had always believed existed only in fairy tales. But whatever it was he felt for her made it impossible to imagine his life without her now.

And so he handed her up into the carriage and climbed up beside her, pulling her against him once inside just to feel the warmth of her next to him. And he did his best to block out the small voice in the back of his mind that reminded him over and over she would never forgive him if she ever found out the truth.

The wedding had been a small affair, with only the pastor, Martha and Mrs. Kent as witnesses to their union. But he wouldn't have wanted it any other way. He wanted her all to himself, and the fewer people he had to share the day with, the better. He wondered though, if he'd been too busy greeting well-wishers if he would have had less time to focus on the tumultuous emotions roiling inside him.

"You are not already regretting your decision?" she asked, bringing him out of his inward thoughts. But she smiled at him happily; she was only teasing.

"Of course not. With a bride such as you, what man in his right man would be such a fool?"

She laughed, nuzzling her head closer against his chest, and he closed his eyes, relishing in the feel of her so close and the warmth that radiated from her skin.

It wasn't long before they arrived back at the house. He would have liked to take Annika on a honeymoon, like the gentlemen of New England's upper society would have been able to do. And though William's fortune was in his grasp, he hadn't felt comfortable touching any of it since she had arrived. Even before that, he'd only issued the small amount necessary for the advertisements and her passage on the clipper. He'd have to decide what to do with it eventually. Though his guilt made him refrain from spending it, there was so much more he could offer Annika if he overcame his conscience.

Inside the house, it appeared that Martha and Mrs. Kent had been busy readying a wedding breakfast for them long before he and Annika had awoken. The dining table was set and vases of fresh flowers garnished its center.

And surprisingly, once the two women arrived back at the house a few minutes later, the meal was just about underway. Mrs. Kent even managed to surprise him.

"I don't feel comfortable joining you at the table after all this time, but I feel even worse not celebrating your marriage to such a lovely bride. So, I ask that you not get accustomed to my presence. I'll be taking my meals in the kitchen hereafter," Mrs. Kent informed him.

"I'm honored to have you join my wife and I for breakfast. Of course, you will stay too, won't you, Martha?" he asked as the woman began backing slowly from the room.

"Aye, I'll join ye'," she agreed, if reluctantly.

Annika smiled. It seemed his crossing the boundaries between employer and employee pleased her. Though, that didn't surprise him; she didn't seem to view her maid at all in the usual sense, but rather as a mother figure she valued immensely. And though a high-bred lady, she didn't seem terribly fond of the rules of decorum, regardless.

They enjoyed a picnic lunch a few hours later, and then the couple dined alone at dinner. Gabriel could feel the nervous energy that radiated from his bride, but she managed to keep it tightly in check, barely peeking above the surface every so often. With the meal concluded, he took her hand and helped her rise from the table. She looked up at him when he remained there, gazing down at her and savoring the moment of anticipation. Understanding dawned in her eyes a moment later, and though a blush rose high on her cheeks, she lifted her chin toward him. He leaned in, covering her soft lips with a gentle kiss.

And as he guided his young bride down the hall to the larger of the two bedrooms, he knew it would inevitably be the most memorable night of his life.

Chapter 8

More than a month passed, and Annika found it difficult to believe marriage could be such an enjoyable state. Had she known, she never would have postponed it for as long as she had. Of course, she suspected the reason the first weeks of her marriage had been so enjoyable had a great deal to do with the man who had become her husband. He was unlike any man she'd ever met, and while she had come to suspect as much prior to their wedding day, she knew it undoubtedly now.

The women she knew who had become wives had always reinforced her belief that she was better off unwedded, that the state of matrimony was anything but blissful. They complained about every facet of the marital state, even the mere presence of their husbands at the breakfast table. After that first night with Gabriel, she wondered if there was something wrong with her, because she could not possibly be happier. Whatever the reason, she looked forward to the serenity she found every night nestled in her husband's arms.

She had even begun to sleep through the night most nights. And those times when a nightmare managed to slip through the newfound peace that held them back, Gabriel was there. He would pull her closer into his embrace and whisper soothing words in her ear, more aware than most how the tragedies of war could haunt a person.

But that wasn't all there was between them. She looked forward to every facet of their days together. She had imagined that her enthusiastic feelings for him would have cooled quickly. How long could two people be in constant company of one another before growing bored? But now, she feared it was her own company that would bore her to tears after spending so many days and nights with Gabriel.

And she found the more she learned about him, the more she admired the man. She'd probed him so much over the past month that she wondered if there was anything left she did not yet know. He'd been born into a poor family, but his home had been full of love—at least, it had been until his father and brothers perished in the war. A year later, while Gabriel had still been fighting on the battlefield, his mother had passed away, too; he was certain she'd died of a broken heart.

He had no one now. But that wasn't true. He had her, though the more she learned, the more she couldn't fathom why he'd sought out a wife in the manner he had. Certainly, there would have been a multitude of young ladies happy to give up New England luxuries for the affection and companionship Gabriel had to offer. Nevertheless, she was glad he had.

In the days leading up to their wedding, she'd questioned the rationality of their situation. From his first letter, he'd been everything she could possibly want in a man, and that perfection had scared her. She had to be missing something, or at least she'd nearly convinced herself of it by the time she stood at the altar. But she'd traveled all that way, leaving behind her old life in favor of a new one with Gabriel, and she was ever more grateful for the courage that compelled her to follow through with their marriage.

She stretched then, opening her eyes to the morning's bright sun streaming in through the window next to the bed. He'd positioned his house beautifully, ensuring the bedroom window would capture the earliest rays, making it seldom that they would awake to a darkened sky, even early in the morning. It was only on those days when the cloud cover was heavy that the room was still dark when she awoke, but she didn't mind. She'd simply snuggle closer against Gabriel.

She looked over at the other side of the bed then, finding it odd that she wasn't pressed up close against him, but the reason became apparent quickly—he wasn't there. She must have slept far later than she'd expected.

In a hurry to see him, she sat up and wrapped her dressing gown around her body, but the moment she rose from the bed and turned to go in search of her husband, her stomach roiled. She sat back down, thinking she must have risen too quickly. She waited for the waves of nausea to pass, but they only grew stronger and she was forced to make a dash across the room.

"Are ye' all right, my dear?" Martha asked as she came into the room to find Annika bent over the wash basin at the table in the corner.

"I don't think so, Martha. I fear I've come down with something," she replied, remaining where she was for another moment, but as she stood there, the nausea began to pass.

"Is that so?" Martha came up behind her then and placed a cool cloth against the back of her neck. It seemed to help cool her body quickly and her stomach settled. "I think ye' ought to get back into bed then."

"No, no. I'm sure I'll be fine. I'm already starting to feel better. I likely allowed myself to go too long without food. It always did upset my stomach when food rations were tight at the hospital." Still, she sat back down on the bed for a moment just to be certain. She didn't want to end up having a recurrence at the dining table.

Martha stared down at her for a moment, but she didn't say a word. "Would ye' like me to see about yer breakfast, my dear?" she asked finally.

She did feel hungry, which she hadn't been expecting, given the tumultuous state of her stomach just moments before. "I suppose so, Martha. Thank you."

The woman nodded then and left the room, but she was back before Annika had finished washing and dressing. She came in bearing a tray laden with food. "Why don't ye' just rest and have yer breakfast here. Yer husband's gone out for the morning."

She wasn't surprised by the wave of disappointment that rushed through her; there hadn't been a morning since their wedding she hadn't looked forward to seeing his handsome face and talking with him over breakfast. Still, it wasn't as if he'd gone off to some foreign country. He'd be back soon. And though lazy of her to even entertain the idea, the notion of a relaxing morning in bed wasn't altogether unpleasant.

She eased back against the headboard of the bed and Martha placed the tray on her lap. Instead of leaving the room or sitting down on the chair next to the bed, she continued to stand there, eyeing her like she had a few moments before.

"Is there something wrong, Martha?" she asked when she felt the urge to fidget beneath the woman's stare.

"Nay, I suspect nothin's wrong, my dear."

"Good then." But Martha continued to stand there silently while Annika sweetened her tea, and although her sudden appetite bid her to dive into the meal, she couldn't. Something was definitely wrong with Martha. She set down her tea on the tray and looked up at the woman once again.

"What is it, Martha? Certainly, there must be something

vexing you this morning."

"It's just yer bout of nausea on my mind, Miss Annika..."

"Please, do not worry yourself about it. I'm certain I'm quite fine."

"My dear..." Martha began.

"Out with it, Martha," she laughed suddenly as she spoke, bemused by the woman's discomfiture despite the gleam in her eyes. What mischief was this woman up to now?

"Having been raised by yer father, there's certain things ye' might not be aware of..."

What on Earth was the woman talking about? "My father was a very intelligent man, Martha. You know that."

"Aye, he was. Well, the thing of it is...have ye' had yer monthly flow since yer wedding?"

Martha opened her eyes wide as if she was trying to convey some silent message in them as she spoke, and within seconds it dawned on her—what Martha had been trying to suggest. Her last had been about two weeks prior to her wedding, and given that more than a month had passed since then, well, she'd been so caught up in her new husband she hadn't even noticed. But that meant...

"Martha, I hadn't even considered...it had never crossed my mind. Do you really think...?"

"Aye, my dear, I do."

"Martha, I'm...pregnant!" she told the woman—as if she didn't already know. How long would it have taken her to figure it out if Martha hadn't been there? Would her mind have waited until her belly was well-rounded before it realized the miracle that was taking place inside of her?

"Aye, that ye' are." Martha smiled then, the brightest smile she'd ever seen lit up the woman's face.

She was going to be a mother. She was going to be the mother of Gabriel's child. Not so long ago, her life had been in shambles—her father gone and her home soon to follow, and here she was married to an outstanding husband and carrying his child. Life couldn't possibly have anything more wonderful to offer.

She'd never been a terribly verbose woman, but suddenly she felt the urge to ramble endlessly, to talk infinitely over her excitement. But Gabriel...she had to tell Gabriel. Wasn't it fitting that the Lord would slip in a lesson in patience at that moment, forcing her to keep her new knowledge to herself until he returned home? Hopefully, he wouldn't be gone long.

Though relaxing had seemed like a fine idea a few moments ago, she needed to move now, to pace the floors or wander the house. She felt so full of energy it seemed nigh impossible to contain it.

She moved to rise, but Martha gently stayed her action. "Ye' need to eat to keep up yer strength, my dear. Ye' have the baby to feed now, don't forget," she admonished, though the way she smiled down at her lightened her instruction.

She didn't want to sit still, but she couldn't argue with the woman; after all, she was responsible for another life now. And so, she settled the tray back on her lap and delved into her breakfast, now almost cold. She feared the queasiness would return, but it kept itself at bay the entire time she ate.

Thankfully, when she rose afterwards, she experienced none of the same nausea she had before. Martha took the tray ahead of her to the kitchen while Annika wandered aimlessly through the house. It would be a boy, she decided. Not that she opposed the idea of a daughter, but rather she relished the thought of a smaller version of Gabriel in the house. She would love the child, just as she loved the man.

A half hour later, and Gabriel still hadn't returned. Although she'd only known about the child a brief amount of time herself, she was anxious to share the news with him. They'd never discussed it, but she had a feeling he would be pleased to discover he was to become a father. Men seemed to take great pride in their offspring, she remembered, thinking back to the countless soldiers who had regaled her with tales of their own progeny. Though, most of them seemed to take far more pride in their sons than their daughters, but she would change that, at least in her small family, if the baby was to be a girl.

Another hour, and still Gabriel had not returned. Eager to see him, she wandered into his study, and she was immediately glad that she had. It was a room that reflected the man perfectly. The floors and walls needed no colorful stains to reflect their beauty; they were handsome entirely on their own, just like Gabriel. She wandered about the room, running her hands over the woodwork, toying with the paperweights and writing implements that laid across the desk.

A stack of papers in the corner caught her attention. Her name on the top page stood out and drew her nearer. Her father's name further down the page peaked her curiosity, and she scanned through the page, wondering over the topic of the official-looking papers.

Her breath caught in her throat and she grasped the edge of the desk to support her knees, suddenly weak enough to give out on her. The papers were official, indeed, the legal will of her father—William Neville. Reading page after page, she learned he'd bequeathed nearly all of his wealth to Gabriel—everything from the interests he had in businesses in New England and across the Atlantic, to the manor in Boston. The manor that had been her home. The manor she'd been told would be torn away from her.

Something was seriously wrong. Why would her father have left everything he owned to Gabriel? She hadn't even had any contact with her husband until after the war had ended, long after she'd received word on that terrible day that her father had been presumed dead.

She scanned through one page after another, searching for something...anything that would explain what she'd found. All the while, a small, scared voice in the back of her head told her she didn't want to know the answer. But she wasn't a coward. And what good would it do her to turn away now? She already knew something wasn't right.

As she came to the last page—a page not drawn up by lawyers, but written in her father's own hand, she finally understood. She knew what had driven her father to bestow upon Gabriel his entire estate. Her heart clenched tight in her chest.

Gabriel and her father had known each other previously. They had fought together in the war, during which her father had offered Gabriel his fortune all for one purpose. There had been only one thing he had to do in order to reap the vast riches her father had been offering. All Gabriel had to do was marry his daughter, to woo her in newspaper advertisements and letters, and convince her to agree to his proposal of marriage.

All the hours they'd spent engaged in conversation, they all flashed through her mind at once. He had never wanted her.

She'd been such a fool.

The only two men she had ever loved had conspired to deceive her. Her father had treated her as no more than a little child, forever assuming he knew what was best for her. And her husband...he'd married her for her father's money. He'd let her believe his feelings for her were genuine. He'd let her fall in love with him despite the cold, unfeeling nature of his wedding vows. He didn't love her. He didn't care for her. She was nothing more than a means to a very lucrative end to him.

But what was she to do now? She hadn't only been naïve and married the man, she'd been foolish enough to become with child. Could she just walk away from him? Turn her back on her marriage vows?

Yes, she could—she had to—because the vows she'd made had been nothing more than the lines in a script, a script in Gabriel's deceitful play. Oh, what a good actor he'd been. She had been thoroughly fooled. The words had meant so much to her when she'd spoken them aloud in the church, but they were suddenly devoid of meaning.

She had to leave. It was the only option. She couldn't possibly remain there with him, knowing he felt nothing for her, knowing if it hadn't been for her father's fortune he would not be with her now. She would return to Boston, or perhaps investigate to see if there was work for her in the west. It would be more convenient;

there was nothing for her to return to in Boston; no family, no home—her home belonged to Gabriel now. And the price of passage to return would eat up a large portion of what little money she had left.

No wonder Gabriel had been magnanimous enough to offer Martha's passage—it wasn't his money he'd been offering. And having Martha there meant he'd have to invest even less time in his burden of a wife.

Martha. What was she to do about Martha? Could she possibly find work enough to pay for them both as well as the child? She didn't know, but she would try. She'd been left a small amount of money from the will Mr. Fitzpatrick had delivered to her in Boston. It would provide her with enough to get herself and Martha settled. She had no idea if a woman could even buy property in the west, but she would look into it. If not, then there were no doubt inns nearby where she could stay until she figured out what to do next. The port city where she'd first met Gabriel— San Francisco—there would be inns there, no doubt.

All so quickly, her decision had been made. In the span of a few moments, her life had been turned upside down once more. Would it never end?

Yes. Yes, it would. She would take charge of her own future now. She would be nobody's fool ever again, and the tumultuous chaos that had ruled her existence since soon after the start of the war would come to an end.

And then there was nothing left to plan, no decisions left to make, and she was suddenly exhausted. She sat down in the chair behind Gabriel's desk, but it wasn't until she rested her head against her arm that she realized she'd been crying. Her cheeks were soaked in tears and they continued to cascade down her face unbidden. How could she have let herself fall in love with him?

Chapter 9

Annika spent the next hour packing her belongings, stuffing as much as she could into the small sack she would bring with her. She would take no more from Gabriel than she needed. That meant she and Martha would take only one horse, and she didn't want to burden the animal down any more than was necessary.

She had informed Martha of her decision, and despite the way the woman had railed in objection, she'd made it clear she would have no more discussion on the matter. The last thing she needed was for Martha to try to convince her to stay. The woman had good intentions, no doubt, but Annika's mind was made up.

Dog sat at the end of the bed, watching her as she moved back and forth between the closet and the sack opened on the bed.

"It's okay, Dog. You'll have him all to yourself again soon," she spoke soothingly to the animal. Right from the first moment he'd nudged her hand upon his head, he had weaseled his way into her heart. She would miss him, the animal who had been so brave—probably braver than a good number of men. The way he watched her, she was certain he knew something was wrong, but of course there was no way to make an animal understand. Their lives were simpler, entirely without the kind of deception of which humans were capable.

A few short hours ago, she'd been the happiest woman in the world; now, she was nothing more than the shell of the woman she'd been. Her tears had finally let up, and though an overwhelming weight threatened to crush her heart, she refused to let another one fall. Nothingness—that is what she wanted to feel. She pulled it to her and let it surround her like a cloak, staving off the wretched heartache that hovered in the air around her.

She heard the front door open and close quietly a moment later. Her pulse sped up, knowing the confrontation that was about to take place. She could have left before his return, saddled the two horses that remained in the small stable beyond the house and fled the home that had been such a happy place not so long ago. But the thought made her feel like a coward, and she refused to succumb to the fear that wished to escape the fight.

Though, in truth, she wondered if he'd fight her at all. There was no stipulation in her father's will that demanded Gabriel remain married to her. He could have easily filed for divorce the day after they'd spoken their vows and sent her on her way. She wondered why he hadn't done just that. But she wasn't left to consider it for long.

Gabriel appeared in the doorway, a smile turning up the corners of his full lips and a light gleaming in his mesmerizing eyes. How did he put on such a convincing front? If she didn't know better, she'd guess it was love radiating from his gaze.

But she did know better.

"I'm leaving, Gabriel," she announced without preamble. There was no sense in mincing words.

"You're doing what?" he asked in a deceptively quiet tone, the smile he'd worn turning to a frown in a blink of an eye.

"I'm leaving. I do not wish to stay with you."

"Something has upset you," he stated and she fought the urge to blurt out exactly what it was that had "upset" her. She had no wish to bear that humiliation, and it would be for naught. What good would come of it? She'd read the will for herself and the ridiculous agreement drawn up between him and her father.

What could he possibly say to defend himself? Nothing. He'd lied to her all this time; all for her father's money. That made it abundantly clear where his loyalty rested: with William Neville's fortune.

"I've nearly finished packing. I will leave within the hour. I will take Martha with me; there's no reason for her to remain here as your responsibility."

"Whatever it is, certainly there must be a solution, Annika."

She winced, an ache rising in her throat at the way her name rolled off his tongue. It had always done crazy things to her insides, and the effect was no different now, no matter how much she wished it to be.

"*This* is the solution," she forced out and turned her attention back to the pile of clothing she'd draped over the bed, folding it as neatly as her trembling fingers would allow and stuffing it into the suitcase.

"I don't understand. Tell me what has upset you."

Should she tell him? Give him an opportunity to explain why he'd done what he'd done? No, she shouldn't, and yet the words spilled out regardless of her decision.

"I found my father's will in your study."

Understanding dawned in a flash. She could see it in his eyes, and she prayed he would say something...anything that would explain it all away. But she knew there was nothing he could say.

"It was a long time ago, Annika. I didn't know you then. Afterwards, I didn't know how to tell you, but all I can say is it isn't the same now."

"You're right, Gabriel. It isn't. I read the will straight through, and there is absolutely nothing in it that states you must stay married to me in order to retain my father's money. It is all yours—his money, his business investments...his home. And they will remain yours whether I am here or not."

"Stay, Annika," he whispered simply.

"That is ridiculous, Gabriel. You have no more need of me."

Martha appeared in the doorway then, hovering uncomfortably. "I have been informed that I'm to be leavin' here, Mr. Cole. But I want ye' to know I do so under protest."

Under protest? Martha was on his side and was only leaving with Annika because she'd demanded it? It seemed she was utterly alone all of a sudden, but so be it. She wanted no one with her who was only there out of obligation. She fastened the sack, unable to recall a single thing she'd stuffed inside it, and turned to leave. Gabriel moved to block the door and all she could do was glare up at him, silently willing him to move before she broke down and cried like a child right there in front of him.

But a moment passed, and still he stood there, his muscular frame blocking her only exit. "Do you really mean to keep me here as a prisoner in your home?"

He stood firm for another moment, and she began to wonder if he intended precisely that. But then his shoulders slumped as he let out a heavy sigh and he stepped aside.

"I require a horse. Having recently acquired my family's entire fortune, I'm sure you can spare it. As soon as I am able, I will see it returned to you."

Without waiting for a response, she strode out of the room and down the hall. She could hear Martha's footsteps following quietly behind her, but not Gabriel's. He didn't make a single move to stop her.

"I do not want you with me, Martha. I shall have no one with me who is only there under protest," she informed the woman as she reached the front door.

"But my dear, yer condition..."

"Silence, Martha. I trust that you are at least loyal enough to hold your tongue."

Tears brightened Martha's eyes and they tugged on something deep inside her. Within seconds, she was half-tempted to change her mind, but instead, she yanked open the door and dashed out before her heart swayed her to do something foolish.

Chapter 10

Gabriel had wanted to be angry at her. After all, it had been her snooping around his study that had created the mess. He'd wanted to scream in protest when she stormed out the front door and drag her back inside. But he hadn't. He'd stood by silently and let her walk right out of his life.

It had been the right thing to do, hadn't it? He had known from early on that the lie between them would do irrevocable damage if it ever got out. She could never forgive him for what he'd done. She'd seemed certain that he felt nothing toward her, and by the scathing tone of her voice, it was clear he'd only imagined her feelings toward him.

He could have told her that the money no longer mattered to him, that he'd gladly hand it all over, but she wouldn't have believed him. And he couldn't blame her. If the roles were reversed, would he have given her the benefit of the doubt? There was no way to answer that question; he'd learned it was nigh impossible to judge how a man would act until that man were placed in the situation. Otherwise, it was nothing more than theory and conjecture.

But left alone in the small house that suddenly seemed too big for just him, he saw her in everything. She hadn't even been there just a few months prior, but she'd infiltrated every part of his heart and home in such a brief amount of time. His life felt empty since she left, even though he'd spent most of his life unmarried. But since he'd had Annika, he couldn't imagine his life without her.

Of course, it had been the money and his promise to William that had compelled him to marry Annika. But since he'd met her, gotten to know her, he'd fallen in love with her. What a stupid man he'd been.

He'd followed not far behind her the day she left, making sure she arrived at her destination unharmed, and he'd sent Martha to her the following day. He knew once she'd had a chance to calm down, there wasn't any chance she would send the woman away.

And then he'd buried himself in the knowledge William had bestowed upon him, using the wisdom to increase the small amount of money he'd earned as a soldier. Especially now that William's fortune was the reason she was no longer there, he had positively no interest in spending the man's money. He wanted no part of it.

Months later, he sat at his desk, staring curiously at the envelope in his hands. It had been delivered to him just now, and he couldn't tamp down the hope that maybe it was from Annika. He opened it quickly.

"You must go to your wife. She needs you," was all the note said, and panic welled in his chest. What could it mean? Had something happened to Annika? He'd read about the hefty ransoms rich men had been forced to pay to recover their loved ones. Had she been injured—or worse—because of him, ultimately because of his stupid promise to her father?

He had no idea what to expect, but he wouldn't wait a moment longer to find out. Darting out of the house, he saddled his fastest horse and flew off to the city at a breakneck pace.

Once there, he went straight to the only place he could think to go—to the inn where he'd seen her enter on that awful day several months prior. But would she be there now? Had she moved on, or even gone back to Boston without him knowing? He'd felt so guilty for what he'd done and how he'd hurt her that he'd left her alone entirely once he'd seen she had arrived safely at the inn. And after sending Martha to her, he knew the woman wouldn't let anything happen to her charge.

He left the horse with the young groom out in front of the inn and dashed inside, finding the innkeeper quickly and inquiring about his wife. He wasn't sure which name she would have used, his or her father's. "Is there a Mrs. Annika Cole staying at your inn?" he decided to ask.

"And what would you be wanting with the young miss?" the man asked, eyeing him suspiciously.

"I'm her husband, Gabriel Cole."

"Oh, my apologies, sir. Yes, of course your wife is here. I'll show you to her room."

Relief flooded his veins. She was there. All the wretched worries that had flooded his mind upon receiving that note...but she was alright. But then, who had sent the note? And why?

"That won't be necessary. Please just tell me where I can find her." The last thing he wanted was the innkeeper standing there while he banged down the door, not certain Annika would let him in.

"Just up the stairs and down the hall, last door on the left," the man instructed, and Gabriel nodded, thanking him for his help. He turned on his heels and strode across the room, flying up the stairs, nearly racing down the hallway. But instead of pounding on the door, he knocked casually, hoping that she might open it, expecting to find someone other than her husband standing on the other side.

A moment passed, and he heard nothing. He'd wait a moment longer before banging down the door, but his patience was running thin. Something was obviously wrong for someone to have sent him that note, and he needed to make sure she was alright.

He heard her soft, lilting voice then. "I'm coming," she called, and after a few more seconds, the lock turned and the door opened slowly. Her beautiful eyes stared up at him in shock, and her cupid bow lips parted. She didn't appear to be injured. Her face was just as perfect as it had been the last time he saw her, but his gaze continued lower, searching for the source of the anonymous writer's concern.

And then his breath caught in his throat, and it seemed his heart had ceased its beat. Her belly jutted forth in front of her; a belly that could only be so rounded if she were...

"What in the world?" he whispered in stunned disbelief. Was the baby she carried his? Had she welcomed another man into her bed the moment she'd been free of him? No...he knew Annika, even if he wasn't entitled to know her so well. The baby was his. She was carrying his child and hadn't told him. Had she known about the pregnancy the day she'd stormed out of his house? So many thoughts collided all at once that it made his head ache painfully.

"What are you doing here, Gabriel?" she asked coldly, though he noticed she kept her gaze settled on his shoes.

"I received a note...I feared something had happened to you, and indeed something has, though not what I expected. Did you ever intend to tell me about the child?" he asked, not certain how he felt. Was he angry with her? With himself for allowing her to leave? For failing to try to convince her to come home once she had?

"There was no stipulation in my father's will regarding a child. I believed it would not be of interest to you," she said to his shoes.

He stormed into her room then, certain that the anger he felt was winning out at the moment. Still, he was careful to circumvent her swollen frame. Looking around quickly, he noticed there was no sign of Martha there. No sign that she'd ever been there.

"Where's Martha?" he asked, wondering what had happened to the woman who he was certain would never leave her side.

"I fear I do not know."

"You don't know?"

"No, I do not. I awoke to find her gone several months ago. The note she left said only that it was imperative she leave. I have not seen or heard from her since." She'd found a new spot to focus her gaze, a spot somewhere on the floor beyond him, but even with her head downturned, he could see what she clearly fought to hide. Tears.

If he'd known the woman hadn't been there all this time, that Annika had been completely alone...alone and pregnant with his child! All the anger he'd felt fled his veins.

"Annika, I understand that you were angry, and you had every right to be. But I'm your husband, not because I have to be, but because I want to be. It's true that in the beginning, I was making good on my word to your father. I was upholding a promise, Annika, not just trying to get my greedy hands on his fortune. I vowed to marry his daughter should that valiant soldier perish in the war. He was so concerned about you, about how you would cling stubbornly to the life you'd led up to that point and never find happiness of your own."

"And you have made good on that promise. You convinced me to leave the only home I'd known, and changed the course of my life entirely," she replied, her hands moving to rub her stomach as she spoke.

"Good, then it is agreed my promise has been fulfilled. There is nothing further I have to gain from remaining married to you."

She nodded her head slowly and dejectedly as fresh tears trickled down her cheeks.

"Then come home with me, Annika."

Her head shot up at his request, forgetting her need to hide her tears. "What?"

"I miss you terribly and I want you to come home."

"But I thought—"

"I know what you thought, my love. And while I did not know you at first, I do now. I have fallen helplessly in love with my stubborn wife."

"You love me?"

"Is that really so hard to believe? You are a very loveable creature, Annika, I assure you." He pulled her into his embrace then and she went willingly, though she stared up at him the whole time, still searching his gaze.

"I love you, too, Gabriel. When I found those papers, I thought it meant you didn't want me; that you felt nothing for me. I was hasty, but I was so afraid..."

"There is no explanation necessary, dear. It is I who owed it to you."

"You really do love me?"

"Yes, I do, with all my heart. But it seems I'm going to have to find room to love another." He grazed his hands over her swollen belly, and as if to share in his agreement, he felt a tiny thump from inside her. He was going to be a father, and by the looks of Annika, very soon indeed.

Chapter 11

They'd traveled from the city back to his house—their house—that afternoon, and though they rode in silence, Gabriel held her close. Annika thought back over the past few months, thanking God she hadn't had the strength to sail away from San Francisco.

When she had first arrived at the inn, she intended to stay only a few days before making up her mind about a more permanent arrangement. As the days wore on, however, she hadn't been able to commit to any particular path. Plenty of options came to her, but there had only been one that satisfied her heart: running back to Gabriel.

She'd resisted, though the urge to give in had grown stronger each day. She'd tried to refute the love she felt for him, but that had become more difficult to do once the curve of her belly became the physical proof of the child that grew inside her. The child was proof of their union, and if not of their love for one another, then her love for Gabriel.

When she'd opened the door and found him there, all the emotions she had worked so hard to tamp down would not be held back any longer. Annika had been away from him for months, more time than they had even had together, and yet her feelings for him were just as strong. Time had done nothing to lessen the impact the man had on her.

She only wished Martha could be there now to see them reunited. Martha had pestered her to no end that whole first month at the inn, insisting that she had made a dire mistake. With her own conscience questioning her decision, the last thing she'd needed was for Martha to heap on more cause to doubt herself. But then she'd disappeared. She had left sometime during the night with just a few words scrawled haphazardly on a piece of paper to say goodbye.

Annika's loneliness had mounted quickly after that, so many months with no one but herself for company. The nightmares had returned. With no love in her life to cast away the shadows of those dark years, they haunted her with renewed vigor, countless soldiers calling out to her from beyond the grave.

But it had all been her own fault, her hastiness in jumping to the conclusion Gabriel felt nothing for her. She could only thank God that he'd come for her, that he hadn't determined to get on with his life without her.

Just a few short weeks later, she'd been reminded how infinitely grateful she was that he'd come for her when Gabriel helped to bring his son into the world, and it had been both the most terrifying and exhilarating night of her life. She'd woken to the pains early—a full three weeks too soon, and in the middle of the night, there was no help to be found nearby. He'd been so calm and reassuring, staying with her through every moment when most men would have been apt to keep far away. If it hadn't been for his soothing presence, she had no idea how she would have made it through.

The moment he'd placed their son in her arms, she knew without a doubt she was precisely where she was supposed to be. Some place deep inside her told her what she should have realized all along: she was home.

There were only two things that were missing now, she thought to herself a few weeks later as she laid Brandon William Cole in the bed Gabriel had crafted for him by hand. Annika missed her father terribly and wished he had the chance to meet his angelic grandson. She wasn't even angry with him anymore for having plotted to deceive her. How could she be? She had to admit if it hadn't been for her father's hand in it, she never would have found the man she loved so dearly now.

And then there was Martha. She couldn't help but wonder about her—where she'd gone and why. Had she decided the west wasn't for her and hadn't wanted to confront Annika on the subject? And if so, had she gotten home safely? She'd written to her at her father's manor, hoping she'd returned there, but she received no response.

Martha seemed to have disappeared. It stung, thinking that the woman she'd cherished like a mother could have abandoned her when she did—alone in a strange city and with child. But she couldn't be angry with Martha, not when it had been the woman's presence that had given her the courage to venture to the west in search of a better life. Thanks to Martha, she'd found it.

Just then, she heard the sound of horses approaching quickly outside. Gabriel had been at home all morning; who else would be coming to the house? Martha sprung to mind, but she tamped down the thought quickly, not willing to let herself respond to such hope.

Still, she tiptoed out of the bedroom as quietly as she could and swiftly made her way down the hall. Gabriel was already at the door, looking at her strangely. "Annika, I... I didn't want to raise your hopes, which is why I did not tell you."

"Tell me what?"

"I began making inquiries shortly after we were married. It was ridiculous, of course, but nevertheless, I felt a few well-placed letters could not hurt. At first, it seemed naught would come of my inquiries, but after you left, and I had a little bit of money to my name, I offered a reward for information..."

"What inquiries, Gabriel? What information? I don't understand."

"Apparently, letters in response to my inquiries had been sent to Neville Manor in error. I only just received them a week ago."

"Gabriel, do you mean to be speaking in riddles?" She cracked a smile, but the serious glint in his eyes told her this was no laughing matter.

"Take a deep breath, my love, and please try not to be too angry with me."

He opened the door then and she saw a carriage come to a halt ten yards from the house. A man swung down, placed a footstep at the base of the carriage and opened the carriage door.

Martha stepped out, taking the man's hand as she descended the steps. Annika squealed in delight and dashed toward the woman, wondering all the while how on earth Gabriel could think she would be angry. He'd sent out inquiries—he must have been trying to find Martha. What a wonderful man her husband was!

But Annika stopped abruptly, nearly tripping over her own feet just a step away from Martha's open arms. What on Earth? It couldn't be. It wasn't possible. A sob caught in her throat, wondering what trick her eyes were playing on her. Had all those years of nightmares finally driven her to lose her sanity altogether?

Gabriel came up behind her, and placed his steadying hands around her waist, not lifting her, just supporting her, and she was grateful for she didn't know if her legs would hold her up much longer. "You are not imagining things, my love. I promise you," he told her as if he'd been able to read her thoughts.

Martha closed the distance between them and hugged her quickly, placing a kiss on her cheek before moving aside. Annika swallowed hard and tried to take a deep breath, afraid her heart might pound clear out of her chest.

"Father..." she whispered finally as the man in the carriage stepped down with some help. She leaned into Gabriel for support as disbelief warred against exquisite hope.

"Hello, Annika," the man spoke, the words stilted as if he forced them out through a tall wave of emotion.

He sounded just like her father, and when he smiled at her and stretched his arms open, it couldn't be anyone else. Her legs that were weak just a moment before carried her swiftly towards the man, and she threw her arms around him, not entirely certain he wouldn't disappear in a puff of smoke at any moment.

But he didn't disappear. He hugged her back, and her disbelief gave way as tears of joy cascaded down her cheeks.

That's what Gabriel had been trying to tell her. He'd sent out inquiries about her father's whereabouts, not willing to conclude he was dead as the military had.

She held her father for so long, she wondered if her arms had grown numb, but she didn't care. Suddenly, every person she loved was right there with her, but just then, she noticed that Martha looked worried, a frown furrowing her brow.

"I had hoped we'd make it back in time," Martha began, and quickly Annika understood what was bothering the woman. She'd tried to bring her father back to her in time for the birth of his grandson, and because it was still a full week before Annika had been due to give birth, Martha worried she'd lost the child.

She noticed then that Gabriel was no longer standing behind her, but as she turned around, she saw him reappear from the front doorway, carrying her beautiful son.

"Colonel Neville, may we present to you, your grandson, Brandon William Cole," he announced proudly.

Tears gathered in her father's eyes, the eyes of a man who did not easily succumb to crying. He opened his mouth to speak, but no words could escape; he gave up, stretching out his arms to hold the infant instead.

Her father was standing before her, holding her son. It could be considered nothing short of a miracle from God.

"How in the world did you end up with father, Martha?"

"I found the letters from people responding to yer Mr. Cole lettin' 'im know where yer father'd been seen while I was stayin' at the manor. I was there hagglin' with that Mr. Fitzpatrick for the name of the other law firm yer father'd used."

"You were trying to secure the manor for me? Martha, I don't know what to say."

"Say nothin', my dear. I was only concerned ye'd follow through on that leavin' business you were up to. And I couldna' stand the thought of yer child bein' raised in that inn. I had to do somethin'."

"Thank you, Martha," she said simply.

"When it comes to ye', there's nothin' I wouldna' do."

"Gabriel, there is something I must ask you," her father started, stroking the soft golden curls on Brandon's head.

"What is that, Sir?"

"What are you doing living in this shack when I'd left you enough to build a veritable castle?"

"I worried a castle would look out of place in California, William, or else I would have been sorely tempted," he joked. His voice grew somber then, "Money was not the only thing you bestowed upon me, William. Your good business sense proved infinitely valuable. I have made a few good investments with the small amount of money I had left from my years as a soldier. They have done quite well, and I anticipate they will continue to flourish for some time. I am happy to say I do not require your fortune, my friend, but I'm afraid it is only the money I can return. I have no intention of returning your daughter to you."

"Yes, I thought you might feel that way. I know it was wrong of Martha and I to meddle the way we did, but I knew in my heart the two of you were made for each other."

Martha had meddled, too? But how?

"Martha..." Annika eyed her suspiciously, though with not an ounce of animosity.

"Aye, my dear. 'Tis true. Yer father made his wishes quite clear to me in his letters while he was away at war. 'Twas my job to help steer ye' in the direction he saw fit for ye'."

It seemed all the people in her life had conspired together. But they hadn't conspired against her, they'd conspired to make her life as happy as it could be. She knew that. She knew that none of them would ever want to hurt her, and though in any other circumstance, she wouldn't relish so many people trying to take charge of her life, Annika loved them all the more now for how much it proved they cared.

She'd just have to work extra hard to make sure every one of them was well aware she could be a strong, independent woman, too. She smiled to herself then, thinking of how much fun she was going to have along the way.

THE END

Mail Order Bride: Grace's Second Chance

City Point, Virginia - 1865

Chapter 1

Soldier upon soldier was rushed into the operating tent until the small space appeared to be ready to burst with wounded bodies. Never had there been so many men in need of serious medical attention at one time in the Virginia hospital. Groans of agony assaulted Grace's ears and the bloody scene before her made tears well in her eyes and churned her stomach violently. But she'd grown accustomed to the visceral response.

Steadying herself, she surveyed the room in search of the man most in need of attention. She found him quickly: the man who entered the room last, who stood wobbling against a fellow soldier's gurney, bleeding from wounds to his arm, his chest and his side. He was dangerously pale, and the way he balanced precariously told her he'd also suffered trauma to at least one leg as well, even if she couldn't see the injured extremity at the moment.

It wasn't only his injuries that drew her attention. Despite them, he stood firm, his shoulders straight, rejecting the care of all the doctors and nurses surrounding him, and his voice rose loudly above the rest of the noise in the room.

"You will see to my men right now," he demanded, and his tone brooked no refusal.

He was seriously injured and struggling to remain on his feet, but she knew right then the man would not back down.

Still, the staff continued to hover around him, reaching to get him onto a gurney, not recognizing the steely determination in his eyes. They did move more warily now, though, waiting perhaps for the soldier to strike out at them.

"Major Cade, I give the orders around here. You will submit to my staff this instant," the ever-arrogant Dr. Kiloran demanded in a voice that sounded weak in comparison to the soldier's, despite the unruly Major's perilous condition.

If someone didn't do something soon, the whole lot of freshly wounded soldiers would perish due to neglect.

"Major Cade," Grace spoke up, surprised by the strength of her own voice. "If we treat your men, you'll then submit to our care, correct? And not one moment before?"

"Yes, Ma'am."

"Then you heard the Major; we haven't a moment to spare." Every set of eyes in the room was on her, and she felt the urge to cower away from the heated gazes. If looks could kill, then Dr. Kiloran's would certainly have drained the life from her body.

Regardless, she sprung to action and the room followed suit, removing bullets, bandaging and stitching wounds. One poor soldier's arm was so badly mangled that there was no hope for it. And while Grace wasn't one to condone the frequent practice of amputation she so often observed, she couldn't deny Dr. Kiloran's diagnosis in this particular case—not that he would have listened to her if she hadn't. A mere nurse knew nothing in comparison to the great and mighty doctor.

When finally, every one of his men had been tended to, she turned her attention to the obstinate soldier who'd demanded the treatment of his men before his own.

"Shall we see if enough blood remains in your body to bother stitching you up," she tried to tease, wiping her damp brow as she approached the unapproachable figure that oversaw the goings-on in the room.

He nodded, but as he took a step away from his perch at the edge of the gurney, he stumbled, and it became quite clear he was in very poor condition. She cursed herself silently for taking up the Major's insistence that his men be seen first. She'd known he was in a bad way, and the time that had passed hadn't done anything to improve his situation.

It wasn't that she hadn't cared; it was quite the opposite, in fact. She understood what he was doing and sympathized with his plight, seeing his wounded men all around him. If it were her sister, Rebecca, who'd been wounded with limited people available to help her, Grace wouldn't have accepted any care either until Rebecca had been tended to.

She closed the distance between them in one long stride, wrapped his arm around her shoulder to keep him from falling over, and guided him to the empty gurney a few steps away.

Seeing her success in getting the soldier to acquiesce, Dr. Kiloran strode across the room, the same angry look on his face. The other nurses thought he was attractive. She thought he was arrogant. He surveyed the soldier's wounds briefly, settling his attention on the grim-looking gash on his leg.

"I hope you're pleased with yourself, Miss Williams," he said grimly before turning his attention back to the soldier. "I'm afraid I'm going to have to take that leg, Major."

"Pity, because I have no intention of giving it to you."

"It is unavoidable. Though it is unlikely it could have been saved an hour ago, it is impossible now," he told the soldier plainly, though he glared at Grace as he spoke.

"You'll do no such thing! I like my leg perfectly fine where it is, and I have no wish to have it removed."

"It is not your decision. I am the doctor here, and you'll defer to my better judgment."

"You will keep your hands away from me, Doctor," he sneered, "or else I'll be forced to remove those hands you hack away with. I think perhaps you would gladly take death over the loss of those limbs, would you not? How else would you maim and mutilate your patients?"

"Dr. Kiloran," Grace spoke, her voice barely more than a whisper. It was unwise of her to stir up trouble, but she'd always felt the doctors there were too quick to lop off arms and legs, not sensitive to the fact that a man might need those appendages after the war.

"If the Major wishes to keep his leg, I believe we may be able to save it. We have seen soldiers with worse wounds recover…"

It wasn't entirely true. The Major's wounds were severe, but she'd seen enough soldiers perish after having their limbs removed that she couldn't imagine it was far from the truth. Despite her insistence of the importance of sterilizing surgical equipment since her arrival, the doctors were still just as quick to use the same soiled instruments on one patient after another.

And little surprise, infection after such surgeries ran rampant in the hospital. Even if the doctor could convince the Major to submit to his verdict—which she highly doubted he would—there was a very real chance he would waste away in the days that followed from a raging infection to the wound site.

The doctor's face grew so red, she thought he might set ablaze at any moment. She watched as a vein throbbed violently in his neck while his jaw clenched so tightly, it shook from the force of it. He was certainly not pleased with her observation, and she had a feeling she'd feel the brunt of her insubordination for some time to come.

He was quiet for so long, Grace wondered if his clenched jaw had locked permanently in its position, but then he swallowed hard and looked at her. "Fine then, have it your way. Clean it out and patch him up, Miss Williams. And don't take too long with it; Major Cade won't be long for this world anyway with you tending to him."

He strode away before she could say another word, and she tried to tuck away the feeling of dread that settled low in her stomach. The Major needed her full attention now, and she prayed she hadn't just condemned the brave soldier to his death. Squaring her soldiers, she grabbed a stack of cotton cloths and arranged them over the bleeding wound on his side, the most severe looking injury aside from the one to his leg.

"Hold this down hard," she ordered, and he did as she bid without complaint. "I need to tend to these as well, but your leg has to be my top priority at the moment. And as you can see, I'm not going to have any help from the rest of the staff."

"Do what you must, Miss Williams," he replied, his voice almost normal except for a deep strain that rose through the tone.

Suddenly, she was having serious misgivings, realizing that she would need to employ his help in order to have any hope of accomplishing this enormous task. "I don't think you understand, Major. I...I cannot do this on my own. I need your help, and that means I cannot give you chloroform. It is going to be very painful."

"I understand. As I said, do what you must. I will assist in any way I can. I'll do my best not to move and thwart your efforts, if that is your worry."

Actually, she was more concerned about causing him agonizing pain. His was a valid point, nonetheless, and she nodded in acknowledgement of his promise. Still, she couldn't help but wonder briefly if the man would have acquiesced to the doctor's insistence had she not interfered. Based on his performance since he'd strode into the room, she'd calculated that he would be too stubborn to give in, but what if her calculations had been wrong? Deciding the fate of a man based on a mere hour of observation?

"Are you certain this is what you want, Major?" she whispered, trying to convey the seriousness of his condition without coming right out with the words.

"Yes," he replied easily.

Alright. She'd committed to this, and she would not cower away now. It was unlikely that Dr. Kiloran would return to treat her patient now, even if she begged him to. Still, she bit her lip hard, trying to calm her quaking fear. Though his hand shook, he kept the bandage pressed over his side and she forced her attention to his leg.

It was even worse than it had first appeared, and on closer inspection, she could see that there was something lodged in it. Panicked whirled in her head. Perhaps the doctor had been right!

"Major, it is worse than I thought. I'm not sure...I must confess I have never..."

"Tell me something, Miss Williams. Why did you stand up for me?"

"You have fought for our country; quite bravely, I imagine. You have been made aware of the risks. Even if I do not fully agree with Dr. Kiloran, how you choose for us to proceed should be your decision. It is the least we can offer in repayment for your bravery, Major."

He smiled despite his pain. It was a small smile, barely turning up the corners of his full lips, but perhaps the most genuine she had seen since this mess of war had begun, and certainly the most attractive smile she'd seen in her entire life.

"I have the utmost faith in you, Miss Williams. Now why don't we get on with it," he urged in a voice weaker than it had been before. If she didn't do something quickly, the Major's death would forever rest on her conscience.

"Grace. My name is Grace, and I want you to focus on my voice Major, and nothing else, alright?" She pulled up a story from her childhood in her mind and prepared to share the tale, finding it was often a useful way to distract her patients from what was happening to them.

"Grace," he repeated her name. "No lady has ever given me leave so quickly to address her so informally. Grace...it is the most beautiful name I have ever heard. Fitting, given the exquisite lady who bears it," he murmured, and she knew she could delay no longer. Major Cade was beginning to take leave of his senses.

And so she got to work, sterilizing the wound and the implement she would use to retrieve the shard of metal, a step the doctors and her fellow nurses felt was unnecessary. Though she couldn't administer chloroform, she discreetly handed the man a bottle of whiskey kept in the room for this purpose. He took a long swig as she steadied her hand, and then she retrieved the shard, reiterating a time from her youth when she and her sister had scared her parents half to death, hiding in the grove beyond the house for an entire afternoon—a place they were strictly forbidden to go.

The soldier was true to his word. Though sweat poured from his brow, his fists clenched and his body tremored slightly, he remained fairly still. She disinfected the empty wound once more and stitched it up, and then reached for the chloroform. With his leg mended, she no longer needed his help in staunching the flow from other wounds.

"You will not let them take my leg, will you, my beautiful Grace?"

She looked up in response, and realized then the Major had downed a good portion of the whiskey bottle—not that she could blame him. Still, he was delirious with pain and more than a little inebriated at this point due to the blood loss he suffered.

"After all the work I've just done?" she teased, but she could see he needed more than that, even in his altered state. "I promise that so long as there is breath in my body, I will do everything I can to ensure no harm comes to you," she told him solemnly, and that seemed to be enough. He leaned back and allowed her to administer the drug that would send him careening into blissful unconsciousness.

As soon as his eyes closed, she moved on to address his other wounds. Her assessment had been correct; his leg had been the worst of his injuries. She was able to stitch up the rest of him with much less effort, and was hopeful he would recover.

Though she had no idea how much time passed, it had felt like an eternity before she was able to breathe that small breath of relief. While the Major was not yet out of danger, at least she was confident he had a better chance at recovery than he would have had if the doctor had taken his leg with his grimy tools and dirty hands.

Chapter 2

The tent was much quieter when Grace entered it the next morning, and far emptier. She'd sat by the soldier's bedside for hours, checking his forehead nearly every fifteen minutes. He'd awoken only once during that time, raising himself up just enough to check that his leg was, in fact, still attached to the rest of his body. She'd managed to get him to take a few sips of water—a good sign—but he'd fallen back to sleep shortly after.

Two hours later, Annika—a fellow nurse and the only one who didn't seem to shoot daggers from her eyes when she looked in her direction—had shooed her out of the room, promising to alert her should anything change with the Major's condition. It seemed nothing had changed since she'd left.

He still lay there fast asleep, but she noticed right away that his face was not flushed as was common in fever. It was a handsome face; a strong jaw, straight nose, full lips, and though his eyes were closed now, she knew from the night before that they were the most extraordinary color she'd ever seen—so much like the amber of the whiskey her father had drank on occasion.

Still a full hour before her shift, she crossed the room to where he laid. She was anxious to check beneath the layers of bandages to see that his wounds held no sign of infection, but since he was still sleeping, she settled herself in the small chair next to the bed. His eyes darted open before she'd sat, but they didn't grow wide in panic the way some of the other soldiers' were prone to, waking up in a strange place after so much violence. Instead, his gaze settled directly on her.

"Good morning, Miss Williams. It seems I have made it through the night." His voice was hoarse as if he'd been screaming for far too long, even though he'd barely made a noise. But she'd seen the way he'd been fighting it back, and that likely had caused the irritation.

"Yes, I am surprised. It was stupid of you to refuse our assistance for so long, though perhaps a little brave, too. Your men are fortunate to have a leader with so much concern for their well-being."

"'Twas nothing, I merely did not want to have to listen to their whining while I recovered," he said easily, brushing off her thinly veiled compliment. "It is I who should be commending *your* bravery. I am aware that without your assistance, I would not be here. Either I'd be dead, or your doctor would have had me thrown out once I'd chopped off his wretched hands."

Since he was awake anyway, she set about her original purpose, checking first the wound on his leg, then his side, and then the more superficial injuries on his chest and arm. It was obvious the man had already sustained a number of injuries by the scars that marked his body, several white lines across his broad chest, a thicker one down the length of his arm and one more just above his hip. He was either extremely brave in battle, or else extremely clumsy or ill-fortuned to have so many wounds.

She was hesitantly pleased with her survey of yesterday's wounds. Not even the deep wound in his leg showed any signs of reddening, but she'd brought along an ointment she'd learned about long ago to help keep it that way. It was tucked in the pocket of her skirt and she pulled it out surreptitiously, knowing the doctors weren't fond of her penchant for natural medicine, even if it had been proven useful for centuries before them.

"Major, I have an ointment that will help, but I'm afraid most of the people here don't approve of its use."

"Then by all means, Miss Williams," he replied without hesitating. Despite him having placed his life in her hands the night before, it still surprised her to hear him put his faith in her so easily.

"You are too trusting, perhaps," she teased, though she'd already begun to apply a thick layer of the ointment over his wounds. Not only did it help to stave off infection, it also provided some measure of pain relief, and the effect was evident nearly upon contact. The tension that surrounded his eyes and furrowed his brow began to relax quickly.

"With ointments like that, can you blame me? You are a miracle worker, I think."

She smiled, knowing it was only the pain relief talking, but pleased with his opinion of her, nonetheless.

"So, what is the verdict? Do you suppose I'll live?"

"I'll be honest with you, Major, I am not a doctor, and I have no formal training aside from what I have received firsthand here. But I did learn to tend wounds and to recognize signs of infection and poor healing. Thus far, I would tentatively say there is a decent chance you will recover, though I daresay you'll have several nasty scars to commemorate your brush with death."

"I owe you my life, Miss Williams. I can only hope to repay you one day."

"You owe me nothing. It is my honor to do what I can to help our country's brave soldiers. And you are by far the bravest—or at least, the most stubborn—I have ever seen."

"Can you tell me how my men have fared? I see several of them are missing from the room." His tone had turned somber, and she was glad she had thought to ask about the Major's men on her way to see him.

"They have all made it through the night, and most are resting comfortably. As you know, one lost an arm, though even I agree it could not be helped. We will have to wait and see if he recovers from his wounds."

He nodded, though he was not entirely pleased. Even though most of his men would recover just fine, she could sense that his thoughts lingered on the one still in danger.

"You should get some rest, Major. I will be here should you have need of me. There is morphine for the pain, but I caution you to use it carefully. It seems men who have used it liberally become quite dependent on it, even after they're recovered."

He nodded as his eyes began to droop. "I shall avoid it as much as possible then," he murmured as he drifted off to sleep. It took a lot out of a man to recover from such an ordeal. It no longer surprised her that a patient could sleep for twenty or more hours of the day.

As she rose to leave him in peace, he opened his eyes again. "What is it, Major?"

"You must tell me how your story ends."

She raised an eyebrow inquisitively, not following his meaning.

"The story of you and your sister in the grove."

"You were listening?"

"Of course I was."

"My sister was wiser, I'm afraid. She hid on the ground, concealed in the bushes when my father came looking for us. I was foolish enough to hide far up in a tree. My father's booming voice startled me and I fell out of my hiding place to the ground below."

"Were you injured?"

He should be sleeping, not posing questions about my silly story, she thought. Why was he so interested in the tale she'd told at least a hundred times to soldiers who seemed more mollified by the sound of her voice than the contents of her story? It was difficult to focus on details when one's body was consumed by pain, but apparently, it wasn't as much of a problem for this man.

"Indeed, I was. I broke my leg, in fact. A wretchedly painful experience, if I may say so. But on a brighter note, my father believed I'd been adequately punished for my misdeeds and did not feel the need to discipline me further, even after I'd recovered. He felt I'd learned my lesson."

"And had you?"

She smiled sheepishly, never having been probed on the outcome of her story before. "Well, no, not exactly."

"How long was it before you were sneaking back to the grove?"

"Precisely two days after I was deemed fit to walk again." She laughed, recalling her mother's exasperated expression when she found her there again.

Despite the Major's pained and tired state, he laughed along with her. "It pleases me to no end to hear that, Miss Williams." He yawned then, wincing as he moved to stretch his sore body.

"Get some rest, Major Cade. It will be your turn to share some of your own childhood antics when I come back to check on you."

"I will do my best to find a story as entertaining as yours."

"I look forward to it," she whispered as he closed his eyes. She stood there for a moment longer, but they remained closed this time. Against her better judgment, she reached out, brushing back the errant strands of dark hair that had fallen onto his forehead.

Indeed, she was looking forward to it; far more than she should.

Chapter 3

A day passed, and then several more, and her patient seemed to have started on the path to recovery. He was sleeping less than he had those first few days, and though he could not yet move about on his own, he had nurses and even other patients looking in on his soldiers and reporting back on their progress.

"Tell me about your family," she suggested as she sat next to him on the sixth morning, trying to distract him as she went about checking his wounds and applying a fresh coat of the ointment. She'd noticed he had refused all offers of morphine since she mentioned the potential dangers of it, so she had no doubt he was already in a substantial amount of pain, amplified by even her gentle ministrations. The first few days, she'd urged him to tell her about his men, but they'd exhausted that subject, having covered every single one of the men under his command.

"My mother is back home in Indiana and my brother, John, is at West Point, though he is chomping at the bit to join the soldiers here." He rolled his eyes as he spoke, feigning annoyance with his younger sibling, but she could see through it.

"You don't want to worry about him. You fear he will end up injured just like you, or worse." Grace posed it as a statement, not a question.

"Yes, if you want the truth of it, I suppose."

"I can't say I blame you."

"What of your family?" he asked as she moved from his leg to the wound at his side.

"I'm afraid it is just my sister and I. She is three years my senior, but incredibly squeamish. At least I did not have to worry that she would follow after me. She thinks it quite foolish of me, actually, but the plight of our country and its soldiers did not affect her as much. And money and employment are things that I always worried about more than her. I suppose I kept her too sheltered in that regard. The poor thing's most unwise in the way of the world, I'm afraid."

"It sounds as if you are speaking of a younger sister, not one three years your senior. Why is that?"

"Oh, but she's bright in so many other ways. She's beautiful, and she excels in the schoolroom. And my sister is far more accomplished in the kitchen, even after my years of cooking our suppers."

"The younger sister responsible for cooking suppers? It sounds like you care for her perhaps a little too much."

"She makes my toils worth the effort," she replied, smiling. "I would have no one if it weren't for Rebecca. She was always more sensitive than I, so it only made sense that I take on what I did. Oh, she objected plenty, I assure you, but in the end, we both knew this was better."

"It also sounds like you've been alone for quite some time. You can't possibly be old enough to have been responsible for your sister all on your own."

"Oh, well, there was an uncle for a while there, and before him, my parents, of course. My uncle wasn't of much use, though it's rude of me to say, but true, nonetheless."

She finished re-bandaging the last of his wounds then and slipped the ointment back in her pocket. It was best if she left. It was nearly time for her shift to begin, and the Major looked in need of sleep.

More than that, she couldn't believe the words that had spilled from her lips as she'd worked. She'd never spoken to anyone there about her family, aside from the occasional tale to distract a patient. What on Earth had possessed her to speak so freely with her patient?

"You cannot leave it there," he interrupted her silent contemplation. He smiled at her with a boyish grin, and she had no doubt he knew precisely what he was doing: using his devastating good looks to compel more information from her. "Please tell me more, Miss Williams."

Even worse was she knew exactly what he was doing, and still could not help herself.

"What is it you'd like to know, Major?"

"Tell me about your parents, and how you came to live with your uncle. And how was your uncle of little use to you?"

"You're certainly full of questions today."

"I fear lying abed with nothing to do all day but think gives one's mind room to wander. In truth, though, I would also very much like to know."

"Alright. Let's see...my parents passed away when I was quite young. My sister was fifteen years old at the time, and I only just turned twelve. It was not possible for the two of us to take care of each other on our own; at least, so I thought. We were sent to live with my uncle."

She remembered the day she and Rebecca arrived on Uncle Horace's doorstep, delivered there courtesy of her parents' lawyer. Her uncle had not even seen it fit to collect them himself. His house was dirty and smelled something awful. The man himself had been no better, his skin and clothes covered with dirt, the pungent odors of alcohol and decay on his breath.

Rebecca had taken a turn for the worse when their parents died. While always the weaker sibling—according to their mother—it became more and more apparent those first few months, and that was when Grace felt it necessary to take over; to take on the responsibility of seeing that Rebecca was cared for.

"I'm sorry, I shouldn't have pried," he said softly, pulling her back to the present as he gently laid his hand upon hers.

"'Tis quite alright. I learned to fend for myself and Rebecca quickly, and for Uncle Horace, too. I took whatever odd jobs I could find: washing laundry, scrubbing floors, and the like. I wasn't paid much for my efforts, but it was enough to keep us fed. And that is the sum of it. My uncle passed away three years later, but by then, I was more than able to manage on my own, even saving up enough to send Rebecca to school. I thought perhaps if she were to engross herself in studies, to see the strengths she possessed there, it would help her to regain her footing she'd lost long before."

"You are a very strong woman, Miss Williams. Your sister is very lucky to have you."

She scoffed lightly at that. "If only my sister was of the same mind as you. I'm afraid she sees things a little differently."

"How do you mean?"

"Honestly, we had a fight the day before I left. She was quite opposed to my leaving, thinking it foolish of me. We said things I'm sure the both of us have come to regret, and that was the end of it. I have written to her often, but she has not yet found the forgiveness necessary to send a letter in return."

"I'm sure your sister will come around." His hand had not left hers, and it had begun to brush lightly across her fingers in a soothing gesture. It was having quite the opposite effect, however, sending tiny ripples of warmth up her entire arm. She pulled her hand away quickly, unaccustomed to the odd sensation.

"I must get to work now, Major. Please rest." She stood and left without a backward glance, too riled to remain there a moment longer.

No matter the chaos it caused her body, it did not stop her from returning to him several hours later, re-checking his wounds, though it wasn't necessary for her to tend to them quite so often. In truth, she wanted to be near him; she wanted to see his whiskey eyes and boyish grin.

But it was more than that, too. She genuinely enjoyed the Major's company, and wanted to learn all there was to know about him. She'd spent every free moment she had with him— under the guise of tending to his wounds and keeping him from the insanities of boredom.

****

"We were a world unto ourselves," the Major explained of his time at West Point several evenings later as she sat next to his bed like she'd done every evening since he arrived. He'd spent each night probing her for more information: more tales from her childhood, an inquiry into her reasons for becoming a nurse, a thorough examination of how she came about her seemingly vast knowledge of natural medicine. But she'd deemed it her turn this particular evening, and upon discovering the Major had spent several years mastering the skills necessary of a soldier at West Point, she'd been curious what his time there had been like.

"A world unto yourselves?"

"Yes, well, all of our time was spent there, of course. And being cut off from the world like that paves the way for comradery to develop like nowhere else. We were all men who shared the same experiences, and as such, overcame social and political differences."

It was fascinating, and not inconceivable to imagine the bonds that could be formed under such circumstances.

"We were nearly unaffected by the upheaval going on in the country before the war. My last year there, we trained together and depended on one another, no matter whether the man standing next to you was from the North or South."

"It sounds wonderful. Had you always intended to go to West Point...to become a soldier, I mean?"

"No, actually. I had it in my mind to try my luck further out West."

"What made you change your mind?"

"My father told me it was over his dead body that I'd abandon his plan for me. And seeing as I didn't think I had it in me to meet his requisite, I figured he had me bested there," he laughed, seemingly without animosity.

"You seem to have accepted it well."

"He was right, as much as I hate to admit it. Nothing had ever felt so much like second nature. I suppose it was in the blood."

"So, you are happy with your decision?"

He was silent for a moment, as if her question required deep deliberation. "I could not be anywhere else," he replied eventually, though she couldn't decide whether he had answered her question with that statement or not.

"I confess I don't know a great deal about the military, but it seems to me you are by far the youngest Major I have seen. Why is that? Certainly, you must have done something to be worthy of such a promotion."

"It was really nothing, Miss Williams. The Iron Brigade—my men and I included—designated 1st Brigade, 1st division, I Corps were there fighting that first day at Gettysburg. We all fought hard, but my commanders saw it fit that I be promoted, that's all."

"You must have been very proud," she led, though she did not sense that was what he felt. He did not seem like the type of man who would be quick to seek praise or recognition for himself.

"Proud? No. In truth, I remember the night more than the battle. It was an unseasonably cold night. My men had fought bravely but both sides had suffered many casualties. We were forced to take shelter right there on the battlefield with little more than the shirts on our backs to keep us warm. Some men huddled amid the dead, using them as shields from the wretched wind, while others sought out whatever clothing could be recovered from those no longer in need of it."

He paused, but she could see he was remembering and she didn't try to rush him, leaving him to go back there in his mind until he was ready to come back to her.

It only seemed to take a moment. "Watching one of my men, struggling to remove a dead man's coat, I saw it—his arm flailing feebly in protest. The man actually was not dead, but not far from it. I had no choice but to do what I could for him and hope he would last until the morning. I ordered my men to search the field as best they could in the dark. In all, there were eleven others. We did what we could. Seven of them made it through the night, and the four that succumbed to their injuries did not die alone."

She fought back a lump of emotion in her throat, imagining the Major rifling through bodies, looking for any sign of life when all other men would have seen only to their own needs. "Indeed, I believe your father was quite right about you, Major. I cannot imagine a more valiant soldier."

He coughed uncomfortably and changed the subject quickly, but the damage had been done. She'd seen Major Cade for the strong, caring, intrepid man he was, and if she'd had any claim left to it before then, her heart was now lost to him forever.

Chapter 4

Another full week passed and the Major had begun to make leaps in his recovery. All but the wound to his leg had healed enough that he could use most of his body unhampered. Though she'd argued with him at first, Grace had given into helping him move around, going for walks around the enormous hospital tent complex to work his muscles and encourage his leg to heal—at least, Major Cade was convinced it would.

Though Grace couldn't deny a certain amount of exercise was good for him, she worried he pushed himself too hard and too often. He'd at least agreed to the use of a walking stick that allowed him to lean his weight off his injured leg when the need arose.

She'd also learned to temper her disapproval quickly. Instead of staying back stubbornly like she had at first, she now went with him to watch over his progress and came up with excuses for him to escort her back if she felt he was exerting himself too much. No doubt, he was cognizant of her ploy, but was also aware of the effort she was making to intrude as little as possible, and humored her accordingly.

She'd left the hospital tent in search of her bed long after dark nearly three weeks after Major Cade had first arrived there, but the longer she laid in bed, the more she thought about him. As he made marked improvements in his recovery each day now, it wouldn't be long before he'd be forced to leave.

She would miss him terribly, but that was not her only concern. A man so stubborn would not take his injuries as a sign to slow down, or to count his blessings and leave the war behind him. She was quite certain he intended to return to active duty where he would be thrust into harm's way once again.

With that thought fresh in her mind, she tossed and turned for at least a full hour before abandoning her quest for sleep. Rising quietly from her bed, she tiptoed out of her quarters and out into the fresh night's air. Nurses weren't permitted to wander about after dark, but it wasn't the first time she'd slipped out unnoticed on all those nights when the atrocities of war kept her from finding restful slumber.

She wandered about the nurse's quarters, keeping to the shadows as much as possible. She could hear others moving about, conversing with one another; some of the voices belonged to a few soldiers who had recovered enough to venture from their beds, but were not yet well enough to return to the battlefields. Other sounds came from men she'd become accustomed to hearing often, like the man from the Ambulance Corps who sat outside his quarters some nights, whistling tunes until the early hours of the morning. It should irritate the staff and patients, but it didn't. It was a soothing constant in a world so full of nothing but uncertainty.

Having completed the circumference around her quarters, she wasn't ready to go back to her bed, so she ventured further with no particular destination in mind. It felt good to move, and she picked up her pace. As physically demanding as her job was, it often required her to remain standing stationary for many hours of the day. Her only reprieve was strolling around the area with Major Cade. Stretching her legs now was a welcome change from the tiresome monotony of standing over gurneys endlessly.

Caught up in her thoughts, she came around the next corner and crashed into the hard wall of a man's chest, forcing the breath to whoosh from her lungs with the impact.

"What have we here?" the familiar voice of Dr. Kiloran asked as she put her hands between them to steady herself. He'd barely spoken to her since she'd intervened that night several weeks prior, but she'd noticed him scowling at her from time to time.

His breath reeked of brandy, and it wasn't until she'd righted herself and taken a step back that she realized Dr. Kiloran wasn't drinking alone.

"It seems the lady'd like to join us for a drink," the other voice spoke from directly behind her. Where had he come from?

She moved to spin around to face the newcomer, but Dr. Kiloran caught her by the arms before she could, and an overwhelming dread settled in her stomach.

"You've been nothing but a thorn in my side since you arrived here, Miss Williams. You, with your ridiculous ideals and medical quackery. It isn't enough you've got all the men here distracted from their work, too busy following the sway of your hips to pay attention to the bleeding soldiers in front of them. But you've got to make things worse, hindering our efforts further with your weeds and potions."

More than the vicelike grip that held her, she worried about the odd look in the doctor's eyes. She'd seen her uncle rail in anger plenty of times, but this was something different. There was something else lurking in his gaze. It formed a lump of terror in her throat and sent an icy shiver down her spine.

"I could fire you, but what use are you to me then? No...I think we could find a far better use for you, couldn't we?"

Without warning, he pulled her hard against the wall of his chest and his lips descended on hers, bruising them beneath the ferocity of his repugnant mouth. She struggled against his hold on her, but he was immoveable.

And then there was no question in her mind what the inebriated doctor intended to do.

She couldn't hope for rescue; the doctor's cruel lips stayed her scream and the man who stood behind her laughed maliciously, a sick anticipation clear in the vile sound.

She struggled harder, knowing she was on her own. There would be no help for her aside from what she could manage herself, but her efforts were for naught.

"Hurry up and get to it, would you?" the man behind her whispered furiously. "I want a turn with her, too!"

And then suddenly she was free. The vice fell away, but she stumbled back into the man behind her and he grabbed her around the waist before she could get away. The doctor let out a wretched cry, drawing her attention back to where he'd been standing, but in the dim light, she could barely make out the motionless figure now lying on the ground. Was that Dr. Kiloran? And if so, how did he get there?

The answer to her question stepped out of the shadows a second later, coming to stand directly in front of her, staring murderously beyond her.

"Release her now, or so help me, my men will be picking up pieces of your wretched corpse for weeks," Major Cade growled, and immediately, the arm that held her fell away.

Before the man could turn and flee, Major Cade had locked onto his arm, and with what seemed like not much more than the flick of his wrist, tossed him into the shadows where Dr. Kiloran still lay, presumably unconscious.

As ferocious as his expression had been just a second before, it changed suddenly, deep concern now permeating his amber gaze. "Grace, are you alright?"

It was the first time he'd used her name since she'd given him leave to the night she'd treated his wounds. Strange though, that would be the only thought in her mind. She searched for words to respond to his question, but her brain couldn't find any. What had almost happened—what *would have* happened if Major Cade had not shown up when he did—kept playing over and over in her mind.

Tears trickled down her cheeks, and her body shook so hard, it was a wonder her legs held her up. He quickly wrapped his arms around her, gently, not like the doctor's cruel embrace. He held her in such a way that told her she could escape his grasp any second she chose. His hand moved to her back, stroking gently, soothingly while he whispered softly in her ear. He spoke so quietly, his words were almost unintelligible, but they served the same purpose.

She was safe. Major Cade had dispatched her would-be assailants, and she was safe.

She felt it as he raised an arm up behind him, and just then, she realized that he'd been signaling his men; two appeared there a moment later. Panic should have risen anew at the sight of the newcomers, but it didn't. Somehow, she knew he would let no harm come to her.

The two soldiers followed their Major's wordless order, dragging away the limp forms of the doctor and his accomplice, presumably to dry out elsewhere.

His full attention was on her again, stroking her back soothingly. She didn't know how long she stood there, wrapped in his muscular arms, but eventually, the tremors that had gripped her body began to subside. Slowly, her pulse returned to something that resembled normal.

It was time she tried her voice. "I...I don't know how to thank you, Major Cade," she whispered shakily, looking up at him for the first time since he'd appeared out of the darkness.

"It's Michael," he told her as he looked down at her, his amber gaze clear despite the dim lighting, and what she saw in his gaze left her even more speechless than the tumultuous events of moments prior. It was possible she misread what she saw; so much emotion seemed to radiate from his gaze that certainly it could only be the result of her own disturbed imagination.

Then she felt his fingers against her lips, moving gently. It took her a moment, but she realized what he was doing—he was trying to brush away what had happened to her, or at the least, replace the vile touch of the doctor's lips with his gentle caress. And it was working. So quickly, her memory of Dr. Kiloran's kiss was giving way to Michael's tender ministrations.

He leaned in ever so slowly, until no more than a hair's

breadth separated them. She could feel his warm breath on her lips, and everything else faded away—the doctor, the past two years of mending broken bodies, the years of toiling relentlessly to keep her small family fed. There was nothing but Michael—his full lips and amber eyes, his tender embrace. He hovered there, so close, but he didn't move. And she understood; he was silently telling her it was her choice. He wasn't like them; he wouldn't force her.

She leaned up, touching her lips to his, and when he responded in kind, meeting her brush for brush, the world stood still and twisted wildly on its axis at the same time.

Chapter 5

The night had taken her on wild turns, first plunging her into the depths of darkness and then soaring her to the heavens. She laid in bed, arriving there safely thanks to her brave soldier, and if her thoughts had been taken with him before, they were thoroughly enraptured by him now.

For the first time in so long, she closed her eyes and slept. Real sleep. Not the kind that had left her tossing and turning fitfully since she'd arrived at the hospital. When she awoke, there was only one thought in her mind: Michael. She'd been uncertain all these weeks if he returned her feelings, but last night had proven it.

She sat up, stretching contentedly, but as she moved to stand, she caught sight of an envelope perched neatly at the foot of the bed. She hadn't noticed it there when she'd wearily flopped in bed late the night before, nor when she'd returned to her bed after her tumultuous ordeal. But with the early morning's sun peeking in through the open door of the tent, she saw it there.

It only took her a moment to recognize her sister's writing. After such a long time, and despairing she would not hear from her sister at all, Rebecca had written to her. Exuberance filled her heart as she tore open the envelope and pulled out the single piece of paper inside.

Dear Grace,

I hope this letter finds you well. I want to apologize for my behavior when you left two years ago. It was irrational of me, and I do hope you can find it in your heart to forgive me. But there is one more thing for which I must beg your forgiveness, dear sister.

I have gone about finding myself a husband in the most unusual way—through the matrimonial advertisements, if you can believe it. I will be leaving New York henceforth to join my betrothed in the West. It is an exciting opportunity for me, so much better than the drudgery of life in New York. I fear I was too cowardly to ask your blessing beforehand for fear that you would reject it, and so I have left it to now to write and tell you of my decision.

When the time is right, and if I am able, I will find you again, dear Grace. Until then, may the Lord bring you as much happiness as he has given to me.

With All My Love,

Rebecca

She read the short letter over and over as a cold, heavy weight burdened her soul. Rebecca had not provided one bit of information about her destination, nor her betrothed. How ever would she find her? She had always imagined that once she returned home, there would be an opportunity to smooth this rift between them, but there would be no such thing now. Her sister was gone. The only family she had left had deliberately disappeared.

Suddenly, she could feel the tears hot behind her eyes, and she fought them back. It would do her no good to cry.

She would figure it out. If this war ever ended, she would find a way to locate Rebecca, and they would be as close as they'd once been, once again. She tucked the letter beneath her pillow and rose from the bed. Her shift started in just a few minutes, and she hadn't the time to dwell on her own issues at the moment.

She hurried out of her quarters quickly, intending to seek out Michael, though she hoped to find him resting. She would be eternally grateful for his assistance the night before, but the force it must have taken to do away with those men...she worried it might have done something to set him back with his recovery, though, she couldn't deny he was well-healed now. Still, she needed to thank him once again, and in truth, she'd wanted nothing more since he left her at the entrance to her tent late last night than to return to him, to the man who was not only her rescuer, but something so much more.

Still, she approached the tent uneasily, knowing she could run into Dr. Kiloran at any moment, not knowing how to handle that particular encounter. Steeling her nerves, she walked in. As she looked around, she was immediately gratified to find the doctor nowhere in sight. Unfortunately, he was not the only man missing from the room; Michael was not there either. Perhaps he was out wandering, too cooped up to stay confined to his bed any longer. Hopefully, that meant he hadn't injured himself too badly last night.

"He's gone," a soft voice spoke from behind her. It was Annika, the only nurse she'd managed to befriend during her stay at the hospital.

"Gone where?" she asked, denying the finality in the woman's words.

"I don't know, Grace. Another soldier arrived for him this morning, perhaps an hour ago. He demanded to know where Major Cade was, and left with him not five minutes later. I debated waking you—I know you and the Major have become...acquainted with one another during his stay here, but I did not understand what was going on until it was too late. Please forgive me."

"Of course. No, that's quite alright. Thank you," she managed, trying to ignore the crushing pain inside her chest as she wandered back to her quarters, willing back the tears that sprung to her eyes and threatened to spill over.

It was absurd of her to feel betrayed by the Major's departure; to be angry with him for leaving her. She had absolutely no claim on him. What reason did he have to be bound to her, or to even say goodbye? They'd not spoken of emotion or romantic attachment. It was strange, she mused, since they had spoken of nearly everything else. But perhaps that should have been warning enough.

He'd never held any part of himself back. He'd shared with her his childhood, his time at West Point and the part he played in the war. If there had been some romantic interest on his side, would he not have said so?

She'd foolishly thought last night had been confirmation of it, of the only things they had not yet said to one another. Perhaps what it had really been was nothing more than a chivalrous soldier coming to the aid of a woman in trouble. He had held her because she needed to be held, and he'd kissed her for the same reason, because a tender kiss would help to blur the memory of one taken with violence. She rubbed her arms idly, cognizant of the deep purplish marks that marred her flesh there. If it hadn't been for Michael, how much more violence would she have suffered at the hands of the drunken doctor and his vile friend?

And what kind of selfish wretch of a woman was she to be angry with him after what he'd done for her? She was angry that he was gone, and angry that she'd been fool enough to believe he had felt anything for her but the amicable friendship that arose from their weeks together with nary else to occupy his time. But even so, should he not have had the decency to say goodbye?

Was that really so much to ask?

Reaching her quarters, she collapsed on her bed then, for the first time grateful for the thin curtains that hung between the rows and provided a modicum of privacy. She laid there, staring blindly at the curtain in front of her. He was gone.

She remembered the first moment she'd seen him, torn and bloodied, completely oblivious to his own perilous state. He was so concerned for the welfare of his men, seeing to his own wounds had not crossed his mind. And then his ornery objection to the doctor's diagnosis. The man was stubborn and willful. And wonderful.

Nothing stood in his way. If he'd wanted to say goodbye to her, he would have no matter the obstacle. If he cared for her, he would have told her. He had done neither.

He was gone, and there was nothing she could do about it, no different than all the other things in her life she'd been powerless to control. And like them, she'd find a way to move past. She didn't have a choice.

But for the first time in her life, she was utterly and completely alone. There was no one in the world to share in her heartaches and joys, and no one she could turn to for comfort when the heartaches vastly outnumbered the joys. Her parents had left, through no fault of their own, her uncle had only added to her sense of loneliness, her sister had run off to the West, and now, a man she'd fancied herself in love with, had left without a word.

In love? What a ridiculous notion. As if such a thing existed! Of course there was love in the world—the kind of love a mother felt for her child, a sister felt for her sibling—but to fancy oneself in love with another human being? This was the stuff of fairy tales and nothing more. She wasn't in love with Major Cade, she had simply grown fond of their time together. That time was over.

And with that truth fresh in her mind, she tucked her soldier away in the back of her mind, though she could quickly tell her memories of him would threaten to spill over the floodgates should she not remain vigilant. It was time to go to work, to earn a living, to help another soldier who had given his blood in devotion to his country. It was time to forget about Michael, and to remember he had been nothing more than a patient, another soldier who had given his blood, that she'd helped nurse back to health.

It was what life had given her. What more could she do?

Chapter 6

The war was over. In the beginning, no one had thought it would last so long, but four long years after it had begun, it was finally over. And that meant Grace's services were no longer necessary. It was time for her to return to New York.

The tents had been dismantled in what felt like a blink of an eye and the grounds that had been home to the hospital—her home for two and a half years—were once again empty. The image of the barren land stayed in her mind the entire trip home. Perhaps if she kept it there long enough, it would erase the plethora of abhorrent memories of wounded soldiers, raging fevers, and cold, lifeless eyes. And more importantly, perhaps it would wipe away the memory of the one soldier she wished most to forget, the man whose image seemed permanently etched in her mind, there in startling detail every time she closed her eyes.

The trip home had been pleasant enough with the early signs of spring beginning to blossom all around her. She approached the small house slowly, eyeing the overgrowth of the yard, the dusty windows and the roof in even poorer repair than it had been when she'd left. There hadn't been much she could do at the time for the roof, but she'd always maintained the house and tended to the yard as best she could, planting flowers and keeping pesky weeds at bay.

But there seemed to be no proof of her efforts here. If there were flowers still there, they were hidden far beneath the tangles of brush. It reminded her of the day she and Rebecca had arrived on her uncle's doorstep, repelled by the unkempt property and objectionable odors. She only hoped when she opened the door, she wasn't overwhelmed by the same stench.

Sighing heavily, she forced her legs to move, and was moderately appeased by the dank smell that greeted her inside. It was warm outside for the season and the house hadn't been aired in quite some time, but that was nothing a few open windows and a good cleaning wouldn't remedy. And finding nothing more pressing to occupy her time, she set herself to work, leaving her luggage at the door and going in search of rags and buckets. She'd no sooner gotten to her knees and started to scrub the worn wood floors when a knock sounded at the door. Tossing the wet rag into the bucket, she stood and tiptoed back across the wet floor to the front door.

"Oh, I knew it was you, Grace," the plump woman greeted her from the other side, smiling brightly as she opened the door. Her hair was whiter now, only the occasional chestnut strand peppered her stringent up-do, and the lines surrounding her eyes had grown a bit deeper. But her gray eyes still twinkled with her smile.

"Hello, Mrs. Fraser. It's good to see you again."

"Good to see me? Why, what kind of greeting is that? Come here, child," the woman spoke in mock indignation, and then pulled Grace against her ample frame.

To her shame, tears welled in her eyes at the comforting feel of the woman's fleshy arms around her, but she would not let them fall. She wouldn't. She breathed in and out slowly, forcing every emotion back, but the watery glistening in her eyes gave her away.

"Oh child, come now," the matronly figure soothed, apparently recognizing her turmoil, and she maneuvered them inside the house, closing the door behind them. All the while, she held Grace close to her. It wasn't the same as Major Cade's tender embrace, but it was familiar.

Mrs. Fraser had been the kindly neighbor who had taught her to cook where her mother's instruction had left off. She had helped Grace find work, recommending her to more than a few families and helping to mind Rebecca often. Mrs. Fraser had also been the one to teach her all she knew about medical care, from the importance of disinfecting wounds and washing hands between patients to old poultices and tinctures that were invaluable—like the ointment that had likely contributed to saving Michael's life.

No, she wouldn't think about him. She would think only of the woman with her now. The knowledge Mrs. Fraser bestowed upon her was no doubt responsible for the recovery of countless men who would otherwise have perished amid the filth of the hospital, and this is how she gave her thanks? On the verge of tears in the woman's arms the moment she appears on her doorstep?

That was enough to help Grace rein it in, and she forced her lungs to take more deep breaths of air, settling herself more every time she exhaled. "I'm sorry, Mrs. Fraser. I don't know what's wrong with me," she told her when she was calm enough to speak.

"There's nothing wrong with you child. You've no doubt had quite a hard time of it these past two years. And coming home to an empty house made it all the harder on you."

Hard, yes, but it would not break her down. Outside of that one tumultuous night Michael had rescued her, she hadn't shed a single tear since she left New York for the hospital. She couldn't. From her first day, she'd known if she let even one tear fall, a torrential downpour would have followed and it would never have ceased; such were the horrors and heartaches of seeing one good man after another go to his grave.

Far away from the hospital now, and the war finally over, it was inevitable it would catch up with her eventually. Though, in truth, she'd tucked each fallen soldier away in the back of her mind, a memorial to each of them there, but it was the Major's face that had sprung to mind and threatened to send tears cascading like a waterfall. Of course, she couldn't tell Mrs. Fraser that, and so she just nodded.

"Let's get you cleaned up, and I'll make you a good, hot cup of tea. I've plenty of chamomile, so you just sit right here," she motioned to one of the chairs at the tiny table in the kitchen. "I'll be back in a flash."

****

Mrs. Fraser had been right; the chamomile tea did help, though the woman's presence was equally comforting. How many evenings had the two of them sat at this very table and talked about everything...or sometimes nothing at all? How many times alone in her quarters had she longed for Mrs. Fraser's comforting presence? Perhaps she wasn't as alone as she'd thought after all. Still, the woman's presence did little to ease the wretched way her heart ached for Michael. But it was enough; it would have to be.

In the weeks that followed, she told herself the same thing, over and over again. She tried to ignore the way she missed her sister, to stop herself from imagining where Rebecca was now and whether her choice had brought her happiness or sorrow. She'd be tempted to chase after her just to ensure her sister was content in her new life, but even if she knew where to look for her, she couldn't possibly afford the trip out West.

As she kept busy righting the house, seeking out work and evening tea with Mrs. Fraser, the Major's face came to her less often than it had before, though every night as darkness settled in, it was the same. He was there in her mind as she laid in bed and he infiltrated her dreams, sometimes coming to her as her brave soldier, and at other times her executioner, sentencing her to the slowest, most tortuous death she could imagine—an execution by heartache that slowly drained the life from her. She had known him for such a brief amount of time, not much more than the space of a deep, cleansing breath, but he'd etched himself onto her heart and she could not wipe it clean, no matter how she tried.

"I think it's time you consider a change," Mrs. Fraser told her without preamble one evening, sitting at the table, swirling her spoon in her tea idly.

"Is that so? Well, I considered joining the British monarchy—a princess, I think—but it seems all the positions were filled," she teased. Whatever the woman meant, it was an absurd idea. Women in Grace's position in life weren't foolish enough to hope for anything to change.

Mrs. Fraser chuckled. "If anyone deserves to be treated like a lady of gentle birth, I daresay it is you, my child. But I would not wish that your life were subjected to a crown. You can do good things with your life. Why, just look at all the good you did at that hospital. A princess can do nothing but what she is told. I think that would not be the life for you."

"I suppose I cannot argue with you there."

"What I meant is I think you are in need of an adventure in your life. There is something you have not told me about your time as a nurse, and while I would not pry, I cannot help but notice how it has changed you. It's as if you've been walking with a cloud over your head since your return. It's time for some sunshine, child."

"And what have you in mind?" she asked, though it was only for curiosity's sake. She knew her lot in life.

"This," Mrs. Fraser handed her a newspaper she'd been holding on her lap.

"You think I should go into the business of writing newspapers? Or reading them?"

"No, silly. I think you should take a look at the advertisements on that page. Choose one, and let life take you on a new course."

She looked down at the newspaper in her hand, trying to understand the woman's meaning. The newspaper had been opened to the matrimonial advertisements. Mrs. Fraser thought she should seek out a husband?

"You think I'm in need of a husband?"

"Well, I don't think it could hurt, but it's not my only thought."

"I appreciate your suggestion, but I don't think..."

"Don't be so quick to reject the idea. I am a woman, and I know the look of a woman who's had her heart broken. The only way to move on is to do exactly that—move on. You are too young, and far too beautiful to condemn yourself to spinsterhood for this man, whoever he was. Do not take my advice lightly,

Grace. You are not the first to have her heart broken, and I will not stand by and watch you follow in my footsteps."

Mrs. Fraser had lost her heart to a man? She'd always imagined the woman had chosen the life of a spinster. She'd not once considered why she would have done so.

"I don't think it's that easy—"

"Of course it's not easy. Nothing worth having in life ever is. But it is time to move on, Grace; as difficult a task as it might be."

She scanned the advertisements in front of her, not really expecting to find anything worth considering, but trying to appease Mrs. Fraser. And then her eyes settled on one, just a few lines of text not much different from all the others, but there was something about the ad that struck her differently than the rest. As impossible as it was, it almost seemed like the spaces between the letters were sad...hopeless...resigned. It was precisely the way she felt. Could it be there was a kindred spirit out there somewhere, or was it nothing more than her mind playing tricks on her?

She needed to know if it was just her. "Mrs. Fraser, can...can you read this one, please?" She pointed to the box of text that looked no different from all the others, and yet had spoken to her in a way no other words ever had.

Mrs. Fraser scanned the words briefly and then looked up at her, a slight frown furrowing her brow. "Well, it's a perfectly fine ad, but do you not think the man sounds...I don't know...rather cold?"

Cold? Maybe she'd read her own feelings in the spaces between the words. But then, was "cold" such a terrible thing? The more she thought about Mrs. Fraser's idea, the more it appealed to her, though not for the purpose of healing her heart.

Rebecca was out there somewhere, and until Mrs. Fraser's matrimonial ads, she'd had absolutely no hope of ever reaching her. But all of a sudden...if she married a man out West, perhaps it wouldn't be so difficult to find her sister. Certainly, the West was a large place, but at least it would bring her somewhat closer. And if she was going to commit to the plan, she didn't want a husband in search of some deep, emotional connection. No, she didn't want that at all. That must be why the advertisement had appealed to her. It was perfect.

"I think perhaps there is some merit to your idea after all, Mrs. Fraser."

"Good, good, my dear. But do you really think this one is the best choice for you?" she asked uncertainly.

"I do. I believe this one would suit me just fine. Splendidly, in fact."

"Oh," the woman smiled tremulously, though the corners of her lips barely turned up at all, and the wariness in her eyes told Grace the woman was having second thoughts about her proposal.

"Do not trouble yourself, Mrs. Fraser. You are quite right. I am in need of a change; an adventure, as you call it."

"I only want to see you happy, Grace."

"I know, and I am grateful for that. You've been like a mother to me since the day I arrived here on my uncle's front steps. I don't know how I would have survived if it were not for you."

"Yes, well, I only hope you won't someday come to wish you'd never listened to this foolish old woman."

"I believe you are quite safe from that." Of course the woman was safe. How could any choice Grace made make her any more miserable than she'd been these past few months?

"Then this one as well," Mrs. Fraser pointed to an advertisement further down the page. "There's no harm in sending out more than one reply, and you can make your choice when you've had a chance to correspond with the gentlemen."

She read the ad next to Mrs. Fraser's finger, and couldn't deny that the writer seemed eloquent, interested in a woman with more than just an attractive face and handsome fortune. He was in search of a helpmate, a friend; an amicable woman with whom to share his life. Had her life experiences or her purpose for suddenly seeking a husband been different than they were, perhaps he would have appealed to her as a viable match.

But she wasn't interested in a husband, only the proximity one could place her to Rebecca. Still, Mrs. Fraser appeared quite concerned over her interest in the first advertisement. Perhaps, if it would appease the woman, she would do as Mrs. Fraser suggested and send a letter in reply to both. What harm could come of it?

Chapter 7

Grace sent the letters out in the mail the very next day. At first, she'd been concerned she might change her mind if she took too long, but as she walked with the envelopes in her hand, no part of her had questioned her decision. If this meant she may eventually cross paths with Rebecca, then it was worth whatever she gave up here, and whatever hardships she might find out West.

Once the letters were sent, she endeavored to put them from her mind. As much as she'd committed herself, there was no guarantee either man would respond. She found any odd jobs she could, but with the war over, it appeared she wasn't the only young woman in search of work. Worse than before, her earnings were barely enough to keep herself fed.

Several weeks passed and she'd all but given up hope of a response; so much, that she'd scanned idly through the latest matrimonial advertisements in search of another gentleman. Though she peered intently between the words, not a single one of them spoke to her the way the first had, and none of them corresponded with Mrs. Fraser's idea of a suitable match, either. It wasn't such a difficult task, was it? She didn't foster any misguided hope for anything beyond an amicable acquaintance with the gentleman, so why could she not bring herself to write to another? It was the uncertainty that inhibited her—that must be it. She'd already sent out two letters; how could she endeavor to send out more until she was certain she would not receive a response from those?

And then it came. At least, she presumed the letter she held in her hand was from one of the gentleman in the West. The envelope bore her name, written in a script she did not recognize. But instead of opening it, she placed it down on the table in front of her and went to boil water for a cup of tea. This was what she'd been waiting for, wasn't it? Why then was she procrastinating?

No answer came to her, and once her tea was poured and lightly sweetened with the honey Mrs. Fraser had given her, she forced herself onto one of the wobbly chairs.

Which gentleman had responded to her? The one she had been certain shared a sadness in life no words could have described, or the amicable-sounding gentleman who sought out a harmonious relationship to make his life content? Finding no sure way of answering the question, she opened the letter, skimming through the first few lines on the page. He sounded kind-hearted, intelligent...and hopeful. This was not her kindred spirit; it was the other, for sure.

She finished reading the letter and then closed her eyes, trying to imagine what her life would be like with such a man.

Content. That's what she imagined. There would be no joyous highs or frightful lows. Each day of her life would be the same; pleasant without the swings that set the soul on fire. She couldn't deny it was so much more than she had now, and marriage to this man would set her closer to Rebecca.

Still, she did not respond right away. She waited a day, and then one more, foolishly hoping for a response for the other gentleman.

No response came.

On the third day, she forced it from her mind, and set herself to the task of responding to the letter. She shared with him a few things about herself: her work as a nurse, her fondness for reading and gardening, and how much she really did enjoy helping others through the knowledge she'd gained from Mrs. Fraser. When she was finished, she sent it off before she could change her mind—not quite so certain as she'd been the first time she'd mailed the letters.

Several weeks passed before she received a response, and she recognized the writing on the envelope this time, leaving no room to hope it was a letter from the first advertisement. Still, she smiled as she read the words on the page. The man—Mr. Nathaniel Branscomb—was witty, in addition to his other laudable characteristics. She imagined he would make a good friend, indeed.

Caught up in work, she didn't have an opportunity to reply to Mr. Branscomb's letter that day, but she set it aside and planned to write to him the following afternoon. But come morning, his letter remained on the worn desk in the small parlor. A letter had arrived for her, the writing on which wasn't the least bit familiar. It was not Rebecca's eloquent script, nor the neat and functional writing of Mr. Branscomb.

It was him; the man who had spoken to her in the blank spaces between his words. She'd given up hope of a response from him, and yet it could be no one else, could it?

There was a lump in the center of the envelope, she observed idly. But instead of opening it up, she ran her fingers along the swollen surface, wondering what was inside. Of course she was being foolish. If she wanted to know what was inside, she need only open it up to find out. But still she hesitated, her pulse racing and her heart thudding in her chest. Why she was so nervous, she did not know.

Instead of opening the letter, she guessed at its contents, wondering what he could possibly have to say to her from the few short paragraphs she'd written to him. Would he want to learn more about her? Would he tell her about himself? Would she sense the same sadness from him as she had in his advertisement? And would he give any hint to what had made him that way?

Enough! It was entirely possible the gentleman had written to her for no other reason than to kindly let her know he'd chosen another lady. After all, it had been quite some time since she'd sent her letter, and he had only gotten around to responding now. Yes, that was probably it.

Taking a deep breath, she forced her fingers to open the letter. As she did, an image of Michael flitted through her mind, making her feel terribly guilty for seeking out another. It was strange; she'd never felt this way about Mr. Branscomb's letters. And it was foolish! What did she have to feel guilty about? He was the one who had left without a word. She'd remained there at the hospital for months afterward, and he never returned. As she'd reminded herself over and over again, he had never shared the feelings she felt for him.

Angry with herself for letting him into this moment when she should have been wrapped up in her future, not her past, she yanked out the thick card of paper inside. Grace was immediately baffled; it was not a letter she held in her hand.

"We have this day issued a Certificate of Passage for Miss Grace Williams from New York to San Francisco on August 9th, 1865."

What kind of response was this? The gentleman had not even felt it necessary to correspond with her, even once? Had she come across to him as so desperate in her letter that he'd assumed she would welcome any offer at all? Or had he received no other responses and was desperate himself?

She was not at all experienced in the matters of these things, but she couldn't imagine that this was the usual way these arrangements were made. She wasn't at all comfortable sailing off to a foreign place with not even the gentleman's name, nor the slightest hint toward an offer of marriage. She could arrive there with no means of returning home, only to find she'd committed herself to a scoundrel who had no intent to marry at all. And by accepting, she would cut off the possibility of furthering her acquaintance with Mr. Branscomb.

No, it was best to return the passage certificate to the gentleman and be done with it. As much as she longed to make amends with Rebecca, dashing off in such a hurry to San Francisco could end in disaster and squelch any hope of finding her sister.

She went in search of pen and paper. It was best to get this over with as quickly as possible, but when she returned to the table, her eyes were drawn to the lump in the envelope that had piqued her curiosity before. Though it was irrelevant now, she couldn't help but wonder what else the gentleman had sent. It made no difference, but still, she slipped her fingers inside the envelope and pulled out the small mound inside. Her heart began to thud wildly in her chest.

It was a flower. A dried bluebell, one that looked like it had been pressed and preserved. She squeezed her eyes shut against the onslaught of emotions. Hope. Joy. *Love.*

It looked just like the type of flower she used to gather from behind her quarters to fill the vase she'd kept next to Major's Cade's bed.

Was the man who had sent this none other than the man who'd stolen her heart and run away with it without a word? Was that why she'd felt so compelled by his advertisement?

It was impossible. It was nothing more than a cruel reminder.

All the hurt she'd kept buried rocketed to the surface. Frustration and hopelessness converged inside her and she squeezed with all her might, crushing the delicate bud in her hand. And when she could crush it no more, she hurled it across the room, a trail of broken petals fluttering to the ground behind it. The remnants of the bud fell soundlessly to the floor and she stared at it. She stood there staring at the fragments for so long that they began to blur before her eyes.

It wasn't until a tear had trickled down her cheek that she realized the scene before her wasn't blurred, it was her eyes filled with tears that distorted her vision. And once one had fallen, she couldn't stop the next, or the next after that. They welled over, cascading down her cheeks; the torrential downpour she'd feared for so long. A violent sob racked her body and she collapsed to the floor, so overwhelmed by what she'd sought to hold back for all this time.

She'd tried desperately to forget him, reminding herself repeatedly that their time together had been too brief to come to feel anything as profound as what she imagined herself feeling, and certainly not the love one found only in fairy tales.

She didn't know how long she sat there, on the floor in the middle of her tiny kitchen, but eventually, the tears subsided and the force of her sobs had diminished to nothing more than a tremble. Reaching out in front of her, she picked up the mangled bud and closed her hand tightly around it.

When her legs were able, she stood and retrieved the passage certificate from the table. Perhaps the flower was not meant as a torment, but a sign. A sign that this man in the West might help her to overcome what she had lost and find some semblance of the happiness she'd known with Michael.

Of course she was grasping, but what difference did it make? There was nothing for her here; nothing but reminders of her sister in every room in the house, and her mind always so full of memories of the man who was equally out of reach. At least by taking this step, there was some small hope she would find Rebecca.

It was enough. It would have to be.

The ship would set sail in less than a week, and she would be on it.

Chapter 8

The ship turned out to be a clipper—a very fast one at that, set to reach its destination in a little more than three months. It took other larger ships at least a month more to cover the same distance. The gentleman from the matrimonial ad had spared no expense. She'd expected the passage to provide her with steerage accommodations at best, but that was not the case.

She'd been provided with a first-class cabin of her own, dining at the captain's table every evening, and free to wander about and make use of the ship's extensive library at her leisure. And though small, she'd never known such fine accommodations before. Her cabin was profusely decorated, and the bed was the most comfortable she'd ever slept on. While she'd worried the unfamiliar motion of the boat might make her journey a less than pleasant one, it had no such ill effect. In fact, she rather fancied her time at sea, spending a great deal of it on deck, looking out over the churning waters around the ship.

She heard many of the first-class passengers complain about the dinner fare and a lack of entertainment. Though Mrs. Fraser had given her a lovely dress the day before her departure, she felt every set of eyes on her as she walked into a room, and she couldn't help but wonder if the gossipy women complained about her when her back was turned as well.

Aside from the ladies' derogatory sneers and the gentlemen's inappropriate leers, she didn't harbor a single complaint about the voyage. The long trip gave her plenty of time to think about what might await her on the docks of San Francisco.

She'd brought the crumbled remains of the dried bluebell with her, and she'd wondered often what had possessed the gentleman to send it. More than likely, it was a kindly attempt at sending his future bride flowers—dried flowers being the most practical means, given the long travel between the East and West. The type of flower was nothing more than an unfortunate coincidence.

She tried to resist, but she pulled it out often, alone late at night in her cabin. And it wasn't to the mysterious man in San Francisco that her thoughts would turn, but to the other man; the man who had left her and the bluebells behind in Virginia.

Precisely three months and one day after she boarded the sleek boat, it pulled into port, concluding the long journey and heralding the start of whatever new life awaited her. She paced back and forth across the short length of her cabin long after the clipper had ceased its movement. Though she knew she was expected to disembark in relative haste, the multitude of doubts that had swirled in her mind over the past several months whirled like a cyclone now.

Within moments of stepping off the boat, she would come face to face with the man who had sent her the passage. But she hadn't a clue how she'd recognize him, nor how he would recognize her in return. She had provided no description of her physical person in her letter. But then, she'd become vaguely acquainted with the other first-class passengers, and none of them had traveled to San Francisco for the sake of marrying a complete stranger. Many were venturing to meet with their husbands who had gone out West ahead of them, while others were husbands and wives traveling together.

That would be how she would know: once all the other passengers had left the boat, she would be the only one still remaining. Keeping her mind focused on the task of locating the mysterious man and off the many doubts that surrounded their impending meeting, she left her cabin, and followed the few passengers remaining off the boat.

A man approached her within moments, but she took a hesitant step back, and then another, hoping this man was not the one who had sent for her. It wasn't that he was unattractive, but from the moment she spotted him, his eyes were more intent on eyeing her person than meeting her own. A shiver of disgust raced down her spine as an image of the wretched Dr. Kiloran sprung to the forefront of her mind. The man continued undaunted until he stood no more than a yard from her. She looked to the left and right of her, making sure there were plenty of the crew still milling around.

"You look a bit out of place. May I be of assistance to you, Ma'am?" he asked.

It couldn't be him, or perhaps she couldn't accept the possibility. There was nothing in particular that stood out about the gentleman, but everything about him made her skin crawl. "Are...are you waiting for anyone, sir?" It was the only way she could think of to gauge whether or not he was the man who had paid for her passage.

"No. No one in particular. But it looks like you could use a companion. Someone to show you around this fine city?"

"That is very kind of you, but it is not necessary. I thank you for the offer, though."

She took another step back and turned her attention elsewhere, hoping to convey the end of the conversation.

Just then, her breath caught in her throat.

It couldn't be.

It wasn't possible. She forced her lungs to resume their work because it was nothing more than her imagination.

But the way he moved, she would know his confident stride anywhere. Even recovering from a deep wound, he had moved in a lithe manner that bespoke a quiet, indisputable authority.

Vaguely, she noticed that the man in front of her had turned to follow her gaze. "Good day to you, Ma'am," he spoke quickly and excused himself, but she was so caught up in the figment of her imagination that she barely noticed.

He continued toward her and her heartbeat sped up. No matter how she tried to rationalize what she saw, her heart would not listen. And then he was close enough that she could see his amber eyes shining clearly in the dazzling sunlight, just the way she remembered them each night in her dreams.

The bluebell in her pocket...she'd denied the possibility every time it had risen to the surface...

He didn't stop. He came close...so close.

"Grace..." he whispered huskily and she could have sworn she felt his warm breath against her cheek as he spoke.

"Michael..." Tears welled in her eyes as she fought against the proof before them. It was him. It was Michael. Unless she'd completely taken leave of her senses, it could be no other standing in front of her.

"Yes. It's good to know you haven't forgotten my name," he teased lightly as he brushed a stray curl back from her forehead.

"But you left..."

"Yes, so I did. And I am eternally sorry for having done so in such haste, Miss Williams. It could not be helped."

She nodded as if she understood, but she didn't. No part of

what was happening made any sense. Part of her, still certain he must be nothing more than a figment of her imagination, wanted to run fleeing from the docks, climb back on board the boat and sail home. But even if he was a delusion, she could not have resisted, not when he offered her his arm, the arm she'd mended and moved now as if it had never been injured. And the look in his eyes…it was as if he was willing her to agree, to give him a chance to explain.

She could do nothing else; no part of her would allow it. She took his arm and sighed as she felt its muscular firmness beneath her hand. Tiny sensations trembled up her arm while a small voice deep inside her told her she was suddenly right where she belonged. Questions whirled around her head: why had he left; why had he never come back to her; how could he have moved on and sought out a wife so easily; and why, when he'd received her letter, had he sent for her when he'd walked away so easily?

But she didn't say a word. Instead, she let him lead her away from the clipper, further and further from the docks until they arrived at a simple carriage. It was a fine enough looking carriage, but it did not boast of extravagance. And though he looked positively dashing in his clothing—of course he did—none of it bespoke of great wealth, either. Yet he'd secured first-class passage for her as if she were some gently-bred lady, and he, an affluent lord.

He helped her up into the carriage where there was room enough for the both of them, and surprisingly, it was far more comfortable than the rigid seats of the one that had brought her home from Virginia. He placed her luggage behind them while the two horses that pulled the carriage stomped lightly, as if they were anxious to be on their way. He stepped up to sit beside her and motioned for the driver to give them leave to stretch their powerful legs a moment later.

Silence prevailed for another minute as she continued to wonder what on Earth was going on.

"My brother...I learned he had joined the war, despite my urging him against it. The lieutenant who came to fetch me that day was there because my brother had been deemed missing in action—his first battle, in fact. I had to find him," he looked at her then, his eyes imploring her to understand. "But it was unnecessary. His body was recovered shortly after my departure from the hospital, though I would not know it until I arrived there several days later."

Guilt for her selfishness threatened to overwhelm her. All this time she hadn't understood why he'd left in such haste, even angry with him for it, when it had been concern for his brother that had called him away. "I'm so sorry, I thought—"

"That I did not wish to return to you?"

The fact that he knew her thoughts should not have surprised her, and there was no sense in denying it. He'd been able to read her so well. Grace nodded, tugging nervously at her bottom lip.

"I wished for nothing else, Miss Williams."

No, it couldn't be. If he'd wanted to return to her, what force could possibly have kept him away?

Silence resumed, nothing but the sound of the horses' hooves plodding against the ground while the distant noise from the docks grew quieter with their every step.

She'd stopped herself from considering the possibility it could be him there waiting for her, so much that she felt completely unprepared for it now. So many emotions roiled within her, but despite the reason he'd left—more than understandable now—it didn't negate the fact he'd never returned, and he'd gone on to seek out a wife, making it clear he had not seen her in that regard.

Was it merely a convenient coincidence for him that she'd been the one to respond to his advertisement? Had he taken so long to respond because he'd been hoping that some other woman might write to him? Was there any point in continuing to come up with theories and conjectures when the source was sitting next to her? She just needed to be brave enough to pose the questions.

"You never did come back, Major—"

"The war is over, Miss Williams," he cut in quickly. "And I have resigned my commission. Please, call me Michael."

"You resigned?" What could have compelled him to do such a thing? Hadn't he been the one to say it was in his blood? "I thought...I couldn't imagine a better soldier..."

He exhaled heavily and looked as if he might say something, but then he swallowed it down and the carriage was silent once again. Still, there had been more she'd been meaning to say, and if she didn't say it quickly, she feared she might never get the words out.

"Nevertheless, you did not come back, and it took you so long to respond to my letter...if you were perhaps hoping for a different woman—"

"I hoped for no such thing," he cut in, as a look somewhere between anger and frustration flitted across his handsome face, but he covered it quickly. "I apologize, Miss Williams."

He'd been quiet for another moment when he motioned for the driver to stop the carriage. The man guided the horses to the edge of the trail, and she only realized then they had long since left the bustling streets of San Francisco. She had no idea where they were now.

He held up his hand to her, encouraging her to join him. "We will not go far, Miss Williams. My driver should serve as an adequate chaperone for propriety's sake, though I daresay we were far more alone quite often in Virginia, were we not?"

She hadn't even considered the impropriety of leaving with him unchaperoned. What he said was quite true, so it seemed almost ridiculous to worry over such things now. Besides, looking to her left and right, there was no one around but for the driver and horses. She took his hand, the tingle in her hand and up her arm an all so familiar sensation.

Once out of the carriage, he started away from it, but only seemed to venture far enough to keep the driver from overhearing their conversation.

"In truth, Miss Williams, I took so long to respond to you because I did not want to," he confessed.

She looked down swiftly to hide the sting that made her eyes water. So, she had been correct. He'd hoped another lady would reply to his advertisement, and only when he was sure that no other would did he seek her out. "I see," she said, hoping her tone sounded less pitiful to him than it did to her own ears.

"I did search for you," he spoke with a gentle fire in his voice and stopped to look at her, taking her hands in his own. "I inquired with the Sanitary Commission about the nursing staff in Virginia during the last quarter of the war. But I gave up the effort quickly," he confessed, though he looked pained. "I'd never imagined when I put out that advertisement you would be the one to respond."

She felt silly, standing there with his hands enfolding hers.

"We never discussed our feelings, Miss Williams. I had no assurance you would want to hear from me again, and it wouldn't have been fair of me to pressure you. You are so young, too young to be so burdened after spending so much of your life responsible for another."

"Burdened?" She didn't understand. He believed she thought of him as a burden? Could anything have ever been more untrue?

"I stopped searching because I could not fathom asking so much of you. You are young and beautiful. I saw the way every soldier's eyes followed you; you could have had your pick of any of them."

She shivered, remembering one particular set of eyes that had leered at her, sending terror to her core.

"But when I received your letter, I couldn't bring myself to dispose of it. I kept it with me for so long, but always resisted the urge to respond. I thought of you so often, I thought I was going mad, but still you would not leave me alone. Memories of you...your letter...they all haunted me until I could ignore them no longer. I am ashamed to admit that I succumbed to my own selfish desire. Even then, I did not know what to say to you, though, and that's why there was nothing but the passage in the envelope. That, and the one token of you I took with me from the hospital."

She was desperately trying to make sense of what he was saying, but it came back to the same question over and over again: what burden? He'd searched for her, but had given up. She'd written to him, but he'd refrained from responding. Why? What was it he felt would burden her so deeply?

"I know," he added, seeing the confusion in her eyes. "And I suppose I should tell you now so you might have me turn this carriage around and bring you back to the docks." His shoulders slumped in weary defeat, something she'd never seen in him before. This was the man who had stood stock straight while blood seeped from multiple wounds in his body. He'd remained that way the whole time they had treated the soldiers under his command.

"My brother's death was not the only tragedy I discovered upon my arrival. He was a good young man, but with no one there to guide him, he hadn't the moral constitution I expected of him. He'd gotten a young lady with child while I was at war—soon after I left, actually. And not with one child, but *two*. The twins were already two years old when I was informed their mother had succumbed to a fever. There was no one left to care for them. If I did not assume the responsibility, they would have been sent to an orphanage. What did I know of raising a child? Two of them!" he scoffed lightly. "But I could not allow the alternative."

"It must have been terribly difficult for you." She laid a comforting hand on his arm, all of the anger and confusion she'd felt dissipating. Her heart ached for him, imagining what it must have been like to have so much to deal with so suddenly, and on the heels of learning of his brother's death.

Perhaps he did not know much about raising children, but she had a feeling he'd done a fine job. Once he'd committed himself to the care and welfare of the young children, there would have been nothing that could have stopped him in his task. Yes, she imagined he'd done a fine job.

But he pulled his arm away quickly. "You do not understand, Miss Williams. You are what? Barely twenty years old? You did not come here to marry only me, but to take on a whole family, two boys who are now my sons as well, nearly three years old now. And they are a handful, I tell you. I do not know how mothers do it, raising children and keeping their wits about them at the same time."

She laughed. She couldn't help it. "And that is what you sought to save me from? You thought the burden of raising two young boys would be too great for me? Had you married me then, many months ago, do you not think I'd be swollen with child already?" she asked, and then covered her mouth, her cheeks turning a bright shade of crimson at the boldness of her speech. But she had to continue.

"When I'd found you had left that morning, I would have given anything to have you back with me. I thought I had misinterpreted our time together, that you cared for me as nothing more than an acquaintance with whom you'd been forced to spend a great deal of time. What else could explain how you had been able to leave so suddenly, and without a word?"

"I had thought the night prior, when..." he trailed off, anger blazing quickly in his eyes, but he blinked hard and turned to her once more. "After, when I held you in my arms, nothing in this world could ever have felt so right. I thought you felt it, too. I thought you knew how much you meant to me."

"I did not. I presumed you had come to my aid because you are far too gallant and brave to have done anything else. I believed you held me because you knew it was what I needed. And I thought you kissed me because it was a far gentler memory to replace..."

She hesitated, swallowing hard against the knot of emotion in her throat, though it was not fear or sadness that had welled up. Remembering the feel of his arms around her and his lips against hers had roused the recollection of the tenderness of those brief moments.

"And all these months since," she forced out. "You are not the only one who has gone near-mad. You, Major Cade, are quite an impossible man to forget, and in truth, as much as it pained me, I did not *want* to forget."

"I did not know your feelings. I was aware you had grown fond of me, but no more than that."

"And all this time, it turns out you were merely trying to save me from the burden of caring for a few children?" She shook her head, smiling, and then started back toward the carriage, lifting herself up and waiting for him to join her. "Shall we go then? I am anxious to see my new home," she announced, her heart growing lighter, and yet fuller by the moment.

He hesitated though. "Are you certain, Miss Williams? I wouldn't want you to come to regret your decision."

She merely laughed and held out a hand to him, urging him to join her. She'd never been more certain of anything in her life.

Chapter 9

The carriage came to a halt in front of a small house. Though it wasn't large—similar in size to Uncle Horace's home—it had been immaculately tended to, the windows sparkling clean, the roof in good repair and the yard neatly kept. It looked welcoming, so unlike Uncle Horace's house ever had. A structure about twice the length of the house stood about twenty yards back; obviously, those were the stables. By the size of the building, it must have held a great number of horses. Beyond that, Grace could see other small buildings further in the distance, though she could not guess their purposes.

"I was good at being a soldier, but it was no life for a new father of two young boys. The war over, and I supposed they needed me more than my men," he told her as he helped her step down from the carriage.

"And so you thought you'd try your hand out West," she reiterated the words he'd told her so many months before. He'd resigned his commission and now she understood why he'd gone out West. While his father had been correct in predicting what a fine soldier he would be, Major Cade was not without ambitions to fall back on, and that explained the expansive stables—he'd become a horse breeder. She recalled him mentioning in one of their conversations that his father had bequeathed to him a good stable back home. He must have brought the horses with him, circumventing the usually high cost of such an endeavor.

"You remember?"

"Of course, I remember," she answered softly.

He took a step toward her, his eyes never leaving hers, but before he had closed the distance between them, the front door to the house flew open and two tiny boys came toddling out. He looked to them and smiled, but then she could feel his gaze on her as they pattered across the yard to where she stood.

They were beautiful—there was no other way to describe them. Both dark-haired, one boy bore the same amber eyes she'd stared into hundreds of times, and the other a bit shorter with deep brown eyes, so dark she swore she could see her own reflection in his enormous orbs. It was easy to see the resemblance, but she wondered if the smaller child had taken the color from his mother or father's eyes.

"My brother's eyes," he whispered, reading her thoughts like he'd always been able to do so easily.

The beautiful, tiny people reached them then, and Grace smiled brightly while they each hugged their arms around one of Major Cade's legs. Once there, they eyed her with open curiosity and turned their inquisitive expressions to the man they knew as their father.

"This is Miss Williams, the lady I was telling you about. Miss Williams, I'd like to introduce to you to John and Adam." He bent first one leg and then the other, indicating to which leg each child belonged. Apparently, John was the child with the deep brown eyes; fitting, given it was his father's name.

Each child murmured something that would have been incoherent had she not recognized their attempt to pronounce her name.

"Hello there, John. How do you do, Adam? It's a pleasure to make your acquaintance," she lilted, and didn't feel the least bit silly as she bent down, practically kneeling in the dirt and greeting two children who could barely pronounce her name.

The amber-eyed boy, Adam, reached out a hand to her then, not taking her own, but moving toward her face instead. Even having just met them, it was obvious he was definitely the braver of the two.

He reached further until his chubby, little fingers made contact with her cheek. She eyed him curiously but did not pull away.

"Pre-tty la-dy," the boy annunciated slowly. Perfect—another young man who would make the ladies swoon one day, so much like his adopted father.

"Yes, Adam. Miss Williams is the pretty lady I spoke of to you, but let's not make her uncomfortable, shall we?" he admonished lightly and smiled ruefully at her. She could tell that even with the smile on his face, his eyes were assessing, taking in every nuance of her reaction to the boys.

"It's quite alright, Major." John hung back, clinging tightly to his father's leg, and she attempted to draw him out. "Might I say, John, that you have the biggest, most wonderful brown eyes I have ever seen."

He didn't release his hold, but he did loosen it some and took one, small, shy step toward her.

"Me?" Adam probed bravely, waiting for his own compliment.

"Adam, yours eyes are the exact same color as your father's," she whispered to him conspiratorially, and if there had been any doubt, that won him over.

He grasped her hand in his—well, he wrapped his small hand around two of her fingers—and pulled her along with him. "Come," he told her in way of explanation and started back toward the house.

She laughed helplessly, unable to resist the boy any more than she'd been able to resist Michael on the docks. But as she stood up straight and turned to follow him, she froze.

She turned back to Michael who was leaning down to scoop John up into his arms, and he smiled, as if to say, "your eyes are not playing tricks on you."

She whipped her head around once more, and she could hear Adam laugh merrily at her strange response, as if she were playing some game with him. But Michael had been right—her eyes were seeing clearly, and what she saw brought tears to her eyes, blurring her vision, but not so much that she couldn't see the woman who stood there in his doorway, and a man she'd never met standing behind her.

"Rebecca..."

She hadn't seen her in three long years, but she was nearly unchanged; the same cherub cheeks that she was quite certain would keep her forever appearing youthful; the same blonde hair, so much in contrast to her own shimmering, dark tresses; and her ocean blue eyes—the only tie that bound them together in any overtly familial way. Her sister's eyes were filled with tears as well, but the moment they first spilled over, she took a tentative step forward and then another. Adam began tugging on the fingers he still held in his own, and she let him lead her forward. Was this what Adam had had in mind when he'd latched onto her fingers? Had he known she would be overjoyed to see her sister?

"S'prise!" he announced gleefully, answering her question before she asked it, just like his father had done so many times before. He had found Rebecca. She'd talked about her often at the hospital, but at the time, she hadn't known her sister had left the East in pursuit of love. How could he possibly have known?

She glanced back briefly to Major Cade, and he smiled wryly. "I feared your sensibilities might be offended if I did not provide you with an adequate chaperone...until I can make arrangements for our wedding day."

"How..."

"Quite by accident, to tell you the truth," he answered the question before she'd asked, just like Adam. "I happened upon Mrs. Rebecca Jones in San Francisco. Of course, the relation was not immediately apparent, but her eyes...they reminded me so much of yours that I knew it could not be anyone else, though I had no idea at the time what she was doing in the West. I thought at first, maybe you had...you both were...well, I had to introduce myself and when I discovered she'd come to marry her betrothed, I feared...I thought maybe you had done the same."

She was torn. She wanted simultaneously to pull her sister tight into her embrace, and throw her arms around Michael in gratitude, in tenderness...in love.

Love. There was that word again, but this time, with him standing right there in front of her, so close, she could not deny the existence of such an emotion.

Respect...admiration...tenderness; these words were all too small to describe what she felt for him. They needed to be summed up in an enormous, profound description, and there was only one that came to mind, one that came anywhere close to describing the overwhelming emotion that filled every fiber of her being—love.

Rebecca reached where she stood then, and Adam hopped around excitedly. "S'prise! S'prise!" he shouted gleefully.

"I had been angry, but I was wrong. When Mr. Cade spoke of you, of how you had saved his life and the lives of countless soldiers in Virginia, I knew I had been wrong. He talked about how heavily the war and its victims weighed on you, though he was certain you'd never admit it, and it was then that I realized you had not merely gone in search of adventure. That is what I had thought, that you were bored with our simple, little existence, and you were hoping to find excitement that life with me could not offer. I thought you were tired of having to take care of your older sister."

"Oh, Rebecca," she cried, flinging her arms around her for the first time in so long. She'd never even imagined Rebecca had felt that way. It must have been terrible to think herself so abandoned by a sister off on selfish pursuits. "I never wanted to leave you, Darling. Never. I had only sought to support our country, and to financially support the continuation of your schooling."

"I know that now," Rebecca sobbed against her shoulder. "I should have known it all along. Can you ever forgive me?"

"Of course," she replied without hesitation. How could she not?

Rebecca snorted most unladylike and leaned back. "You were always far too good a sister," she teased, swiping at the tears that had begun to slow. She looked back and forth between her and Major Cade, and then down at the two boys, one in his father's arms, and the other still dancing merrily about her skirts.

"But look at me, being selfish once again," Rebecca said after a brief moment. "Come along, Adam. Come, John," she told them as she gathered the latter up in her arms and took Adam's hand. "I owe a great debt to you both, the least I can do is give you a moment's privacy. Lord help you, with these two running about, you'll get precious little of it afterward."

Grace was not eager to see Rebecca walking away from her after missing her for so long, even if it was only toward the house, but she didn't object. She turned to Michael instead as Rebecca and the boys reached the front door to the house. "I...I don't know what to say..."

"Tell me honestly what you are thinking, Miss Williams."

"Honestly, I'm thinking that I gave you leave to call me Grace many months ago, and you have seldom seen it fit to do so," she laughed.

"Tell me what you are thinking, Grace. I had sought to avoid burdening you for so long, I feel guilty even now for bringing you here."

"Guilty? You cannot be serious, Major."

"I believe I made my wish clear also, Grace, that you do me the same honor of using my given name. And I am quite serious. You should be gracing ballrooms, shopping for pretty things and enjoying the attention of a dozen young fops. You have been responsible for far too much, for far too long. Rebecca is delightful, truly, but she should have been the one to take care of you all those years after your parents died, not the other way around."

"Do you not suppose I should have some say in what I should, and should not be doing?"

"Yes, of course you should. But I fear you are being blinded by a wayward affection for me that will pass in time."

"Pass in time? When, Michael? Day after day I have longed for you, night after night I have dreamed of you. I see your face every time I close my eyes, and it is your voice I hear inside my head in place of my own."

"Yes," he exhaled heavily, "I know the feeling. But life here is not easy. The work is hard and the boys are tiring. You deserve a rest, Grace."

"Life here might not be easy, but nothing worth having in life ever is," she reiterated the words Mrs. Fraser had spoken to her, seeing the truthfulness in them now more than ever before. Certainly, minding two toddlers, tending to a house and helping Michael in any way she could would be tiring, and not the least bit easy...and she couldn't imagine anything she would like more.

He pulled her to him then, as he had that night so many months ago, but there was no vileness or violence to overcome this time. It was just the two of them there, and love and joy overwhelmed her heart. He leaned down to her, so slowly it felt like an eternity before his lips pressed gently against hers. With the first gentle brush, she sighed in delight.

She was home.

THE END

Mail Order Bride: Cate's Change Of Heart

South Bend, Indiana - 1867

Chapter 1

Catriona massaged the aching spot between her eyes as Violet, the young woman sitting next to her, driveled on and on about the gentleman who'd made an offer of marriage to her from out West. He was charming and eloquent, kind and warm-hearted, and a plethora of other characteristics that made him the most wonderful catch this side of the Atlantic—at least according to Violet. Catriona—or Cate, as she preferred—had smiled politely and nodded her head at the proper intervals. But after seven hours of listening to countless variations of the same praise for a man she would never meet, her head ached and she wondered just how much trouble it would be to walk the rest of the way.

Her own match was not so amorous, but she wasn't jealous. She'd had no interest in seeking out something as trivial as a love match. In fact, she thought it unwise of the young girl next to her to have made such a terrible decision. A man's eloquent words and silly pet names weren't going to put food on her table or a roof over her head.

Cate, well-accustomed to an empty stomach and questionable accommodations, would not base her future on such frivolities. She had sought out and acquired an offer of marriage from a young, hard-working gentleman who had well-established himself in the West. He was not rich, by any stretch of the word, but she would not know hunger ever again, and her family back home would no longer be burdened with another mouth to feed. It was a smart match, if not the stuff of fairy tales, but she would choose a full stomach over sweet nothings any day of the week. Violet, though only two years her junior but having come from a comfortable existence, could not possibly comprehend the need to make a choice between the two.

And that was precisely why she had nodded politely and allowed the woman to continue rambling ad nauseam. Violet was a bright-eyed, innocent and eager to share her romantic excitement with someone; anyone—even if that was only a stranger sitting next to her on a train. Cate would not take that away from her. It might be the last time the young girl felt full of so much hope and anticipation over her future. Soon, cold reality was apt to steal away that childlike innocence.

"...and the house is not even furnished yet, which means he and I can tackle the task together," Violet exclaimed.

Not furnished yet? That most likely meant that in reality, he couldn't afford the furniture, but it didn't matter; the girl was so enthralled, it would probably take months before she noticed there wasn't a seat in the whole house.

Just then, the train came to a grinding halt and she lurched forward, bracing her hands against the seat in front of her to prevent hitting her head against its hard back. What on Earth was going on? Though not a frequent traveler, she was quite certain the train's stop should be gentler than that. But then she heard it, the distant din of voices from the cars in front of them.

The commotion quickly grew louder, and soon, screams rent the air. Cate stood, looking first out the window, and then at the door to the car ahead. She could see nothing, but there was no doubt in her mind they were in trouble.

And then, the resounding *bang!* rang out; a sound she knew all too well.

The other passengers in the car sat frozen in their seats, and Violet looked up at her with terror in her eyes. Apparently, one did not need to be familiar with the sound of gunfire to recognize it.

The screams ahead of them grew louder, and she understood why. Whatever trouble had come aboard was working its way toward them. The rest of the passengers in her car had moved from their frozen tableau, scrambling to duck behind seats—like that would somehow make them invisible to whatever was about to come through that door. But Violet remained frozen, too terrified to do anything but stare up at her.

Cate had to act fast. Making her decision, she grabbed Violet's arm and yanked with all her might, forcing the girl out of her seat. Holding onto her small traveling bag, she pulled the girl to the back of the car, opening the door and dragging her through to the car behind them. There were a few passengers here, all hiding—albeit poorly—like those in the car ahead, but Cate didn't stop.

Keeping Violet in tow, she headed for the back of the car and into the one behind them. Once more through the back of the next, she came across the first of the cars holding cargo. Looking around for what she sought, she found it quickly; it was there in the corner behind a tall stack of crates. She quickly shoved Violet into the small hiding place and grabbed an armful of the burlap sacks she saw peeking out from an open crate nearby.

"I'm going to cover you up. You just stay here and be as quiet as you can. I know it's scary, but I want you to focus on your Mr. Greenfield, and wait. When it's safe, I'll come for you. But you do not come out; not for anyone."

Another wave of screams and gunshots came from no more than two cars away. She was out of time. "Do you understand, Violet?" she urged, pleading with her eyes for the girl to realize her life depended on her ability not to scream. Finally, Violet nodded, and Cate tossed the burlap sacks on top of her, spreading them out to look like a large stack of the sacks shoved in the corner.

She drew a deep breath, steeling her nerves against what she must do next. There wasn't room for her to hide there as well, and if she lingered any longer, she risked giving away Violet's hiding spot. If she could make it to the previous car before the men were upon them, she would not draw undue attention to where she'd been.

Looking over the unmoving stack of burlap sacks once more, she darted back to the previous car, knowing she had just sacrificed her own life to save a veritable stranger. But there had been no choice. She could not have left the terrified girl who had sat next to her there in her seat to die while she ran to cower away in the cargo car.

She'd made it a few steps into the car when the door at the front opened, admitting a dangerous-looking lot of men, five of them in total, looking all the more threatening with the pistols they held in their hands. At the same time her eyes took in the menacing sight in front of her, she recognized something more: the eerie silence from the cars that had been filled with screams moments before. There was no sound because everyone was dead, their screams silenced for all eternity.

Suddenly, her heart pounded wildly, knowing with absolute certainty, she was about to die. Blood whooshed in her ears so loud, it drowned out the sounds coming from the mouths of the murderers in front of her. And though she couldn't quell the sound, she squared her shoulders, looking the man closest to her straight in the eye. If she was going to die, and there was no way out of it, she would not die a coward.

Just then, something snaked around her waist from behind and she froze in stunned shock. She hadn't anticipated an attacker from behind. He must have boarded the train between cars and entered the same door she'd come through seconds before. Had he seen her run back from the car behind them? Did he know Violet hid there?

Her senses returning, she struggled violently. She could hear the voice of her assailant rising above the other noise in the car, but the blood pounding in her ears made it impossible to make out the words. And then he spun, darting through the open door as the sound of a gunshot rang out once more. She waited to feel the impact of the ball, but it never came. At least, she didn't think it did, and she would certainly feel it, wouldn't she?

The man who held her over his shoulder jumped to the ground, jarring her and making her jaws slam together violently. He dashed the few steps to a horse who stood there unmoving while she flailed wildly, but as he turned, she saw a scene in front of her that chilled her to the bone.

All the passengers were not dead. Many of them had been taken off the train where they knelt on the ground now, sobbing, begging, crying while their assailants waved guns and knives in front of their terror-stricken faces. Her attacker threw her up across the horse as a *bang!* reverberated through the air. She could do nothing but watch in horror as a young man on his knees in the long grass fell forward, lifeless on the ground.

And then there was a heavy weight behind her, holding her down while he turned his horse and darted away from the gruesome scene. No matter how she struggled, she was held there in a vice grip between the horse and its rider, her strength no match for his. The ground blurred beneath her as the horse galloped away, and the cries of the men and women about to die behind her grew quieter. An icy shiver of fear raced through her body as she wondered why this man had taken her. What did he intend; why couldn't he have just left her there to die with the rest? Certainly, it would have been a gentler end than whatever this vile fiend had planned.

She grew tired from her struggle, but still the man continued to ride away. Minutes passed—or was it hours, or maybe days? It could have been either; it had felt like just seconds since she'd watched a man die right in front of her, but a lifetime since she'd begun her struggle against the assailant who held her pinned to his horse.

Suddenly, she felt him pull hard on the reins and the horse came to a graceful stop. He'd dismounted, leaving her there unbound. And though terrified beyond words, her temper flared as she dropped herself onto the ground and whirled on the man.

"How dare you, you filthy, pigeon-livered ratbag!" She drew upon a handful of vulgarities she could remember from the multitude of soldiers she'd met during her time as a nurse in a Virginia hospital.

"Well, there's nothing wrong with your cursing, is there, darling?" he drawled.

He came around to where she stood near the horse and she skittered away out of his reach. He chuckled lightly and rummaged for one of the sacks attached to the saddle. Finding whatever he sought, he stepped back but seemed to sway unsteadily.

She noticed then he didn't look the same color he'd been. In fact, he was nearly stark white, and as she glanced down, she quickly understood why. The left side of him, from his abdomen to his thigh, was saturated with blood, and as he wobbled precariously, he reached for the horse and she saw the back of him, soaked in nearly as much blood as his front.

He'd been shot. The ball she'd expected to feel penetrate her own flesh as he'd stepped through the door of the train must have gone astray.

That was just great. He'd kidnapped her, and now he was going to die after whisking her off to the middle of nowhere, where she might not have any hope of making it to civilization before she died of starvation. What did she know of surviving in the wild? Nothing. And that meant she was going to have to try to save his life and hope he ended up taking her somewhere she might be able to cry out for help—assuming he didn't kill her first.

But looking in his eyes, hooded with pain and filled with something else...something sad...some small part of her, so small it wasn't worth considering, didn't want to leave him as near-death as he was.

She looked around for the best place to lay him down. The closest she could find to a comfortable place was a patch of creeping vines that twisted into a bed of semi-plush greenery a few feet away.

"Lie down," she instructed, taking his arm gruffly and starting him in the direction she was pointing. "What did you have in mind, hmm? Drag me out into the wilderness and let me die slowly? Fine good it would have done you. With a wound like that, you would have been long dead before starvation claimed me."

"I had no such plan, I assure you," he murmured, his voice deep and husky, but weaker than she'd thought it had been before.

Ignoring him, she helped him lie down amid the vines and got down beside him, pulling his clothes out of the way as best she could to get a look at the wound. There were two, as she'd expected: an entry wound through his back and the exit wound in his abdomen, near his hip. At least the bullet had gone clean through. If it had lodged inside him, there would have been little she could have done, having no way of retrieving the bullet.

She lunged to her feet and went to rummage through his packs as quickly as she could, looking for anything that would help her. She needed clean cloths, alcohol, a suture needle, and a plethora of the herbs, poultices and tinctures she'd been forced to leave on the train. Those would be invaluable now, but there was no point in dwelling on it.

Among other things in his packs, she found a small bottle of whiskey, a shirt that appeared clean, a sewing needle, fishing line, tinderbox and sulphur-tipped matches, and a small knife. The man had a strange assortment of things in his sacks, but at least they might serve her purpose now. Bringing them back, he looked up at her oddly.

"And what do you intend to do with those?" he asked, paying particular attention to the sewing needle and the fishing line dangling from her hand.

"I intend to give you some hope of seeing tomorrow, if that's alright with you," she snapped. "This is going to hurt, but you deserve it, so don't worry that I'll feel too badly about it," she announced as she placed the items next to her and opened the whiskey. Pouring it over the open wound on his abdomen, he sucked in his breath and drops of sweat sprung up on his brow, but he didn't cry out. She wished he had.

Maneuvering him so she could reach the wound on his back, she poured more whiskey, and this time a small, strangled noise escaped his lips. She could only imagine the pain that it caused and the effort that it took to keep it for the most part hidden, and she regretted wishing he'd shown more proof of it.

The first of her tasks accomplished, she set the bottle aside, thought better of it and held it to his lips, tipping it up as his lips parted. She watched his throat work as he swallowed several times before she took the bottle back and placed it on the ground next to her. He nodded in appreciation, and tight-lipped, she nodded back in acknowledgement.

Scanning the area once more, she gathered twigs and branches, using the tinderbox and matches to start the fire. And once the flames burned bright enough, she held the tip of the knife within it, letting it get good and hot before bending the steel of the needle with it. It wasn't perfect, but it crudely resembled a suturing needle. It would have to do.

It took another minute to cut the fishing line into short pieces and then disinfect the pieces with a bit of whiskey, but all the while, she could feel his eyes on her, and his gaze turned wary as she scooted over to him with the items ready.

"Would you prefer I stitch you up, or leave you open to bleed to death?" she asked as he leaned away from her. She didn't wait for an answer before threading the first length of line through the bent needle. She staunched the slow trickle of blood with the clean shirt, doused in alcohol, and then pinched the open ends of flesh together before hooking him with the needle and tying the ends of the first stitch together. He remained silent through it, as well as each of the others, though sweat now poured from his brow.

She stopped for a brief moment when she'd finished stitching the wound on his abdomen and once again held the whiskey bottle to his lips. He swallowed eagerly and she watched again as his throat worked to take down the fiery liquid.

"I'm sorry, it's the best I can do," she heard herself apologizing and then chastised herself silently for the moment of weakness. "I'm going to turn you over," she told him more briskly, and did just that, though she was careful to avoid putting pressure on the wound she just stitched.

It took less time to finish tending to the wound on his back since the entry wound was smaller than the exit, and she breathed a sigh of relief the moment she was finished. It hadn't been often she'd been left to stitch up a man; it was not proper work for a nurse, she'd been told. But for having nothing to work with but a makeshift needle and fishing line for thread, she'd done a decent job.

"Thank you," he whispered ruggedly as she sat down a few feet from him.

She was about to tell him he wasn't out of trouble just yet, but she hesitated. It was true enough—the wound was stitched, but she'd have to wait and pray that no infection appeared. It was probably too much to hope that the bullet had been clean and no debris had gotten into the wound before she got to it. But she couldn't bring herself to tell him that right then, as he looked up at her, pain still etching his features and gratitude in his eyes. She nodded instead. "Get some rest. Your body will thank you for it."

He eyed the knife she'd left laying carelessly on the ground as if he was deliberating the chances of her stabbing him with it while he slept. She hadn't gone to all the trouble of stitching him up just to render her own effort wasted.

"You're safe enough," she told him. "I'm not in the habit of butchering my patients in their sleep."

Questions seemed to form in his eyes in response to what she'd said, but he didn't say a word. After a moment, his eyes closed, the dark lashes splaying across his cheeks as his mouth slackened seconds later, telling her he'd gone straight to sleep.

Chapter 2

Michael awoke slowly, the ache that pounded all through the left side of his torso drawing him out of sleep. He forced himself to remain still, listening to the sounds around him; he heard nothing but the quiet breathing of the woman he'd forced from the train and a strange grinding sound, wood against rock, over and over again. It almost forced him to open his eyes, but he resisted. Not yet. He needed a moment to think, to gather his wits about him.

He'd expected to wake up to find her long gone. While he had been conscious, she might have feared what he would do, even in his weakened state, if she tried to run. But while he'd slept, surely it had crossed her mind that she could easily have slipped away. He could think of no reason why she stayed, and having no way to learn the reason on his own, he opened his eyes, blinking against the brightness of the morning sun. He'd slept clear yesterday evening and the entire night.

"You're still here?" he asked as his eyes lost the blur of sleep and settled on her slim form a few yards from him, bent over a rock and repeatedly pressing on it with a blunt stick. Well, he understood what the noise was now, though he had no idea what she was doing.

"And what exactly was it you expected me to do? Walk to the nearest town? For your information, I don't make a habit of trekking out into the middle of nowhere on a whim. So, I will see you recovered, and then you will take me to the nearest town and leave me there."

She could have been a royal princess commanding her subjects by the way she spoke, but he could tell the haughtiness in her tone was deliberate and forced.

"And if I don't recover?"

"I will leave your rotting corpse to the birds and try my hand at surviving in the wilderness until civilization can be found."

He wondered just how far he should push her, but figured he might as well find out just what she was made of. "And if I refuse?"

"Well then, I suppose I might be sorely tempted to let your body fill with a nasty infection and let the vultures take you."

She went back to whatever she was doing with the stick and rock, and he couldn't help but be impressed by her answer. She had nerve.

"How is it you know so much about treating gunshot wounds?" he asked her as he tried to sit upright and then thought better of it as a sharp pain tore through his abdomen.

"I was a nurse during the war, though little good this knowledge did me," she motioned to whatever she was grinding on the rock. "The physicians—an educated lot of arrogant butchers—they'd sooner lop off limbs than listen to a lowly nurse—and a poor one, at that."

A poor one? He wouldn't have suspected that by the way she carried herself or by the way she spoke. Then again, few pampered ladies were likely to have done what he'd stood outside the train and watched her do the day prior.

"It's too bad, really," he heard her continue. "They weren't bad men, not all of them, but even the basic necessity of handwashing was beyond them. But then, it isn't the way of things, is it? I suppose it's unfortunate you were shot," she eyed him dubiously as if she questioned her own statement, "but you're likely to make a much better recovery here in the forest than you would have in some filthy hospital."

Well, the woman wasn't modest—at least not when it came to her healing skills. And he supposed he should count himself lucky. Though what she didn't seem to realize was that if he hadn't been whisking her off that train, he would never have been shot in the first place.

He laid there, watching her silently, and he could tell she was aware of it, though she continued on as if she wasn't. She was a pleasure to watch; the delicate way she used her hands, the way she worried her bottom lip with her teeth when she was particularly engrossed in something in front of her. She was soothing to watch, but he found his eyes growing heavy already. He fought it, though, with relative success, doing little more than dozing off for a few minutes at a time here and there. She would be right there in front of him when he opened his eyes sometimes, while at others, he could only hear her moving about, the quiet swish of her skirts telling him precisely where she was.

At one of the times he awoke, he remembered the brief conversation they'd had earlier, about her opinion of doctors. He propped his head up and glanced down at the wound he could see near his hip, and he had to admit she'd done a good job. Heck, the stitches looked better than those he'd gotten when he had been injured in the war. Was she right, then? Were the physicians who had cared for countless soldiers no better than butchers?

His brother, Nathan, came to mind. He'd been injured in the war as well, afflicted by a gunshot to the leg. According to the surgeon, it had shattered the bone in his calf irreparably and nothing could be done but to remove it. The stump became infected shortly after and had nearly taken him, but slowly, he recovered. Of course, he had recovered only to be sent home. A soldier without two legs to stand on wasn't much use on the battlefield, he'd been told. Nathan hadn't been the same after that.

"You said the doctors remove limbs too eagerly. Do you honestly believe that to be the case?"

She looked up, as if the question had surprised her. "Yes, of course."

"Then, do you think a man who'd taken a gunshot to his shin, shattered the bone there, supposedly...do you think such a leg could have been saved?"

She glanced down at his leg, assuming he'd been referring to himself, but her eyes dismissed the assumption. "You could move—and ride—like a man with two legs. I do not think you speak of yourself?"

"No, not me. My brother, Nathan. He was injured in the war and the doctor took his leg below his knee. The infection that followed nearly killed him—what was left of him, anyway. He wasn't the same, you know?"

She was silent for a moment, as if contemplating her answer. "I wish I could tell you, but I do not know. In truth, there were many times when it could not be helped. And though difficult, you say your brother maintained his knee joint. He could function almost normally compared to the men I've seen lose the leg above the knee. It is more of a blow to the mind than to the body, though, isn't it?"

He nodded in agreement, remembering the shell of a man Nathan had been ever since.

"Now, the infection, that blame you could probably lay at the feet of his surgeon. The filthy hackers; that's what my aunt called them."

Suddenly, she was silent, as if she'd only just realized she'd been conversing with the man she thought had kidnapped her. Well, that is what he'd done, wasn't it? Not a lot of choice in the matter, though.

"You should get some rest," she told him despite the fact he'd been awake for mere minutes.

He noticed then that the sun had already begun to set. Had he really slept so much and left her to her own devices the entire day? He should make a fire. Still early in the season, it got quite cold at night. He gritted his teeth as he struggled to sit up, but she jumped to her feet in a flash.

"What do you think you're doing? I spend all this time stitching you up and you're going to rip yourself open to show your gratitude? I think not. Do you really wish for me to leave you to the vultures?"

"I was...I was going to make a fire," he rasped as waves of pain tremored through his torso with his effort. "It gets cold at night, and you'll freeze without it."

"I've gathered sticks already, and some fallen pieces of wood. They'll have to do. So, as you can see, I shall be just fine. Now, go to sleep."

Surprised by just how tired he was, he closed his eyes, listening to the quiet brush of her skirts as she moved around.

He'd just thrown away any hope of finding his brother for her...and here she was threatening to leave him to be pecked away by birds. And worse, the only thing he could think was, *Gosh, what a woman!*

Chapter 3

A day passed and she kept an eye on his wounds; all the while, she considered making a run for it. He slept so much, she'd be miles away before he noticed. But each time it came to mind, something held her there, whether it was preservation of self— fearing a trek through the forest by herself—or concern for her kidnapper, she didn't know. Nevertheless, she was still there the following evening, and she woke after dozing off for a few hours. She stretched her limbs and stood to cross the small space between them to check his wounds once again.

He was sleeping fitfully, writhing lightly while his brow furrowed unhappily. He looked different than he had when she'd last checked on him a few hours prior. His face was flush and the skin was drawn tight over his smooth, high cheekbones. A quick check of his brow against the inside of her wrist and her heart began to race. He was burning up.

She moved to his side and peered beneath the fabric pads. The wound on his back was healing as expected, but the one above his hip...it looked angry and red.

As much as she'd tried to stave it off, infection had come, and it had come quickly. She'd managed to retrieve some helpful items since she'd first stitched up his wound, but would they be enough?

She was going to have to open up the wound and pack it with the provisions she'd managed to gather. She would worry about re-stitching it later when he recovered—*if* he recovered.

His eyes opened slowly, wincing as she tested the flesh around the wound with her fingers. "I'm sorry, but this is not healing as I'd like. You've come down with a fever. I'm going to have to apply a poultice, packing it into the wound to let it destroy the infection."

He nodded, coming awake enough to understand her words, it seemed.

"This isn't going to be pleasant," she whispered, reaching for the whiskey and holding it to his lips, but she couldn't wait for the alcohol to wind its way through his body and take the edge off the pain. She reached for the small knife to slice through each of the stitches that so neatly held the wound closed. Her fingers shook though as she hovered above his abdomen.

"It's okay. Just do it," he whispered, closing his eyes and gritting his teeth in clear demonstration that he was ready.

And she did, tearing them open as quickly as she could while avoiding any more damage. Once the wound was open, she reached for the poultice she'd made, though she'd hoped it wouldn't be necessary.

Even when the wound was packed, her job wasn't finished. He wasn't going to survive long enough to heal from the infection if she didn't bring down his raging fever. Looking around for what she could use, and coming up with nothing, she reached under her dress and tore at the thin layers of her petticoats. She ripped them into rags and made a quick trip to the stream she'd found not far away, soaking all of them and bringing them back to put on his brow, under his arms, on his chest.

He was already unconscious by the time she'd returned, but she lifted his head then, and urged him to take a few sips of water.

And then she waited, sitting by and watching as he writhed uncomfortably. Each time she checked, his fever had gotten no better, and she remembered the countless soldiers she'd watched go to their graves the very same way—and many of them looking in a good deal better condition than this man. She didn't know why she should care so much—the man was a thief, a kidnapper, and no doubt a murderer as well. But when he'd spoken about his brother, he'd been human. She wasn't going to let him die.

She spent the day and night toiling, dousing the petticoat cloths with fresh, cool water over and over again, wiping down his arms and legs, forcing him to take sips of water as often as she could, and replacing the poultice every few hours. She was frustrated to tears more than once. It all seemed to be for naught;

he did not seem to be getting any better. In fact, his fever seemed to rage even hotter. He mumbled incoherently each time she woke him, and he writhed in fiery heat while he slept.

Changing the cloths once more, she laid down for just a moment, a moment's reprieve for her tired, aching limbs. She listened to his restless movements and the uneven rhythm of his breathing as her eyes grew heavy. She would close them for just a minute. Just...one...minute...

Cate's eyes opened to the bright light of day, and she instantly knew she'd slept far too long, but she lingered for just a moment in the warm cocoon that surrounded her. Then she realized where she was—in the crook of his arm, with her head against his chest.

Panic coursed through her body, but then she felt it: the warmth beneath her cheek. It wasn't raging heat; his chest was warm. She sat upright, moving quickly to check his forehead. It was warm, and his skin was slightly damp, perspiring from the heat of the morning sun. Relief flooded her veins, but she halted it and moved to check his wound. The breath she hadn't realized she'd been holding escaped in a rush. The ugly redness had left.

The infection was gone.

Chapter 4

He'd awoken shortly before the woman, feeling her warm body pressed against his, her head on his chest and her hand on his shoulder. He had a faint memory of her shivering there beside him some time while it was still dark. He had pulled her toward him gently and she had come the rest of the way, nuzzling at first into the crook of his arm and then against his chest. He'd closed his eyes and reveled in the feel of her so warm, so close, and must have fallen back to sleep a short while later.

So caught up in the woman, he hadn't realized it then, but with her checking his brow and his wound, he recognized it now: he felt better, much better than he had the night before when he'd been certain he was on the brink of death. And suddenly, finding himself on the path to recovery, he realized he would have died had it not been for her.

Heck, he was baffled to learn she'd lost even *one* man in the war. The woman was so darn stubborn, it wouldn't have surprised him to discover she'd brought him and many other men back to good health by sheer force of will. Not that he was complaining; quite the opposite, in fact. She was unlike any woman he'd ever known.

Who else would have tended to the wounds of her captor? Fought so determinedly to make sure he survived? He'd seen her tears intermittently the day prior. He knew she didn't weep for him specifically. It had been her sheer determination that had frustrated her when her efforts had appeared to be for naught.

Before he'd grown ill with fever, he'd had no intention of returning to any town; he couldn't be caught near one for fear of being arrested. Certainly, sketches of his face must be plastered everywhere by now. And all for nothing; after so many months, he'd failed. But what was the alternative? To keep her out in the wild indefinitely? No, the woman who had saved his life deserved more than that, didn't she?

"What's your name?" he finally asked once she'd finished checking his wounds and had sat back a few feet from him.

She looked up at him warily, "Catriona McLachlan."

"Well, Miss McLachlan, it seems I owe you a great deal of thanks."

"Please, call me Catriona; Cate, actually. I think there is little need for civilities out here, don't you agree?"

"I suppose you're right. I'm Michael. Michael Westen."

"I would say it is a pleasure to make your acquaintance, Michael, but I think not."

"Why were you on that train?" he asked, more roughly than he'd intended.

Her eyes darted up to meet his, and she held his gaze, as if she were trying to see further, deeper.

"I was on my way to meet a man out West—my betrothed, in fact," she confessed, making him feel even worse than he had when he'd started. She'd been on her way to meet her fiancé—possibly to her own wedding—when that horrid event had taken place.

"Where?"

"Nebraska."

She must have been on the Chicago-bound train to a stagecoach that would take her that far out West. Perhaps, in a few days' time, he could bring her there—to Chicago, or at least a stagecoach stop nearby it. But part of him didn't want to. He didn't want to hand over the lovely, fiery woman to another man. He wanted her all to himself...but could he be that selfish?

No, he couldn't. Even if they'd met under better circumstances and she didn't think of him as nothing more than a vile and violent thief and kidnapper, he couldn't.

"I'll take you to the stagecoach," he whispered, barely breaking into the silence. She'd grown so quiet, he was quite certain she must have gotten caught up in thoughts of the man, whoever he was.

"You kidnapped me...only to deliver me to my destination yourself? I question your logic, sir, so please forgive me if I'm not inclined to believe you."

He just nodded. What could he say to refute that? What did he want to say when it seemed she'd made up her mind about him?

"You need rest. You've been very ill and recovering from a gunshot wound. You can promise me whatever you'd like once you've recovered. For now, go to sleep."

He could see in her expression that it wasn't entirely for his benefit that she wanted him to go to sleep. She seemed uncomfortable and not the least bit interested in continuing this conversation. And if the only thing he could do for her for the moment was to close his eyes and pretend that he was fast asleep, then so be it, that's what he would do.

Chapter 5

Did he really mean it? Cate wondered as she meandered away from their makeshift site, looking for more medicinal supplies and firewood. There had been a genuineness in his eyes as he'd spoken, but perhaps he was simply well-versed in the art of lying. He was a thief and a kidnapper, after all.

Regardless of what he was or wasn't, the both of them were soon going to run out of food. There was little left in his sack, although she'd been trying to ration it as best she could.

But she was about to rectify that. She'd brought the small knife and the rest of the fishing line with her. Long ago, her father had taught her how to fish with a spear—the things a man would teach a daughter when in want of a son. Still, the knowledge would come in useful now. She found a long stick, used the fishing line to secure the knife to it, and waded into the stream, tucking her skirt up in the neckline of her gown to keep from soaking it.

To her surprise, it did not take long for her to re-master the skill she'd learned long ago. She stood still in the water, watching one small group of fish and then another wade past her feet, waiting for the perfect moment. And then she found it, thrusting the makeshift spear down into the water in one, swift movement and coming up with a fish on the end. A few more, and that would certainly hold them over for a short amount of time.

Returning to the bank of the stream after spearing four medium-sized fish, she tossed the fish and the spear on the bank and looked back at the water longingly. It had been days since she'd soaked in a bath, washing away the dirt and grime of dusty roads and all the blood, sweat and other vileness since her capture.

Looking back in the direction she'd come, there was no way Michael could see her from where they were camped. Quickly, she disrobed and waded into the deepest part of the water, which only came up to her waist. But it was enough, she washed as best she could and waded back out of the stream, drying off haphazardly and redressing.

With the fish and spear in hand a few moments later, she traipsed back to their camp, moving quietly as she grew closer, not wishing to disturb his sleep—for her benefit, as well as his own. It was too disconcerting to sit there talking with him, and in no small part because she actually liked talking to him, though she refused to linger on that thought. Instead, she turned her attention to the fish once she'd returned, using the small knife to clean away the scales and prepare them for cooking.

She'd cleaned three of them when he stirred and his eyes opened slowly, a piercing set of steel blue orbs that surveyed her activity quickly, his eyes widening just the slightest upon realizing what she'd done.

"I'm beginning to think you kept me alive merely for your entertainment. Is there anything you can't do?"

"Yes, apparently. It seems I'm unable to save myself from repugnant train robbers."

"Since I've given you my word that I'll take you to your destination, I think you've managed to do that just fine."

"Your word? I'm to believe the word of a criminal?" She closed her mouth, looking at the fish in front of her while she struggled to get her temper under control. "I do not wish to argue."

He was silent then, as if acquiescing to her request. And with the last of the fish cleaned, she stoked the flames of the dwindling fire and set their dinner to cook. When the simple meal was ready, she divvied it up between them, but he tried to push some of his share on her.

"You must be hungry," he told her. "After all, it could not have been easy having to catch our dinner."

"You need it to recover. Besides, there are always more fish in the stream. I can get more when we have need of it."

Not surprisingly, he fell asleep shortly after they'd eaten, and with nothing left to do and the sky's light fading quickly, she laid down opposite him across the fire and was surprised to realize the depth of her own tiredness, suddenly pulling her under, lulling her into sleepy submission.

Unfortunately, it was not long before she awoke, the ominous sound of a low growl drawing her out of slumber. Her eyes shot open, but she saw Michael there across the fire. His eyes were wide open, too, a knife already in his hand. He was still laying down, but she could feel a tightly coiled energy radiating from him.

"Don't move," he whispered slowly, and she resisted the urge to nod in understanding. Her panic made her heart pound violently and made her limbs wish to flee, but she did as he said, not moving a muscle. She heard the quiet sound of brush and twigs crushing beneath the wolf's feet. That's what it was, wasn't it? It had to be a wolf. She was about to die.

"It's okay, Cate," he whispered so quietly, if she hadn't seen his mouth form the words, she wouldn't have known he'd spoken.

Suddenly, he was no longer in front of her—he'd sprung from his place and leaped over both her and the fire in a single bound. A shuffling commotion behind her and then a howl shattered the night's silence seconds later.

Then there was no more sound. She was terrified to look, but how could she not. Was it the wolf who had been wounded, or the man? The wolf could be there still, but she couldn't lie there and do nothing. She rolled fast, trying to prepare herself for what she might face. But he was there, standing over the wolf, pulling the blade of his knife from the animal. She breathed a ragged sigh as she came to her knees and tears welled in her eyes. So caught up in panic, she hadn't thought to cry, but now that the moment of terror had passed, her fear and relief mingled and caused the cascade to flow.

He walked back toward her, slowly, stiltedly. It was obvious he'd hurt himself in the fray, so she needed to check his wounds. Yes, she had a job to do, and so she wiped the tears from her cheeks and refused to let another fall.

He settled back down on the vines at her urging, and though it was dark, she could see that he had not torn either of his wounds open. A little bit of blood trickled from the wound in his abdomen, but it was not much, not enough to raise significant worry.

Satisfied he was not much worse off, she went to rise, intending to go back to her spot on the ground, but he reached for her arm. She stilled, not certain what he intended, but he looked up at her imploringly.

"Please, stay here, Cate, just in case."

She wanted to argue, to tell him she could take care of herself, but the truth of the matter was she couldn't—not here. If he hadn't attacked and killed that wolf, she would be a meal for it even now. And as she nodded and settled back down on the ground just an arm's length from him, she couldn't deny the relief that flitted through her veins, knowing he was close...knowing he would let no harm come to her while she slept.

Such a strange feeling to hold for her captor.

Chapter 6

It was possible it had been a straggler, but Michael had run into his fair share of wolves, and they almost always traveled in packs, though he hadn't been about to tell her that and terrify her further. Instead, he'd settled down and had her do the same, right near him this time.

He laid there watching, listening...waiting. He'd never taken on a whole pack on his own before, but he wasn't going to lose the battle should it come to him. He eyed the collection of heavy rocks he could use around him, the two knives, one tucked in either hand. Some way, somehow, he'd come out victorious.

He heard hooves approach at a canter from behind him and he breathed a small sigh of relief. He'd not needed to tether Innes when they'd stopped. His stallion was a good and faithful one; he would not go far. Apparently, Innes had been spooked by the wolf, too, but sensed no more danger now and returned to him. That was definitely a good sign. It had been what first awoke him—his horse stepping agitatedly—and that had let him know something was there, even before he'd seen or heard it himself. Michael already had his knife in hand by the time Innes had skittered away and the quiet growl had reached him through the brush beyond.

He'd prayed that Cate would not wake up, not wanting her to feel the terror that came from that low growl. But he'd prayed even harder that she'd keep perfectly still, whether awake or asleep. She'd done well. Incredibly well. She'd remained motionless when he'd told her to, and he'd seen in her eyes that at least a part of her had believed him when he'd told her it would be alright.

The woman was magnificent—there was just no other way to describe her. She could catch fish, make her own medicine and heal wounds. Heck, if he'd been too incapacitated to take care of the wolf, it wouldn't have surprised him to find out she'd done it with her bare hands—though the thought of her forced to face the predator sent a shiver of protective fear down his spine.

She was unbelievably stubborn, but she hadn't been able to leave him there bleeding to death. Then again, she'd also admitted she had stayed because she wasn't sure she could make it on her own. Still, he knew it was more than that. He'd always been fairly good at reading people, and he had a feeling she wouldn't have been able to leave him there to die regardless.

She shifted in her sleep then, rolling toward him like she'd done the previous night, and she continued moving toward him until her body found his warmth, snuggling her head into the crook of his arm and her small hand splayed across his chest, her fingers so delicate looking and yet capable of so much.

He was still awake to see the sun begin to rise above the horizon. By that time, it was safe to assume that any pack that had hovered nearby had fled for the time being. Still, it would be best for them to be long gone come nightfall. His eyes heavy with fatigue, finally he allowed them to close, drifting off into a dead slumber within moments.

Michael awoke before Cate, the bright morning sun high in the sky and her body stirring against him. Her face was turned up toward him but her eyes were still closed. Long, thick lashes, high cheekbones, straight nose, delicately stubborn chin, and cupid bow lips that beckoned him to kiss them.

He must have inadvertently tightened his grip on her though, because her chocolate-colored eyes flew open a moment later, and it took her about three seconds to scoot away, straightening her gown and doing her damnedest to compose herself. It was one thing to wake up in his arms, and think he was fast asleep and none-the-wiser. It was likely quite something else to wake up to find him staring down at her exquisite face.

But she must have succeeded at least to some degree because she came back a few moments later, checking his wounds without a word, and laying her hand against his forehead, no doubt just to assure herself he was still free from fever.

"Thank you," she whispered after another moment had passed, though she kept her eyes carefully focused on the ground.

"It was my honor," he told her, and he meant it.

"Were you...were you awake all night?" she asked almost shyly.

"No, I nodded off at dawn," he answered easily, making light of the situation.

"It seems I should be thanking you for that as well, then."

"There's no need."

Blushing lightly, she turned her attention to tidying the few things on the ground and fiddling with the plants she'd gathered for grinding the day prior. He just watched her, fresh from sleep, color high in her cheeks, blonde tendrils framing her lovely face; she was a sight to behold, one he would never forget for as long as he lived. Why she caught him so at that moment, he didn't know. The mass of contradictions that made up who she was seemed to clash high right then—she was strong and yet fragile, stubborn and kind, brave and also the woman who slept tucked safe against him...was there anything she wasn't?

Yes. The sobering thought came to him, crushing the warmth that had spread through him. She wasn't his.

"We need to leave shortly," he said, more gruffly than he'd intended, but it was true, nonetheless.

"Oh. Right, yes. You're right," she agreed, stopped fidgeting and stood, but before she took a step, she looked down at him, her brow furrowed.

He had the most ridiculous desire to place his fingers there and smooth away whatever troubled her.

"We can't leave," she said simply. "You are in no condition to travel."

"Shouldn't you be in a hurry to return to civilization, regardless of my condition?"

"You're...taking me back?"

"Yes, Cate. It will take us several days, but I promised you I would see you safely to your destination. And it's important that we leave quickly. It would be good if we could cover as much distance by nightfall as we can." He didn't want to say it outright, but he was concerned that if they didn't get far enough away and the rest of the pack honed in on their location...

Her eyes widened in horror, reminiscent of the terror he'd seen in her eyes last night.

"It's okay," he reiterated just as he had then. "I'll do everything in my power to keep you safe." And it was only after the words were out that he realized how truly and deeply he meant those words.

Chapter 7

Michael had insisted that they leave quickly, and though he'd been reluctant to explain why the haste, it had only taken her a moment to realize the truth of the matter. She'd been so relieved the night before when he'd killed the wolf, she hadn't stopped to think there might have been more. Now he was in a hurry to get underway despite his wound and weakened state.

Still, she'd insisted they delay just a while longer. In the stream now, she held her makeshift spear motionless, waiting for her prey. With no guarantee they'd have such readily available food later, it was best to conserve what remained in his pack for when it was needed. A quick breakfast—if somewhat redundant fare—would provide Michael with as much nutrition as possible to help him make it through the long ride.

She bided her time, the muscles of her arm and shoulder coiled tight, ready to spring at just the right moment. A splash seconds later, and she lifted the spear up victoriously. Tossing her winnings on the bank, she resumed her position, waiting for the next plump-looking fish to come close.

Not ten minutes later, she started back with an armful of fish and a handkerchief filled with wild blueberries and red currants. Given that she had no idea what his previous diet had been like, there was no harm in ensuring his body wasn't further plagued with early signs of scurvy. She cleaned and cooked the fish in a hurry and then started packing up the items she'd removed from his sacks just as quickly. She was ready.

"There is absolutely no way I will sit astride this horse while you walk for miles with gunshot wounds, barely fresh from a brush with death," she told him adamantly not five minutes later. "All that work to keep you alive will be for naught when you keel over from exhaustion or worse."

Straddling a horse for hours, no doubt, was no easy feat, but even worse was trying to walk for miles with his wounds so fresh. She wouldn't have it, and there was nothing he could do to change her mind. The look of unenthusiastic resignation in his eyes told her she'd won the battle.

"Fine," he sighed heavily, "Then let's get to it, but let it not be said that I did not offer."

He helped her up into the saddle. She would have refused his help, but since she'd only just had a victory, it was too soon to wage another battle. He swung himself up behind her, and though he didn't make a sound, she could feel the tautness in his body, tensed from the pain of the movement. He settled in a moment later, seemingly more comfortable, and wrapped his arms around her to handle the reins.

They rode for quite some time, neither of them speaking. When they'd first started out, she had been on edge with his body so near. Whether it was the rhythmic jostling from the horse's steps, the serene whispers of the forest around them, or the warm, strong wall of his chest behind her, she didn't know, but her muscles relaxed more and more as time passed and she found herself leaning back against him.

And it was a good thing. Her position made her acutely aware of changes in his posture and position, and she felt it the moment his arms began to slacken around her. The difference was miniscule at first, but quite quickly, it became clear that he was tiring.

He needed to rest, but looking around, she could clearly see why he was in no hurry to stop. Every direction around them looked just as it had the night before—trees, brush and dirt. The only difference was there was no stream in sight now. And with no stream for fishing and no better shelter, they might very well be eaten by wolves with nothing in their bellies but the scraps left in his pack.

And so she remained silent, monitoring his condition by the slackness of his hold. They traveled perhaps an hour more, but his grip had grown weaker and he'd begun to sway forward.

Though their surroundings looked little better, she could see the stream then, wider now like it was nearing its source, which meant he'd kept them on a path that followed it—very wise. There would be fresh water and plenty of fish, at least, and it looked as though there was an outcropping of rocks up ahead that formed a small cave. It certainly looked like it would provide adequate shelter.

And that was a good thing given the ominous appearance of the sky above. It had been dark all day, but the clouds had grown thicker. What dim light remained highlighted the angry looking clouds overhead, gathered and ready to spill forth their fury. It she had any hope of catching their dinner, it had to be soon.

"Michael, we need to stop. I...I've grown quite sore and I think it would be best to stop for a while." She didn't like to lie, but she knew another battle would ensue if she tried to convince him to stop for his own benefit. She could only hope he would feel compelled to stop for hers.

"That cave up ahead, Cate, that's my goal," he spoke, gathering rugged breaths in between words.

Well, it looked like she hadn't needed to lie after all, but Michael was willing to stop, so she didn't intend to fret over the reasons why. He reined in Innes a few yards from the rocks, leaving him free to wander and graze nearby once he'd swung down and used what little strength he had left to assist Cate down, too.

"Stay here," he told her as he staggered toward the cave, a knife gripped tightly in his hand. It was entirely possible they weren't the first to think the cave would provide shelter from the rain, though she did question whether he'd have the strength to stand against anything he should happen to find inside.

She held her breath as he peered into the wide mouth and tossed small rocks into its short depth. She listened for sounds of shuffling or claws scraping along rock inside, or even worse, the low, portentous growl like they'd heard the night before, but no sound came from within the cave. He disappeared inside its mouth and she held her breath, more afraid for his safety than she should be. He reappeared a moment later and she let out the air in her lungs in a rush, telling herself that his well-being was necessary to her own survival. That was her only concern.

Still, seeing the fatigue and pain etched in his expression, she hastened her step, grabbing the things she'd need from his packs and hurrying him back inside the entrance. Fortunately, she'd thought to bring along a stack of sticks and short pieces of branches she'd collected—as ridiculous as it had seemed at the time. But it meant now that she could get a small fire started, brightening and warming the interior of the cave without having to search around for loose kindling and branches first.

Once that task was accomplished, she looked over Michael, trying to assess his condition. She didn't have time for a thorough examination—not if she hoped to catch their dinner before the storm. He didn't appear well, but he looked like he'd survive, at least until she returned. So, she rummaged for the things she'd need, the knife, fishing line and stick that would make her spear, and turned to leave.

"Where do you think you're going?" he asked incredulously from where he now sat at the back of the cave. He was too pale. They should have stopped hours ago, but there was naught she could do about that now.

"I'm going to catch us dinner before the storm lets loose and we're stuck in here with nothing but what is left in your sack."

"You shouldn't be going out on your own."

"Oh? Shall we sit here and starve together?"

"I'll go," he told her, making to rise from where he sat. She could tell he was trying to infuse his voice with as much sternness as possible, but given his weakened state, his efforts were falling short.

"You'll do no such thing. You can barely stand. You'll end up face first in the water and I'll be forced to cook you for my supper."

"Then I suppose I'll drown with the satisfaction of knowing you'll not want for sustenance."

"Perhaps, but your corpse won't keep me fed indefinitely, nor will it guide me to where I'm going."

"You are beyond stubborn, which you might as well know is a terribly unappealing characteristic in a woman to most men. Your fiancé may not approve."

"Forgive me if I fail to trouble myself with your opinion of my characteristics."

"I didn't say it was my opinion, Cate." The huskiness in his voice made her heart speed up and sent a strange shiver through her body, but she could not let it distract her. She was wasting time and hadn't any more to stand there arguing with the stubborn man. There was only one more approach to try before she gave up, turned on her heels and hoped he didn't follow her out.

"You'll rest now, so that you can uphold your promise to see me safely through."

If he wouldn't be reasonable, maybe she could appeal to his sense of honor. Funny, she'd thought him devoid of such a thing not so long ago, hadn't she? What happened?

Still, it seemed to work. He lowered himself back to the ground and nodded solemnly. He did not like being at her mercy for his mere sustenance, it seemed. Good—she hadn't particularly liked it when he'd hauled her away and she had felt her very life was in his hands.

Chapter 8

He didn't like it, not one bit; sitting idle the past hour while Cate was off catching their dinner. It just seemed wrong. He wasn't against a woman being able to take care of herself, but neither should a man be laying around letting a woman care for his useless self in addition. His mother, God rest her soul, would turn over in her grave if she saw him relaxing while a woman saw to putting food on the table.

The ride had been more exhausting than he'd expected, and after the first few hours, it had taken all he had to keep himself in the saddle. The wounds in his torso had ached something awful, but he wasn't a stranger to pain. Certainly, he would be riding even now if it was nothing more than those that troubled him. More than that, his body had seemed devoid of resources, depleted of all its reserves battling that blasted infection. He had little left for keeping himself astride a horse and leading it through heavy brush and uneven terrain.

The rumble of thunder brought him out of his brooding. He watched as a flash of lightning lit up the sky beyond the cave's mouth and then all of a sudden, the heavens' floodgates let loose their downpour. Cate still had not returned.

He pushed away from the cave's wall and steadied his arms, locking his elbows and digging his palms into the loose earth beneath his hands. He'd waited too long. She was going to come back soaking wet and shivering with cold—if she came back at all.

With a mighty storm brewing, it was unlikely many animals were out hunting, but there was a chance, and even more of a chance she'd fallen and hit her head or suffered some other injury that hampered her return. She could be out there, lying unconscious on the forest floor, and he was sitting there warm inside a cave.

An even more terrifying thought came to him, and he was on his feet in a flash, the pain of his wound and the fatigue of his body forgotten with a violent surge of panic. He wasn't the only man who knew how to use the dense forests to travel from one destination to another, and most of the men who would use such a route were not the reputable sort—his own company not included. What if one of them had come upon Cate, alone and unsuspecting?

"Darn it," he cursed aloud as he strode toward the mouth of the cave, but before he'd made it out, she came into view in front of him, strolling casually through the heavy sheets of rain as if it were a clear and dry day. She had a spear in one hand, his wool-covered canteen slung over her shoulder, and she carried a makeshift sack in the other—presumably filled with the fish she'd gone off to catch.

"What the heck are you doing strolling in the rain?" he ground out, the remnants of his panic making him testy.

"I didn't see the point in racing back once I was already soaked," she smiled. "Besides, I love the rain. It's refreshing, it wipes everything clean, does it not?"

"Yes, and it also chills to the bone when the cold sets in."

"Yes, it does that, too," she admitted without a struggle, and that brought him up short. He'd expected her to argue with him, perhaps to tout the benefits of a thorough drenching out in the cold just to rile him further. He certainly didn't expect her to agree with him complacently.

Inside the cave, she stepped past the fire, moving in a wide circle around it, obviously taking care to avoid dousing it with her dripping skirts. She laid her bundle down near the back of the cave where he'd been sitting a moment before, but as she stood to prop the spear against the rocky wall, he saw that she was already shivering, and in the space of a few seconds, the shivering intensified, making the metal of the spear's knife clang repeatedly against the wall. The cold had already chilled her to the bone.

"Get out of that dress and wrap my blanket around you," he told her, but she only looked up at him with an indignant expression on her face.

"We'll set your dress in front of the fire to dry, but you can't stay in those wet clothes, Cate. You'll never get warm if you do."

She seemed reluctant, but she was also intelligent, knowing he spoke the truth. She reached for the large blanket that laid folded on the ground but then nodded in the direction of the mouth of the cave.

"You want me to go out there and get soaking wet to cater to your sense of propriety?"

"No, I want you to turn around to cater to my sense of propriety. I'm not disrobing with your eyes on me," she replied primly.

He chuckled and turned slowly, admittedly because he didn't want to turn around.

Her dress was laid out by the fire a moment later, a careful distance from the flames. With the blanket wrapped tightly around her, she gathered the fish again and untied the knife from the spear.

Michael took them from her this time. "If you're forced to catch our dinner, the least I can do is ready it for the fire."

It looked as if she was going to argue, but the stubborn set of her jaw relaxed a moment later and she eased herself down next to the fire, reaching out her hands to let the flames warm her cold flesh. By the time he'd finished his task, he was relieved to see that she'd grown significantly warmer. Her body no longer shivered uncontrollably and she'd sat back from the fire, no longer seeking its warmth to thaw her extremities. Still, the occasional tremor seemed to race through her, making her tug the rough blanket more firmly around her and check the state of her dress—which was still quite damp an hour later when they finished eating and she stifled one of her many yawns of the evening, belying just how exhausted she was.

She wasn't alone in her exhaustion. His body ached and he struggled to keep his eyes open. "Shall we retire for the evening?" he asked in mock formality, motioning to the somewhat even terrain at the back of the cave.

She gazed up at him speculatively, her eyes darting back and forth between the mouth of the cave and the proposed sleeping place. No doubt, she was deciding whether to keep her distance and risk unwelcome visitors or sleep close to him once again and risk...unwelcome advances.

Sighing, he seemed to win out against potential intruders, and she made her way over silently, taking up a spot several feet from where he'd reclined against the wall earlier. She looked up at him again, her eyes challenging him to argue the distance she'd placed between them. He was too tired to argue, laying down in his place and gingerly stretching his arms above his head, using them as a makeshift pillow.

She imitated his position—there was no point in trying for anything more comfortable—and closed her eyes. He could see she'd resumed the occasional shiver, now several feet from the fire, but the stubborn set of her posture told him there was no point in suggesting she come closer. So, instead, he closed his eyes, listening to the sound of her breathing, inhaling the light scent of her, and watching the image of her that appeared behind his lids as he drifted off to sleep.

He awoke what must have been several hours later, and though he still felt tired, he felt more relaxed, more comfortable than he often was. He understood why immediately; she was fast asleep next to him, her head once again tucked in the crook of his arm and her body pressed against him for warmth. He wondered if she'd done it deliberately—wriggled closer to him once he was asleep—or if her body had sought his heat while she slept.

He noticed the knife in her hand, too, clutched loosely, but there, nonetheless. Had she intended that as protection against wolves that might happen by, or against him? He chuckled, thinking either could be possible, but he was not very worried she'd use it on him. If she'd wanted him to believe she was a ruthless killer, she shouldn't have gone to such lengths to patch him up and rid his body of infection. Still, he'd feel more comfortable if she couldn't accidentally stab him with it while she slept, so he slipped the knife from her grasp and laid it down next to him.

He listened intently then for any sound of danger approaching. Given the heavy downpour, it was unlikely a pack of wolves would happen upon them during the night. So, aside from the inconvenience of dampness and darkness, the rain was rather a fortunate force of nature at the moment.

Chapter 9

Daily life for Cate followed along much the same course as that first day of lengthy travel. They arose each morning, consumed a quick breakfast and set out to cover as much distance as they could before finding a place to rest for the night. Some nights they found a dry cave, and others, they slept amid the trees and brush of the forest.

The second night had been spent at the foot of a tall oak, and she'd tried in vain to worry over propriety, settling down to sleep several feet from Michael. But always, she would wake up right next to him, usually with her arm flung over his solid chest or her head resting in the crook of his arm. Since then, she'd given up on decorum and the rules of polite society. After all, this wasn't polite society; it was a forest. And the night's cold temperatures could be fought off much more effectively when she had not only her own heat, but Michael's as well, to stave off the chill.

And that's where she found herself now, cradled against Michael's side, her body pressed tightly against his beneath the blanket. It seemed unseasonably cold for the time of year, but then, she'd never spent nights outside with nothing more to warm her than a rough, and somewhat threadbare blanket. Even in the crude construction of the tent she'd slept in as a nurse in

Virginia, there had been a stove for cold nights, and a multitude of exhausted bodies to heat the air.

She remembered that Michael had said he'd been a soldier in the war, both him and his brother. She wondered if either of them had been patients in her hospital, though there had been thousands of soldiers and a multitude of hospitals, making the likelihood slim. Besides, she would most certainly have remembered Michael. He was taller than most men and broader than any soldier she could recall. And the penetrating gaze of his steel blue eyes was something she couldn't imagine one ever being able to forget.

Then again, she'd taken note of as little as possible during her years as a nurse. Her time there had been quite miserable, with the entire lot of so-called doctors looking down their noses at her "quack" theories and "useless" plants. At first, she'd prayed that they would listen to her, would see that her theories weren't crazy at all, nor were the age-old medicines she knew so well. But they didn't listen. No one ever listened. She'd been sent to mop damp brows, clean up pans and basins, and murmur sweet nothings of hope and comfort in the ears of dying patients.

She'd wanted to leave so many times, to run as far away from the senseless death and despair of the place, but she couldn't. The money she'd made as a nurse was what helped to sustain her aunt and uncle back home. And there was always the hope she would make a difference; that just one doctor would listen to her, that even a handful of lives would be saved because of her.

But by that final, horrible year at the hospital, she'd begun to pray for God to make her numb, to make her impenetrable to the guilt and grief that accompanied every death in that wretched place. She'd kept up her fight, striving to make the doctors listen, but by then she knew it was all in vain. They never would.

Michael stirred restlessly in his sleep, drawing her closer to him, and she looked up at him, concerned that somehow his fever had returned. But he didn't appear the least bit flushed, and testing her wrist against his forehead, there was no raging heat there, just a comfortable warmth.

Still, she didn't settle back down right away. She remained propped up, looking down at him as he slept. His lashes against his cheeks and his full lips parted in slumber, it was near-impossible to reconcile the man with a violent criminal. He'd even seemed surprised—and offended—when she'd referred to him as such. And the way he'd treated her since her capture...it didn't make any sense.

"Who are you?" she whispered so quietly he wouldn't have heard her had he been awake.

Cate settled back down then, coming up with no answer that satisfied her. She'd tucked the question neatly away by the time she woke up the next morning, falling into the same well-established routine now. She fished for their breakfast, intending to give Michael a few extra moments of sleep since she knew he was prone to staying up late, listening for unwelcome visitors. He'd taken over the hunting beyond that, doing the fishing himself and setting snares for small game for the rest of the day's food.

The first few days, they had spoken about no more than the forest around them and the hope for a bit of shelter that night, but the conversation had begun to come easier, and as they made their first stop to rest Innes that morning, it took a terribly personal turn—and it was her own doing.

"Do you have a family, Michael? Aside from your brother?"

His head shot up at her unexpected question and he stared at her for a moment, though she could not tell what he was thinking.

"I did. Not a wife, if that's what you mean, but a father and a mother—though that was a very long time ago."

"Will you tell me about them?" If she couldn't reconcile who he was by him alone, perhaps she could understand him better by learning about his family, the people who had helped to shape his life.

"I was born in Boston, my brother as well, and we lived there with my father and mother for several years. My family was very poor, but I suppose what we lacked in wealth, we made up for in other things. Fairly close we all were, you see?" His smile was soft and genuine.

"It sounds lovely," she confessed, warm memories of her own father fresh in her mind.

"I was twelve, perhaps, when my father took us out West. He had heard tales of men striking it rich, making a fortune out there. It was a risk, but given what he had at home, not much of a risk, really. And though he never found the wealth he'd sought, he always managed to put food on the table. It was a good life, for a time. My mother passed while I was away at war, and my father did not long after I returned. He died of heartache, I think."

"From losing your mother?"

"No, though that affected him to no small degree. My brother."

"But did you not say he returned home after he recovered?"

"Yes, he did do that, but he was not the same." His eyes had grown wistful, and she had a feeling his mind had taken him far away from the forest around them. She didn't know what he was thinking, but felt a strange urge to console him, nevertheless. Not thinking about what she was doing, she reached out and laid her hand on his. It seemed to bring him back to the present, and he smiled.

"And what of your family, Cate?"

"It was only my father and I for quite some time. My mother passed away during childbirth along with the baby when I was five. I think perhaps because he knew he could not afford the small family he had, my father never remarried, as difficult as it was for him to raise a strong-willed daughter all on his own."

"It seems to me he's done a fine job," Michael interjected.

"Yes, well, he passed on when I was eleven. I was sent to live with my aunt and uncle—kind and wonderful people, but they could not afford another mouth to feed. I knew it well, despite how they tried to hide it. My aunt was a wise woman, though, from a long line of healers dating back to the sixteenth century. It earned her a bit of money here and there."

"And that is where you gained your vast knowledge of healing and medicine," he stated matter-of-factly.

"Yes, it is, and I thank you for the compliment." It shouldn't, but it pleased her immensely that he viewed her as so knowledgeable, so different than the multitude of people who thought her a fool.

"And that is how you came to be a nurse?"

"I suppose so. We needed the money, certainly, and thinking of all the good I could do for the soldiers who fought for our country...I applied quickly, and persisted even though I was far from thirty, anxious to help and to send money back home."

"There is disappointment in your voice. It was not as much money as you'd hoped?"

"No, no. That wasn't it at all. I was grateful for the income. It's just that...it was not what I had expected. Everything I knew...all the ways I could help..." She took a deep breath, feeling the grief and despair rise high in her throat. "I watched hundreds, maybe thousands of soldiers waste away, many of them from carelessness...ignorance...pride."

He'd placed his hand on top of hers, and he traced soothingly along each knuckle now, but he was quiet, as if he knew there was more for her to say.

"They would not listen to me. They thought I was foolish, that I was ignorant of modern medicine, not fit even to be a nurse."

She blinked hard, fighting back the tears that stung her eyes. She'd hardly ever spoken of her horrible years in Virginia. She hadn't wanted to burden her aunt or uncle with her misery, and there had been no one else to tell. Speaking the words aloud now to Michael somehow made all the emotional wounds of those years painfully raw.

"They were the fools," he whispered assuredly.

"You're right, they were, but it was not my pride that was wounded. Certainly, I could have lived with that. It was standing idly by while doctors hacked away with dirty saws and went from patient to patient with filthy hands. It was being forbidden to treat an infection with the simple things that I used to treat yours. I tried, you know, sneaking what I could to men I knew would die otherwise. But always in secret, and so there were precious few I could help. I was caught more than once and nearly dismissed. So many of those men died, Michael, and there wasn't a thing I could do about it." Tears cascaded down her cheeks as her frustration reached its pinnacle, and she stood swiftly, pacing back and forth across a small patch of flat ground by the stream.

"I kept thinking I could make them listen. I tried being assertive, but was chastised for being an insolent woman. I tried to be coy—feminine wiles and all—and I was deemed a foolish, young girl. I tried everything I could think of and it mattered not one bit. And they died! Not because I didn't know how to help them, but because I wasn't *allowed* to help. You have no idea what it is like to stand idly by while good men—men who bled for us—waste away to nothing more than shells of the men they had been!" she cried so loud, her words echoed through the forest.

Realizing how ridiculous she must appear, pacing and crying and ranting in front of a veritable stranger, she struggled to rein it in, commanding her tears to dry up and her lungs to take in slow, deep breaths of air while he stared at her with an unreadable expression on his handsome face.

"And now you must think I am as crazy as a loon." She tried to smile but her lips quivered instead.

"No, Cate, I don't. I think you're brave and strong; kind, with an overwhelming passion for helping people. You must—you helped me, didn't you? And I do know what it is like. Perhaps not over and over again as you were forced to endure, but I watched my brother, my own flesh and blood, come within inches of the grave. Even though he recovered, he continued to waste away, and I could do nothing for him."

"I'm sorry, Michael. It is similar, as you say, but I cannot imagine the pain of watching that happen to someone you hold so dear."

Seeing the pain in his eyes, she felt an odd connection to Michael and it drew her back to him. She sat down next to him and reached out her hand, placing hers in his and grasping tightly, not in pity, but in unity, feeling joined with him in a way far more intimate than the touching of their skin or the closeness of their bodies.

They remained that way, sitting together, gazing down at the gentle flow of the stream. Her mind should be in turmoil, drawn to this man who had captured her and ridden off with her against her will. But right in that moment, there was no chaos or confusion in her head. She was right where she should be—even if it made no sense at all.

"The man you have waiting for you, Cate, will he be able to provide well for you?" Michael asked suddenly, and she could not think of his reason for asking.

"Yes, of course. That is the point of it, is it not?" Caught off guard, she hadn't known how to respond, and had said the first thing that came to mind.

"The point of it?"

"Yes, of marriage, I mean."

"Is it now?"

"I could find no work when I returned home after the war, nothing that would even cover my own living expenses, never mind help my aunt and uncle in any way. I sought to relieve their burden, and mine as well, I suppose. After a life of not always knowing when the next meal might come, it is a relief; a relief to know there will be food on the table and a place to rest my head each night. Should I have children, it puts my mind at ease to know they will not know hunger like I did."

"The man you are to marry, what kind of man is he?"

"Well, Mr. Abernathy, he isn't wealthy by any means, but he has his own homestead, and it has been growing more stable each year. He hopes to branch into horses next, by the fall perhaps."

"But what is he like?"

How was she to answer that question when she knew so little about the man herself? She tried to remember the letters he'd sent before his offer of marriage. "He's congenial and polite, and has a sound mind it seems."

"Praise, indeed," he muttered under his breath, and then returned to tossing stones into the stream.

Thinking about Mr. Abernathy now, he seemed to pale in comparison to the man sitting next to her. But then, how could she say such a thing when the man sitting next to her was a criminal? The question began to whirl around in her mind yet again, and she could take it no more.

"Michael, I have been trying to figure this out on my own. At first, I was so angry—and still am—but there is more to you, I think. But how could you be both? I cannot reconcile it, no matter how I try. The man who dragged me off that train...that is not you, and yet...it must be."

She didn't know if she was making any sense, and so she stopped and took a deep breath, realizing there was only one question, one thing she desperately needed to know. "You must tell me which man you are," she whispered.

"You do not think I can be both?"

"No, I do not think so. Either you have deceived me well and I know nothing of you, or else, you are not that man from the train. Because the man who has traveled with me all these days and nights is a good man, honorable and courageous. But how is that possible?"

He was silent for so long, she thought he wasn't going to answer, but then his expression changed as if he'd come to a decision.

"I told you my brother was not the same after he recovered; Nathan is his name. Nathan was restless and unhappy. My father told me he would ride off for hours, and then days at a time without a word, and it only grew worse after I returned home. I just happened to overhear talk coming back from the nearby town one day, and I suddenly understood what he'd been up to all this time. He'd gotten himself involved in a great deal of trouble—a gang of trouble, actually. I confronted him on it that very day. At first, he denied it, and when he finally did admit to what he'd been doing, he tried to justify it, saying it was nothing more than a way for him to feel alive again."

"When you say a gang...you mean he got himself involved with a group of criminals?"

"Yes...the same group that stopped your train."

Michael had gotten involved with the same men as his brother? Why would he do such a thing? To keep watch over his brother? Admirable, for sure, but did it justify his crimes? The men on that train had been killing people—innocent people. The thought brought Violet to mind, not for the first time since that awful day, and she couldn't help but wonder if her hiding place had been enough.

How many innocent victims had cowered before Michael only to meet the same fate as those people on the train? And if it were true he was only there for his brother, why had he captured her, riding off from the rest of the men where he could no longer keep watch over Nathan?

"I started out with them several months ago...after my brother failed to return home. I had no idea where he'd gone or what had happened to him. All I knew was he was no longer with the wretched group, but they were likely the last people ever to see him. If he is alive, I thought they might know. And if he's not, then I'm certain they know it."

"That day on the train..." Michael paused as if trying to collect his thoughts. "The men had picked up another man a week prior. I'd never met a man so vile in my life. Before him, the men raided traveling parties and trains under nothing more than the threat of violence. Never...never like what happened on the train. But this man, he riled them up and the men they were gave way to nothing more than savage animals, creatures just as appalling as their new leader."

"You didn't kidnap me. You...you saved me." She voiced her thoughts before she had time to process them, but it suddenly made sense and she somehow knew what he said was the truth.

"I saw you go running with that girl, and I thought you were fleeing, and I silently hoped the two of you would get away. I didn't know how to help you...how to help any of them. I stood there for a minute, trying to figure out what to do, and then I saw you come back, and I knew what you'd done—and why you'd come back. I knew something terrible was going to happen when they started planning that heist, but I had no idea."

He paused for a moment, as if he were trying to force the words up and out of his throat. "I needed to find Nathan, but I couldn't leave you to your fate. You, a woman who had sacrificed herself for another. I could be wrong, but that girl didn't even look anything like you, Cate. I don't think she was your sister—"

"No, she wasn't. Her name was...*is* Violet. I had just met her."

"You were willing to die for a stranger on a train?"

"I didn't want to die. I just...I didn't have any choice."

"But I did."

"But your brother..."

"My brother wouldn't think I am worth the air in my lungs if I let that happen. Neither would I, for that matter."

Another thought occurred to her. "That bullet...it wasn't meant for me, was it? I had thought it had gone astray, but—"

"It hit the target it was meant for, though I imagine it didn't do the damage intended. It would have happened eventually. It was one thing to steal jewelry and coins in pursuit of my brother, but quite another to take a life, and not something I was willing to do. I saw more than enough violence for one lifetime in the war; I certainly didn't want part in committing any more of it."

"And all this time I thought...Michael, I am so sorry," she

whispered, remembering all the awful things she'd thought of him and the hideous things she'd said.

"There is no need for an apology. You could not have known." And he meant it; there was no animosity or accusation in his tone. "Perhaps now you will believe my promise to see you safely to your destination."

"I already did," she confessed. She laid her hand on his then, just as she had done before, and they sat there in silence. An hour passed, perhaps two, and a multitude of thoughts coursed through her mind. Things she hadn't been willing to think about before but couldn't hide from now, like the ridiculous realization that part of her—a very large part—did not want Michael to see her safely to her original destination after all.

It was absurd, but she couldn't deny what it was that part of her wanted—to stay with Michael. But to stay hiding out in a forest with a man who was no doubt considered a criminal by the law? What kind of security could that possibly bring to her life?

Unfortunately, she knew the answer—none.

Chapter 10

They rode little that day, and Michael was glad for it, as selfish of him as that may be. He knew where they were, and that it wouldn't be long before they reached their destination. He also knew that he'd be quite happy if they never reached the stage coach that would take her to the fiancé waiting for her further out West. The truth was he didn't want to uphold his promise. He wanted to turn around and take her with him, somewhere— anywhere. He didn't particularly care where, so long as he could keep Cate with him. He'd never wanted to keep someone close so much in his life.

But he couldn't. She deserved more...so much more. What could he possibly offer her? The homestead that he had inherited from his father had been left in disarray the past several months. Likely the entire year's crop would be wasted by now, and there is no telling how long it would take him to get it re-established— assuming he didn't wind up at the dangling end of the hangman's noose before then.

Cate had made it abundantly clear what she wanted and he couldn't blame her. After a life of uncertainty, knowing starvation and homelessness didn't loom frighteningly overhead was a relief few could understand who hadn't suffered the same upbringing.

Even if she had come to care for him, would she possibly turn away from that certainty for him? And even in a moment of hope that she would, how could he ask it of her? The devastating truth of it was that he couldn't.

So, he would savor these last few precious hours with her, the time between dusk and dawn, and the two or three hours it would take to reach civilization. Those were the only moments he had left with Cate, the woman who he hadn't even known two weeks prior, and now would never forget so long as he lived.

He looked down at her where she slept against him and watched the gentle rise and fall of her back to be certain she was fast asleep before he pulled her closer to him, feeling her soft warmth against him for the last time.

It was funny, really. Had they met under any other circumstances, their proximity and familiarity with one another now would have been deemed outrageous. But it was their very circumstances that had brought him to feel so much for her, so quickly. Had they met in any other time or place, they would have been introduced by a mutual acquaintance and spoken of little more than the weather. Perhaps a brief conversation over a favorite author or a topic in the news, but little more than that. They would never have been free to talk so openly and share so much about themselves. And that being so, would he have seen beyond her pretty face to the unique and fiery woman that laid within? Would he know with such certainty that he would never find another woman like Cate?

And yet, because he'd come to know her as well as he had, he couldn't keep her. Knowing why she'd chosen to marry a man she had never met meant he couldn't ask her to stay. He couldn't ask her to sacrifice the certainty of a comfortable life for one that could be described as unstable at best.

****

She awoke early, as if her body was aware their travel was nearly over, anxious to be on her way. The sun had barely risen above the horizon when she shifted in his arms and stretched her limbs. In the next second, he was staring into her deep brown eyes, and his heart clenched hard in his chest as she smiled up at him sleepily.

It felt so wrong letting her go, but that was precisely what he would have to do, and so he forced a smile on his face and brushed the loose wisps of golden hair back from her forehead one last time. "We should get moving early, Cate. We should be able to reach the stagecoach in just a few hours."

"Just a few hours?" she reiterated.

He hadn't told her how close they were to her destination, as if holding back that piece of information somehow let him prolong the inevitable a little longer. Now that the inevitable had come, he watched her expression, waiting...hoping. But she sat up and turned away before he'd been able to glean anything from her expressive eyes. He sat up slowly, noting that it had become easier each day to move around, that while he could still feel the ache in his side from his wounds, they had diminished substantially each day. He was healing—because of Cate.

"I thought I'd fish for a quick breakfast while you pack up," he suggested as casually as he could.

"Yes, that seems like a good idea. You go ahead and I'll have us ready to go by the time you get back."

There was no hesitation in her voice, no emotion that would lead him to believe she was anything but happy to be on her way. And yet, why wouldn't she turn around and face him?

He grabbed the spear propped against the tree under which they'd slept and gazed back at her once more and left for the stream.

An hour later, they had cooked the fish, packed up their belongings and had headed out for the final leg of the journey. Even though he rode at a canter, the forest seemed to fly by beneath him far too fast. It felt like little time had passed at all when he turned the horse away from the direction of the stream and started up along the path that would take them where they were going.

"It's probably best if we part ways here, Cate," he told her when they were no more than a hundred yards from the small building, visible now through the sparser brush and trees up ahead. "If I accompany you any further, you might find yourself answering a whole lot of questions rather than boarding a stagecoach for Nebraska."

"Yes...yes, I suppose that's probably for the best then."

"I can see the rest of the way up ahead. There should be no danger, but just in case... I'll wait here until you're safely inside."

"I'm sure that's not necessary, Michael," she insisted but he could hear the lack of conviction in her tone.

Could it be that she wasn't so certain, that perhaps a part of her wished to remain with him? He knew that was true; whether a small or large part of her, he didn't know. But he'd felt it, and he'd seen it in her eyes. It didn't matter though. Could he really say that he cared for her if he'd let her throw away a future that would bring her peace and comfort?

"Your Mr. Abernathy will be anxious to see you safe and well. You should be going now, Cate."

She nodded her head but didn't move to leave. She continued to stand there, looking at the ground in front of her while she toyed with her bottom lip. He'd come to learn she did that often, both when she was nervous and when she was deep in thought. Which one was it right now? Regardless, he couldn't let her linger any longer. He wasn't sure just how long he could be upright and honorable before he abandoned it for what he really wanted— Cate. It was hard enough to let her go, and even worse standing so close, waiting for her to leave.

She looked up at him then, and he could see the uncertainty in her eyes. And maybe it was only in his imagination, but she seemed to sway toward him, as if her body was trying to make the call that her mind could not. It was too much temptation. Just too much.

He crossed the small space between them in a single bound, and he pulled her to him like he'd been longing to do for too long. She didn't resist, but maybe he'd just caught her off guard. Perhaps it was surprise that parted her lips. And it was possible she reached out not to touch him, but to steady herself. Still, he couldn't have stopped then if his life had depended on it. In a moment, she would be gone. This was all he would have of her.

He leaned in, covering her soft lips with his own. Instead of pulling away as he'd feared, she leaned in closer, and her fingers twined in the hair at the back of his neck. He wanted to keep her there, holding her in his arms, breathing the same air forever, but too quickly he knew he had to let her go.

Clenching his fists so tight his knuckles turned white, he forced himself to pull away, leaving her lips for the first and last time.

"Go, Cate," he whispered before he no longer could.

"But Michael—"

"Go."

Confusion, doubt and uncertainty flitted through her gaze, but she took hold of them all at once. They disappeared from her eyes and she nodded, this time taking a deep breath and turning away. She seemed to hesitate for only the briefest of moments, but then she started toward her future, leaving him to watch as his walked away.

She didn't look back, not once, and though he wished it with all his might, a small part of him was glad. She hadn't been caught up in him the way he'd gotten caught up in her, which meant she could have her future without regret.

His breath caught in his throat as she walked through the clearing at the edge of the forest and he held it as she opened the door to the small building where she would await the stagecoach. And then she was gone.

He let out the breath with a heavy sigh, his eyes fixed on the place he'd last seen her. A moment passed, and then another. What was he waiting for? For her to come out that door and bounding back to him? That wasn't going to happen. Cate was gone. And just to prove it to himself, he waited another minute, and then several more, and still she did not reappear there in the doorway.

"Come on, Innes. It's a long way home." He stroked the horse's dark mane and swung himself up into the saddle, setting the horse off at an easy pace. There wasn't any hurry. There was nothing waiting for him back home, but home is where he was headed. He'd lost any hope of finding his brother when he'd abandoned that group of hooligans for Cate, but that was a good thing. The images of that day burned bright in his mind, and he couldn't have taken part in their evil schemes, even to find Nathan. No, he would go home now because there wasn't anywhere else for him to go.

An hour passed, and he realized he'd guided Innes back toward the stream. He swung down and set the horse to graze while he sat down on the bank. He could see her so clearly, as if Cate was there now, makeshift spear in hand and standing motionless in the stream. He hadn't wanted to admit it, but the woman could catch fish better than he could. He was reminded of the multitude of other things she could do—from wound-healing and tongue-lashing to weaseling her way into a man's heart and making it unfit for any other. She'd done that last one better than she'd done anything else, though what he'd give for her to have failed miserably instead.

"Should you not be at least another mile away by now?" a lilting voice chastised from several yards behind him, and he thought he must be hearing things. He'd been caught up in thought but he couldn't possibly have tuned out his surroundings so thoroughly that he hadn't even heard her approach. Still, he turned around.

"Cate," he breathed.

Her face was flushed and she was breathing hard as if she'd been running, which he realized she must have been doing to have caught up with him at all, even at Innes's easier pace. But what the hell was she doing there?

"You came back," he said, wondering if he hadn't only been hearing things, but now hallucinating, too.

"Yes...Michael, I know it doesn't make any sense—"

"No, it doesn't. You shouldn't be here. The life you want is back that way," he pointed in the direction from which she'd just come. "I can't offer you any of that."

"I realize that, but I don't want it anymore."

She wasn't thinking clearly. She couldn't be, and yet she was walking toward him and he could see her eyes now, her clear, unwavering gaze that held no uncertainty.

"You let me be *me*, Michael, and you made me feel appreciated for it. Do you suppose Mr. Abernathy will do the same? Do you suppose it will please him that I can fish and make medicines? That I can swear like a soldier and spar verbally like a stubborn mule? And what of him? Do you think my betrothed would endanger his life or sacrifice a single thing to save me from danger? Do you think he is honorable and kind? Intelligent and equally as stubborn as I? Can I tell him that I laid in your arms each night, Michael? That it may have been warmth I sought at first, but then, what I wanted was something so much more?"

"He can offer you a life I cannot," he argued feebly.

"But he can't offer me *you*."

She stood right in front of him, the same stubborn look in her eyes that told him she would not back down from the fight and she was hell bent on winning the battle. Maybe he was too weak to argue; maybe he was too tired to fight. All he knew was she had won the battle the moment she'd begun it because he hadn't an ounce of resistance left in him. He didn't want to fight her. He wanted to kiss her, to hold her, and to never let her go.

So when she crossed the small space left between them, wrapped her arms around his neck and lifted herself up to fit her lips beneath his, he surrendered unequivocally.

It was a long moment before they came up for air, but when they did, she smiled up at him victoriously, and he couldn't help but laugh.

"Well played, my lady," he acquiesced good-naturedly.

She nodded, accepting the compliment, and then she said something he could not have expected. "Let's go find your brother, Michael."

"Nathan? You want to go look for Nathan?"

"I know you care for him very much."

"I do. But I think it is time to go home. If Nathan is still alive, I think he does not wish to be found. When he does, he'll come home, too. All I can do is try to ensure there is still a home for him to return to. And one for you as well, if you'll have it."

"Of course I will. And I will do what I can to restore it to what it was, but...I don't need it. I thought I did; I thought that was what I wanted, but I was wrong. I want you, Michael. So long as I have you in my life, the rest does not matter. You are the only certainty I need."

He smiled. She meant what she said, he could see it in her eyes. She would give up all that had been important to her for him. And he was going to do everything in his power to make sure she never had to do without.

Chapter 11

The trip home was a lengthy one—nearly a full month to make it back to the homestead Michael's father had left for him. Of course, the trip would likely have taken half that amount of time had they been in any hurry. But they stopped often along the way and traveled at a leisurely pace that allowed them to enjoy the peaceful surroundings and the pleasure of each other's company. And it took even longer because of the detour they made not far from his home, but it was the most wonderful detour of her life.

It was the detour that made Cate and Michael husband and wife.

At the end of their journey now, Michael swung down from his horse and helped her to the ground, leaning in to place a gentle kiss on her lips. But he looked up at the house with bewilderment in his eyes, and she could understand his confusion. The house wasn't large at all, but it was in good condition, far too good for a house that had been neglected for nearly eight months.

The grounds surrounding the house were even more perplexing. Tidy, well-managed fields spread out in every direction as if they'd been carefully tended all this time.

"This is home alright, but I can't tell you what's happened to it," he told her when she looked up at him questioningly.

Holding the horse's reins in one hand, and her hand in the other, he led them to the side and beyond the house to where a small stable stood—also in good repair. He opened the stable door and, if it were possible, he looked even more baffled as he guided Innes inside the stable, which was already occupied by three other horses.

Someone—and their horses—had taken over Michael's home? It seemed unlikely, and yet what else could account for what they were seeing now? Just then, a door slammed shut from somewhere not far off. It must have come from the house. Michael had tucked Innes away in one of the few remaining stalls, and he reached for the knife in his back, moving Cate behind him and creeping quietly toward the barn door.

Footsteps approached quickly but they sounded odd to her ears, though she couldn't figure out quite why. Michael had only just situated them behind the stable's open door when a figure walked in, pausing just out of sight.

"Michael?" a voice asked then, and she could feel the breath escape his chest in a sigh of relief. He sheathed the knife and stepped out from behind the door, pulling her along with him.

She came face to face with a man a few inches taller than herself, but still a few inches shorter than Michael. And though it wasn't apparent at first, she picked up on the resemblance after a moment—hair color and strong jaw, breadth of shoulders and easy smile. It could only be one person.

"Nathan," Michael whispered, and she could hear a plethora of emotion in his voice—relief and happiness, confusion and a hint of anger. "What are you doing here?"

"It's a long story, but it seems you have some explanations to make yourself," he nodded in her direction.

"This is Catriona Westen, my wife."

"It is a pleasure to meet you, Mrs. Westen. As my brother pointed out, I'm Nathan Westen, pain in the arse and younger brother to your husband." He smiled and she couldn't help but smile back.

With only the briefest of glances down, she understood why his footsteps had sounded odd to her—his wooden leg had made strange footfalls over the grass and dirt terrain. All things considering, he moved exceptionally well, given the wooden extremity.

"What are you doing here, Nathan? I spent months looking for you. Don't tell me you've been here all this time."

"No, I should have been, but, I haven't. I returned about four weeks ago, and as you can see, I've been working around the clock...to try to make amends. If you'll come inside," he motioned to the house, "I'll explain everything."

"No, I think you can explain everything right here just fine." Apparently, Michael wasn't moving until he'd gotten a full explanation—not that Cate could blame him.

"Alright. I ended up parting ways with that band of trouble I'd gotten caught up with. I wish I could say it was by my own choosing, but it wasn't. At least, not then. We'd been riding hard away from a stagecoach we'd…met with…and I ended up losing the wooden leg. Well, they didn't even bother waiting around for me to get a new one fitted so that left me on my own. I'd been trying to catch up with them ever since—the fool that I was—but always just a bit behind them, you know?"

"I can imagine."

"I didn't end up catching up with them, but I'm damn glad now I didn't. I did stumble upon what they'd done though." He paused then, and moisture gathered in his eyes. He swallowed hard, as if he fought back a great deal of emotion.

"I stumbled upon a train…God, Michael, you can't imagine…"

"Yes, I can. I was there, Nathan. I was with that group of yours, trying to find you, and I was there when they took that train. So, don't tell me I can't imagine. I know very well what happened there."

"Then you know I was not with them, that I had no part in that."

"And if your leg hadn't held you up? You would have stayed

with them. Would you have been part of it? Would you have aimed a pistol at Cate..." he choked on his words, and grit his jaw hard.

She laid a hand against his shoulder, trying to soothe him without words. She didn't have any business in this confrontation between brothers.

"Your wife...she was there?" Nathan started, but the violent look in Michael's eyes quelled his brother's question in that direction. "Michael, I...I don't know what I would have done. It was never like that. God, do you think I would have gotten caught up with them if it had?"

"I don't know what to think, Nathan."

"All I can tell you is I wouldn't be caught dead with them now. When I found that train, I was so tempted to turn around and ride off, but I didn't. I needed to see what they were really capable of, what monsters they really were. I wandered from car to car, fighting with everything I had not to be sick. They were all dead, every last one of them..."

"No!" Cate whispered, thinking of that tiny hiding place near the back of the train. Michael squeezed her hand and she tried not to think of Violet, the innocent girl she'd left hiding beneath burlap sacks.

"I almost got off the train so many times, but I didn't. I made myself walk through every car, past every passenger. And then I wasn't in the passenger cars any more. I heard a faint noise and I froze, thinking it was probably just a rat. But it wasn't a rat."

"Nathan, what are you doing out here?" a woman's voice called from just beyond the stable.

A moment later, Violet was standing next to Nathan, right there in the stable doorway. She was alive! The noise Nathan had heard on the train must have been Violet shifting in her hiding place. He'd found her and must have seen her safely out.

"Violet!"

"Cate!" they exclaimed at the same time, neither expecting to see the other ever again.

"What are you doing here?" she asked the young girl as she hugged her tight.

"I suppose it's a bit of a long story, but I think it can be summed up rather neatly," Violet began. "Nathan intended to see me safely to the stagecoach, but by the time we got there, well, it turns out I wasn't so enraptured with Mr. Greenfield after all." She turned to Nathan then, "This is the woman who saved my life. If it hadn't been for her, I would never have thought to hide from those horrible men."

Nathan's jaw dropped, but he composed himself rather quickly, smiling wryly at himself. "Violet had told me a young woman had helped her, but I never thought I'd have the privilege of meeting her. The way she told it, I presumed..." he let the thought trail off, all of them no doubt knowing well enough what he'd presumed.

"Yes, well, if it wasn't for Michael," Cate replied, looking up at her new husband with love in her eyes.

"Perhaps, but if I recall that wasn't how you viewed it at first, was it, my love?" Michael joked back, breaking the tension and heavy emotion amid the small group.

"So, you've really come home, Nathan?" he said then, his hope that it was the truth evident in his voice.

"Yes," Nathan replied simply.

Michael nodded, and then he wandered past them and out of the stable to look at the house. Cate followed, her hand still clasped in his. He looked at the house and then back at their small group, and then back to the house once more.

"I think we're going to have to build a bigger house since we both now seem to have saddled ourselves with wives," he mused.

"Saddled yourself, have you?" Cate replied with mock incredulity.

It seemed the seriousness of the unexpected reunion between Michael and Nathan had passed. In those few moments, the brothers had made their peace. Perhaps that was just the way it was among siblings. She couldn't know for sure, never having had one of her own.

It didn't escape her notice, though, that suddenly, she had a husband, a brother-in-law and a sister-in-law. She was a world away from the home she'd known, but now found herself suddenly and quite warmly ensconced in a small family of her own.

It wasn't the happily ever after she'd expected. It was a thousand times better.

THE END

ABOUT THE AUTHOR

Faith-Ann Smith has always loved to write. As a child, she enjoyed penning simple tales about prairie life in her home state of Oklahoma. While in college, Faith-Ann became fascinated with American history, particularly of the 19th century, and began to write creative historical fiction in her late twenties. Blessed with a loving husband and two precious children, Faith-Ann enjoys knitting, teaching Sunday School and tending to the flower beds surrounding her home in Nebraska.

To keep up to date with her latest releases, you may visit www.hopemeadowpublishing.com and sign up for her newsletter.

For a FREE sweet historical romance e-book, please sign up for Hope Meadow Publishing's newsletter at **www.hopemeadowpublishing.com**